Beneath Everything

By Suzie Carr

Cover photography: Terry Messerschmidt

Also by Suzie Carr:
The Fiche Room
Two Feet off The Ground
Tangerine Twist
Inner Secrets
A New Leash on Life
The Muse
Staying True
Snowflakes
The Journey Somewhere
Sandcastles
The Dance

Keep up on Suzie's latest news and projects:
www.curveswelcome.com

Follow Suzie on Twitter:
@girl_novelist

For you, my twin soul sister.

Acknowledgements

There are many people I want to thank for helping me to see this book to its completion. Firstly, I'd like to say a great big thank you to my readers for your generous support and feedback. I am thankful for the reviews you leave on your blogs, social media, Amazon, Goodreads, and other platforms, and also for the encouragement you offer me to keep writing.

Next, I want to thank Terry Messerschmidt. Your patience and knowledge as a friend and scuba instructor helped gift my better half and me with the experience of a lifetime. Thank you to your beautiful wife, Lisa, as well for helping to keep me calm and focused under the deep blue sea! Also, thank you for the generous gift of the beautiful cover photo you captured on our memorable Bonaire trip.

I also owe a great deal of gratitude to Jaco Hesseling and Jagga Jagersma for guiding me through the underwater world of Bonaire. Thank you for taking the time to share your insights and knowledge with me.

To my editors, Ashley and JoAnne, thank you for always giving my work your keen eye and generous care. To Jennifer, Deborah, Felicia, and Alak, as always thank you for the gift of your time, honesty, and insights. Your guidance is a true treasure that I will value forever!

And to my twin soul sister, Dorina, thank God for you and our friendship.

Chapter One

Through her typical mad dashes from one meeting to another, Sarah Destin had learned that a good laugh or an extra-large glass of merlot could usually mitigate most stress. Well, on that particular morning, no amount of laughter or merlot could rescue her from the upheaval.

Running ten minutes late for her meeting with the La Chapelle department store, Sarah dashed through the crowded mall, littered with strollers, clumsy toddlers, teenagers, and elderly mall walkers. She zipped around a kiosk advertising La Chapelle's new summer dress line, an ad campaign her team spent months coordinating, and then she skirted around a middle-aged couple sipping Starbucks coffees.

She pushed onward, tossing an apology over her shoulder and drawing a deep breath to stave off the beginning pangs of a headache. The sugary scent of waffle cones in the distance, colliding with the flashing lights of the carousel and wailing screams of an upset child, caused her temples to throb.

The spree towards the escalator ended on a giant sigh when her heels pressed against the first step towards her climb to a victory she hoped to bring back to her team. She placed her laptop case on the step above her, and then she combed her fingers through the ends of her faded amber hair to untangle it.

She leaned her head backwards to take in the sight of pastel eggs decorated with glittery lines and circles hanging from the light fixtures. They

1

sparkled and twirled, and they reminded her that the Cadbury Mini Eggs she favored so much would once again be luring her into gaining another ten pounds before summer. She'd wolf them down, every last morsel of their chocolatey center.

After her meeting that morning, she would visit the Rite Aid near Sears and treat herself to some. She'd buy an eyeliner, notepad or pen, and sneak the bag into the sale. Because of her addiction, by the end of Easter season, she always had a ridiculous collection of Bic ballpoint pens, spiral notebooks, and liners in every imaginable color.

As she approached the top of the escalator, her cell chimed. She bent over and dug it out from the front pocket of her case. As she rose, something pulled at her waist. In a blink, the escalator stairs, while flattening out at the top, began to swallow the bottom of her long skirt.

"No, no, no," she screamed, pulling back on it. The escalator devoured its edges and wouldn't let go.

The cackles coming from the upper landing motivated Sarah to fight the angry teeth of the escalator. She clung to her plush Italian wool knit skirt, but the escalator needled it further into its gluttonous clutch. Next thing she knew, the escalator groaned on a final churn when an older woman, holding the hand of a toddler, pushed the emergency shut-off button.

Sarah's two hundred-dollar J.Jill skirt lay murdered on top of her red Jimmy Choo heels, leaving her exposed in all her nakedness to a crowd gathered around her like drooling vultures on feeding day.

Of all days to not wear undies. The godforsaken things had tortured her with a wedgie from hell on the drive over to the mall.

She crossed her arms in front of her exposed hoo-ha. "Nice ass," a boy called out while pointing his smartphone at her.

She stared in horror at the phone. "Put that away," she shouted, pointing her finger at him. "Right now. Put it away."

He continued capturing her shame, nudging his friend to do the same.

"Stop! Stop filming."

When they didn't listen, she cried, "Please. Stop!"

She scanned the upper landing for someone reasonable. She spotted a middle-aged man covering his mouth in shock. "Please stop them," she begged.

He sprang into action, rushing towards them. Meanwhile, the older woman picked up the toddler and headed up the escalator, wrestling one arm at a time out of her jacket. When she landed next to Sarah, she handed it to her. "You poor thing. Take it. I'm here to buy myself a new one anyway. So, it's yours."

Mortified, Sarah gripped the jacket and backed up against the escalator's glass supports. The hoots and hollers echoed deeper against the cavernous pitched ceilings and endless opened mouths of shocked, stupefied onlookers, branding her with their gawks, points, and mockery. "Thank you," she said, wrapping it around her waist. "Thank you so much."

"No thank you is necessary."

Sarah spun around, looking for shelter from the mob snapping photos of her. Sacrificing all for the sake of finding shelter, she abandoned her favorite skirt and fled, tossing her cell into her laptop case and wrapping the lifesaving jacket tighter around her waist.

Her cell kept dinging.

She galloped like a fool all the way to the parking garage. She pushed through its double doors and, in all her disgrace, landed in its orangey glow, panting and sweating.

Her phone rang again, beeping out its annoying tune in perfect sync with her heels.

A moment later, back in the safety and comfort of the front seat of her Lexus, she brushed her hair back behind her ears. Then, in one controlled and smooth attempt, she composed her next inhale and exhale. She pointed her eyes to her passenger seat, to her new black undies that crawled too far up into her butt to be worn into an important meeting. She narrowed her eyes at them, angry at their impractical beauty.

She reached into her backseat for her Bug-out bag. Sarah, prepared and practical, would not let a little chaos destroy her plans. She would put on her spare outfit, march into that mall as if she owned it, and get the job done.

A moment later, she slipped into her comfortable, sensible pair of white undies and a gray pencil skirt that matched her red blouse and shoes. Then, she searched the pocket of the laptop case for her cell.

Five missed calls from her best friend, Frenchy.

Bypassing her, she dialed the VP of Merchandising at La Chapelle. "It's Sarah Destin, and, I'm in the parking garage. I'm sorry I'm running late. I ran into a traffic jam. Are you still available to meet?"

"Take your time. We'll see you when you get here."

Just like that, everything fell back into its rightful place, undisturbed and smoothed over.

She blew out a sharp breath and thought about the pictures and videos the crowd took of her. As soon as she finished with her meeting, she'd call her assistant, Sam, and ask him to locate and remove any that popped up on social media. If anyone could help her, Sam could.

She pulled on the door handle then toyed with calling Frenchy back. A quick call always turned into an hour, especially when it had been so long since their last chat.

Reluctantly, she pinged her back. "I saw you called. A lot," she added. "Is everything alright?"

"Are you terribly busy?"

"Just a little preoccupied at the moment," she said. Rehashing that hellish detour would cost her too many extra minutes.

"I need your help."

Sarah pressed her forehead against the window, looking ahead to the mall's entrance. Trying on her most patient tone, she said, "With?"

"I'm having a surprise 60th birthday party for Johnny and his twin sister, Maureen, and I'm in over my head."

At forty-seven, Frenchy was smack dab in the middle age-wise between her husband, Johnny, and Sarah. Yet, when it came to planning, Sarah seemed to be the most sensible of the three.

"Just keep it simple," Sarah said.

"No. I want this to be the party of all parties for Johnny. We only have two months to plan it. I need your creative brain, specifically for the invites. I want them to be unique, you know? Something special. I'll need them in like five days, though. Please tell me you can do it?"

The bass from a passing car boomed, causing the concrete supports to moan. Her best friend had no idea the height of the work pile on her plate. She also had no clue that, in the next week, she'd have to rise at one in the morning just to get through the things she put off from the week before. "Email me what you want them to say, and I'll get it done."

"Oh, you're the best, kiddo."

Sarah smiled at the reference, despite having turned thirty-five a few months before.

"Oh, and mark your calendar for May twenty-third," she said.

"Of course."

"I'm going to try to get Maureen's daughter, Jolene, to come too. She lives on an island in the Caribbean and hasn't visited in years, so I'm not sure if I'll be able to make it happen. But, I'll try. Do you remember her from my wedding?"

Sarah lifted her forehead from the window, recalling the memory of Jolene. Sarah had stepped on her toe while dancing the electric slide, and then Jolene winked at her. That wink had traveled from the tip of her head to the middle of her thighs. *Jolene.* The name shifted her lips into an instant smile. "That was ten years ago, my friend. I'm lucky to remember today is Tuesday."

"Well, actually it's Wednesday. Which brings me to my next question."

Sarah bit her lip, vying for more patience. "What's that?"

"Instead of emailing you details for the invites, come over for dinner on Thursday. I'll be dining with little Tony on corn dogs. We can go over the details then. Johnny won't be here, so we can be silly just like old times."

Old times before Sarah got her promotion.

She could've used some time with Frenchy's five-year-old step-grandson. Tony always had a way of simplifying everything. One little flash of his smile brightened the world. But, her work pile. "Can I take a rain check on the corn dog and Tony? This is a tough week. If you email the invite details, I can rush them back to you."

"If it's too much trouble…"

"No," Sarah cut her off on a strained sigh. "Email them. I can do it."

"What's wrong?" Frenchy asked. "You sound like you're panting. Like you're stressed. Everything good?"

"Everything's fine." Sarah pulled at the door handle, climbing out of the

6

front seat. "It's just another day at the office."

Chapter Two

Jolene Aster met with her dive buddy, Neil, for an early morning adventure out at the double reef site of *Alice in Wonderland* to capture glimpses of Bonaire's breathtaking angelfish and parrotfish. One of her favorite sites on the island, its sandy oasis joined two vibrant reefs together in a peaceful union. A few mornings a week, she'd venture out on those personal dives with Neil to hunt the invasive lionfish, a destroyer of not only Bonaire's, but also the entire Caribbean's fragile ecosystem.

They had entered the crystal-clear water and finned out over the reef, hugging it at about twenty-five feet when Jolene's mask strap broke. She tapped her tank with her dive tool then signaled to Neil to ascend. When they surfaced, she had to break the bad news to him that she failed to bring an extra mask strap with her in her dive kit. One little, itty-bitty broken strap ruined a perfectly good morning.

"I don't have one in my dive kit, either," he said as they waded in the water.

Jolene laughed. "Great instructors we are."

"I guess everything happens for a reason," Neil shrugged as they made their way back to the rocky shore.

Ten minutes later, they stowed their gear in the bed of his pickup truck and drove back to the Rainbow Ridge Resort. "We'll try again tomorrow morning?" Neil asked, as he pulled into a parking spot.

"Sounds good." Jolene hopped out of his truck. "I'll see you down at the boats in a little while, then. I heard we have many divers today. We'll be using all three charter boats."

"Best be sure we restock our dive kits, then."

"Yeah." She tapped the truck's side. "See you soon."

She headed to her scooter.

The sun shone brightly over the arid landscape, so she decided to keep her scooter parked at the resort for later and stroll back to her and her girlfriend's apartment. With the extra time on hand before she had to report to dive duty, she figured she'd grab a couple of coffees too.

Shannon had been distracted the night before, so a relaxing wake-up over hot vanilla bean coffee might soothe her. As she carried the tray of coffees down the gravel path of the resort, her mother called.

"Any chance I can talk you into coming for a visit at the end of May?"

"May's tough," Jolene said. "I've got a new team of divers to train. We're getting more charter boats, and we'll need to get them up to speed."

"I'm begging you," her mother whispered.

"You're begging me?"

"More for Frenchy than for me."

Jolene had gotten a message from Frenchy the night before, but didn't return the call. "Is everything alright?"

"Everything's fine. I'm not the only one from home who misses you."

Jolene rolled her eyes. "First of all, I've spoken with Frenchy about ten times in my life. So, missing me is kind of a stretch. And secondly, Bonaire is my home now."

"Maryland will always be your home. When they ask you on a

10

questionnaire what your home state is, you're not going to say Bonaire. You're going to say Maryland because that's where your roots are. That's where your family is. That's where you went to school, where you became a diver, and where you're going to come one day when you have to dig a hole and stick me in the ground."

"You have such a way with words," Jolene said.

"That's the writer in me. Though, I've had some writer's block lately. I don't know what my problem is. It's probably my brain revolting against turning sixty soon."

Her mother would be turning sixty in May. "She's throwing a party for you, isn't she?"

"Shush. It's a surprise."

"I can't do May, Mom. Maybe once the team is trained, I can take a week and go visit. More likely July."

"You'll miss the cicadas if you come much later than mid-summer."

The cicadas. One and a half million emerged on each acre of land every seventeen years. "I do love those cicadas."

"Then, come home and get your cicada fix."

"Sorry, Mom. Maybe next time." Jolene strode past the low-lying shrubs that lined the resort's pathway to the docks, pausing in front of the dive board to see how many guests would be on her boat that day. Eight.

"Sweetheart, what's it about that place you love so much?"

"We don't have traffic lights. We don't need them. There's no traffic."

"I like being a passenger in traffic," her mother said. "I reflect on life when I'm sitting in it. Well, except if I have to pee."

Jolene laughed. "I miss you. I wish you'd come here for a visit."

"I'm the only one who can lay on the guilt trip," she said. "It's a mother's right. Now come for a short visit and put a smile on my old wrinkly face. I've been miserable for years now."

Jolene suspected she meant it. Her mother did lay on the guilt, spreading it across the miles in thick, heavy layers. "Soon."

"I'll cook you onion soup, and I'll get Frenchy to bring home some of those sour dough baguettes from her bakery. She's amazing like that."

Her mother loved Frenchy. She didn't have to put up guards around her. Frenchy took it upon herself to slip in and be that support when something in the house broke down. So, Jolene suspected her mother's esteem of her had less to do with her amazing personality and more to do with her ability to hammer a nail or fix a broken faucet. Something always fell apart back in their home. In her home. In her mother's home.

"How's Frenchy doing?"

"She says she's happy. She isn't, though."

"Why do you say that?" Jolene asked.

"She's going to surprise your uncle with renewing their vows at our party. He didn't want to get married in the first place, let alone have to do it again. She's pushing him, and he's going to push back one of these days."

"That's a terrible thing to say."

"It's true. Your uncle is never home. He's either at the garage working, riding his motorcycle, or at a race at some dusty bowl of a field in Pennsylvania. I love your uncle because he's my twin, but I don't like how he flirts with our neighbor, Eloise. I've seen him talk over the fence to her, and she gets all giggly. Once I overheard him compliment her new haircut. I've never told Frenchy this, though."

"Mom, not everyone is like the characters in your books. Some people compliment others because they're being nice and not because they're trying to get into someone's pants. I doubt Uncle Johnny is the cheating kind. He likes old cars and getting dirty under the hood of them."

"Well, if you ask me, he should stay home more often. By the way, she's planning this big, expensive to-do for the party. It's silly. Don't get me wrong. I'm grateful, but it's so unnecessary. Your uncle will love it, though. He's always been the center of attention, hasn't he? I'm creating a picture of a big, bad monster. He's not a monster. He's my twin. I love him. I do. He's been driving me to the grocery store and the mall in his newly refurbished Cadillac Seville, so why am I complaining about him?"

Her mother talked in circles, always sending Jolene's heart on a wild race. "What happened to your Corolla?"

"I only like being a passenger now, sweetheart. I hate driving. It's too busy on the roads. Everyone's out to kill each other. Nobody wants to go the speed limit. Everyone honks their horns and sticks their middle fingers up at me. No more driving for me. I gave your cousin, Brad, the Corolla."

"I bought it for you."

"He needs it. He's going to be job searching now that he's graduating college, and will need to get to his interviews in something."

"He can buy his own car. You're going to turn into a recluse."

"All I need is my computer to write my novels so I can pay my bills. I live through my characters. That's enough for me. I don't like real people. They're all a bunch of gossipers and backstabbers."

Her mother, a New York Times bestselling novelist, wove stories together of people who lived life in the fast lane. Her fans would be surprised to know their favorite writer actually preferred nightgowns to the elegant outfits of her debutant characters.

Jolene rounded the corner to the beachfront house where she rented the basement apartment from her boss, Max. "Mom, I have to go."

"Please come for a visit soon."

"I will."

"If you come for the party, we'll have fun. We'll dance the salsa. Frenchy will have Latin music playing. She's been taking lessons, you know."

"I don't like to dance, Mom. You know this."

"It's a shame, too, because women love to watch other women dance."

"Is that so?"

"It is," her mother stated. "I'm not even a lesbian, and I love to watch a woman shake her hips. You know, if I liked women in that way, I'd make a fine lesbian."

At that, Jolene rolled her eyes and walked up to her basement apartment door. "I'm soaked from my morning dive, Mom. I've got to dry up and get inside."

"I miss you, sweetheart."

Jolene hesitated on her goodbye, flinching against the pinch in her heart. "I'll be home soon. I promise."

"I wish you didn't live so far away. I miss cooking you eggs."

She missed that, too. Her mother could cook eggs like nobody else with the yolk still a bit runny, but firm enough to stand its ground on top of an English muffin. "We'll cook and eat eggs together soon."

"I hope so."

Jolene pictured her worn and tired mother gripping the tangled cord of her yellow telephone still hanging on her kitchen wall, tears rolling down her drooping cheeks.

"I love you, Mom."

"Love you more," her mother said, and then she hung up leaving Jolene with an uneasy sense of guilt.

Jolene stuck her cell in her backpack then unlocked the front door to her and Shannon's apartment.

She entered their dusky living room and fumbled with the tray of coffees as she placed them on the small wooden end table near her recliner.

She moved towards their bedroom, taking off her wet T-shirt, then her bathing suit top, then her bottoms. She flung them off to the side of the bedroom door then pushed it open on a smile.

The room hung in a shadow, highlighting Shannon's bright green T-shirt as she bent over her drawer. Her large backpack lay next to her feet.

"I'm craving eggs," Jolene said. "Sunny-side up, yolks firm but still a little bit runny."

Shannon jumped back, fumbling a set of socks. They rolled out in front of them. "You're back early."

"My mask broke on me. I figured we could take advantage of the nice morning. Maybe sit on the patio before I have to head over to the docks."

Shannon lowered herself to the bed then dropped her head into her hands. "I'm so sorry," she cried.

"What's wrong?" Jolene rushed to the bedside, her boobs bouncing along the bumpy path as she tripped over shoes and clothes.

Shannon looked up from her hands, and her swollen, dark eyes said it all; they said what Jolene feared the moment Shannon finally agreed to move in with her a few short months before.

"I'm not ready for this." She sighed, glancing around. "The matching towels and my drawers next to yours. It's all too much. We did this too fast."

"But, you said you were ready."

She sucked in a breath, stuttering on the edge of an even deeper exhale.

"Derek called last night to tell me his uncle passed away."

"He called *you,* his ex-girlfriend?"

"His favorite uncle died."

Her whining echoed against the walls, flinging the pungent stench of audacity around. "I don't quite understand why he'd call you."

"He asked me to come home and go to the funeral."

"Are you going to go?"

"I can't not be there for him."

The silence hung between them, littering their space with the sour taste of unreason.

"Yes, you can," Jolene finally said. "He's not your boyfriend anymore."

"You don't get it."

"No," Jolene's voice grew louder. "I don't at all."

"You have no clue how to love someone." Tears streamed from her eyes.

The coldness in Shannon's eyes stabbed her, causing her stomach to plummet into a series of spasms. "I don't?"

"I'm lonely," she whispered. "You never talk."

"I'm a listener. Haven't I established that?"

"I need more than a listener."

The dust trail of her words lingered, leaving a cloud that polluted their once peaceful place. "You still love him, don't you?" Jolene asked.

Shannon avoided Jolene's gaze, focusing back on the socks that lay before them, an innocent to the harsh realities of being human.

Jolene stood before Shannon naked and vulnerable, sandblasted by her silence.

Shannon shoved her clothes into the backpack then pushed past her. "I'm sorry. I want to go home," she said, and then she scurried out the door.

Jolene let her rush away without a fight. No amount of forcing would ever get her to stay.

Minutes later, she dumped their coffees down the drain, showered, and took off to the docks wearing her numbness like a shroud in the ninety-degree blazing sun of her tropical paradise. Jolene finished out her morning work, loading tanks onto the boat and taking a group of eight divers out to offshore sites.

In the course of the following week, Jolene allowed herself to grieve the loss of Shannon. When the week ended with no sign of her, Jolene packaged up her memory of Shannon. She placed it deep inside where it would remain, buried like an old pair of jeans that didn't quite fit right anymore, but ones she couldn't bear to throw away into the stinky garbage.

Then, she dragged Neil out for a shore dive to clear her head.

A strange phenomenon occurred once she opened her eyes and saw the world through a clear lens. No longer would she dangle like a captive fish controlled by the netting of someone whose interests didn't align with her own. Freedom offered the best advantage, breaking her away from the constraints of perils, so foreign and captivating at first, and propelling her up and out of their grip. To be in flow meant to be in harmony with everything around. Jolene embraced that flow and said her final goodbyes to Shannon.

Everything shone brighter and healthier once she did. Fish swam with her, curious and welcoming, guiding her on a new path, one that didn't harness her to an eternity of questions as to whether she deserved love.

When she returned from that cathartic dive, instead of grabbing lunch with Neil, she called her mother. "I can't be there for the birthday party, but I can likely come in the next few weeks, maybe the end of April. Would that work?"

Her mother shrieked. "I would do a happy dance, but you know I'd probably fall and break a finger or two."

"Let's survive one visit without a catastrophe."

"I promise this time around nothing will happen. I'm accident proofing my living room as we speak. I won't end up in the emergency room with another broken nose if I can help it!"

Famous last words. "I'll see you soon."

A Few Weeks Later

Maureen Aster never set out to be a burden to her daughter, Jolene, yet she had become one. Granted life had a funny way of plopping the wrong things in her lap when Jolene visited. Maybe cosmic energy caused those weird fiascos.

She only rear-ended people when Jolene happened to be riding shotgun in the passenger seat. That occurred twice in the past, and all while Jolene fidgeted in the passenger seat like a scared kid waiting on a flu shot.

Then, of course, she had burned through two skillets the year Jolene surprised her for Christmas.

Maureen had to admit, the few trips Jolene took home turned into some kind of mess. No wonder her daughter hated to visit.

Nothing some good home cooking couldn't solve, though. No girlfriend of hers back in that paradise she claimed as home cooked her shepherd's pie or chicken casserole the way she could. No way, because when Jolene flitted through the airport doors, she looked like she'd lost a good ten pounds. She didn't look like someone who enjoyed home-cooked food, or any food for that matter.

"Good Lord, Jolene," Maureen cried when her arms circled around her daughter for a hug. "I'm going to fatten you up."

Their reunion started out as an eating fest. Jolene treated her to buffet after buffet, and each time served herself three whole plates of food.

"Oh, God," she'd moan as she shoveled spoonful after spoonful of drippy, rich, creamy, heart-clogging foods into her mouth. "I miss real food. I eat fish. Lots of fish. But, nothing like this."

Five days into the visit, Maureen relaxed into the idea that their time together would turn into a full success story. Maybe that level of success would even convince Jolene to visit a little sooner next time.

Then, just as they were easing into the busiest day planned, disaster struck.

Maureen pulled her casserole out of the oven while humming *Canon in D* when her phone rang. "Jolene, honey, can you grab that?"

"Mom, we're going to be late for Brad's speaking competition."

Steam covered Maureen's eyeglasses as she pulled out the casserole. "It's done. I'm ready. Just get the phone before they hang up."

Jolene scoffed. "Fine." She picked up the call and mumbled a few words. "I see. Okay. Yeah. She's right here." Jolene turned to face her. "It's your neighbor, Jack."

Jolene extended the cord, and that's when the ground started doing its quirky little shake it always did whenever she came to town. One second the wall stood erect, and the next second, Jolene, with all her skinny biceps, triceps, and what not, pulled the dang phone cord so hard, it took out half the wall.

Jolene parried against the debris and sighed. "This is why you need a cell phone."

Powdery plaster dust swirled around them, landing on the casserole. Maureen tossed a dishrag on top of it then swiped her hands, shooing away the dust particles.

"Well, looks like we're going to have to stop at The Home Depot on the way home," Maureen said as she stole the phone from Jolene's grip. "Maureen here."

"Hey beautiful, it's Jack."

"I'm sorry, the phone is breaking up," she said, shaking the receiver. "Hello?"

"Hello. Can you hear me, Maureen?"

Maureen glanced at Jolene who sighed heavily and stared at the mess.

Maureen warned Jack not to call her during Jolene's visit. Did the man not have ears? "Hello?" Maureen rolled her eyes and twirled her finger around her temple. She covered the phone with her hand and whispered, "He's crazy."

More important things needed her care other than some man who couldn't take direction, like what to do with the new hole in the wall. She hung up, placing the receiver on top of the broken plaster. "We'll deal with all of this later."

Jolene tossed her hands in the air. "I'll be waiting out in the yard."

One tiny mishap. No big deal. At least Jolene caused it that time.

~ ~

Jolene glanced at her mother's smiling face as she watched Brad strut across the stage and present to the large crowd gathered for the public speaking regional competition. Brad bloomed late, ready to earn his degree the following month at the age of thirty-two. Before that, he got himself into

20

trouble selling drugs. Thanks to his son, Tony, Brad smartened up and got his act together. He even managed to gain full custody of his son.

"He's a good man," her mother said on the drive home. "A good man." She wagged her head up and down, and her silvery, manicured layers followed her moves.

"I'm glad I got to see him win the competition," Jolene said. "He's really come a long way."

"He'll be the first one in the family to graduate college."

Jolene nodded. "College isn't for everyone."

"No need to get defensive, dear."

"Just stating a fact, Mother."

As the two-week trip rolled on, Jolene went about fixing all the broken things in her mother's house: the leaky faucet, the blocked air ducts, the broken fence, the squeaky floorboards, and of course that broken wall. Jolene accomplished a lot. She'd leave with a lightness that would hopefully carry her another year or two. She couldn't wait to get back to her Bonaire oasis, soaking up the sun and diving into the clear blue sea.

On one of their last afternoons together, Jolene decided she would focus on her mother, bridging any remaining gaps before she left her again. She would fill the potholes of the broken road that once connected them, smoothing them over and leaving all her impatience, judgments, and immaturity behind. The time to build a better bridge from that old life to her new one stood before her. That bridge dangled naked, ready to be resurfaced and layered in resistant tar that would not falter under the pressure of discontent.

Her mother was wise under all that nervous energy, and Jolene wanted to plug into that precious gift while she still could by disbanding her tough walls and hanging her vulnerability out on the line in the spirit of surrender.

What better way than to bond over something that mattered to her mother? She'd talk with her about love.

"How do you know if you love someone?" she asked as they sat on the back patio.

Her mother drew on her cigarette. The smoke billowed between them. "There's no question. I knew the second I laid eyes on your father."

"The very second?" Jolene swatted the smoke away. "That's not good for my lungs, you know."

"I'm sorry. You're right." Her mother blew another round of smoke away from them, but it still managed to sneak its way back into their space. "Your father saved me from someone trying to ask me on a date."

"Dad, the hero," Jolene joked.

"The best hero. He swooped right in and surprised me with details of a date. A date he would take me on that evening."

Jolene liked the nostalgic glow building on her mother's cheeks. "Well, I want the details."

"Your dad loved fishing. So, he asked me in front of the other guy what time we would meet for our fishing date. Desperate to get away from the creep, naturally I told him six o'clock."

Jolene scooted up on one of her legs, enjoying the trip down memory lane and the intimate peek into her parents' first encounter. "Naturally."

"Seven months later, we married each other then had you in the blink of an eye. I laughed and smiled with him until the day he became our angel."

They sat in comfortable silence. Her mom puffed away on her cigarette while Jolene smiled at the sweet story of her dad. "How did you know you loved him, though?"

"Oh, that's easy. I missed him the moment he turned and waved goodbye on that first day." She drew another long drag. "I had this ache that didn't go away until I saw him again."

Jolene allowed that to marinate. She swallowed it whole and waited for its bitter truth to dissolve and fill her with a profound reality. "I've never ached for someone."

"Because you live on a small island with no hope for prospects."

She batted her mom's hand. "Mom!"

"What? Am I saying something that's untrue?"

Maybe Jolene had something wrong with her. She should've ached for Shannon, right? A pang, jab, hell even a twitch would've indicated she hadn't wasted the last few months of her life convincing Shannon to be more than her friend. Maybe they had grown too used to each other already? "Did your love change over time? You know, like when you got used to him?"

"It only intensified."

Jolene reclined back against the lounger and stared at the sky. A few minutes went by when her mom said, "I noticed you browsing the books in the den the other day. Those were your dad's favorites. He loved reading all that self-help stuff. I prefer romance, as you know. If you want to read any from his collection, feel free."

Jolene had already begun reading one about the power in the present moment. She had started it that morning, and only had another two chapters left. "Sure, yeah."

A few more minutes passed, and the silence started to evolve into a wave, one that began to build and stir the calmness. Jolene punctured its power by diving back into conversation. "What do you want to do tomorrow?"

"Your last day." Her mother groaned. "I'm glad your flight isn't until two o'clock."

"Yeah, we'll have plenty of time to enjoy the morning."

"I'd like to go to D.C. and visit the Vietnam Memorial. It's been two years since I last put flowers in front of Uncle Daniel's name."

"Of course. We'll get there super early, so we don't have to rush. I'd like to get back here and to the airport no later than noon to catch my flight."

~ ~

They borrowed Brad's Corolla and parked it at the rail station, and then they took the commuter ride into D.C. They spent the morning walking through several of the memorials, and even managed a quick trip into the Air and Space Museum as soon as they opened. "We should get back to the metro," Jolene said around ten o'clock.

"I've got to tinkle." Her mother dashed towards the restrooms.

Several minutes later, she emerged and they trekked off to catch their ride.

Once on the metro, Jolene sat back with a freeing smile on her heart, ready to get back to her life. She didn't love Shannon. The trip offered her the space necessary to avoid the disaster of calling her and begging her to stay. If she had agreed, that would've landed them both in a life of misery.

As they approached their station, her mother started to squirm.

"Let me guess. You have to pee."

"Oh dear." A grim look surfaced on her face.

"Oh dear, what?" Jolene asked.

"Oh, you're not going to like this."

Jolene gripped the arms to her seat, bracing for the inevitable. "Come out with it already."

"I made a teeny mistake."

"How teeny?"

"Well, it's a good thing we have some extra time."

"What're you talking about?"

"I left my keys to the house and Brad's car on the sink in the bathroom at the Air and Space Museum."

~ ~

One extensive, silent, grating trek back to the Air and Space Museum resulted in the longest running shared sulk of their relationship as mother and daughter.

"We need to move fast," Jolene said, pulling her mother along the open field of the National Mall. Jolene glanced over her shoulder at her red-faced mom. "Do you see why smoking is so bad for you?"

Her mother flailed behind her, huffing and puffing.

"I'm sorry," she whined. "I told you I'm sorry."

"We're running out of time." Jolene picked up the pace, yanking her mother along. She would not miss her flight.

When they got to the museum and retrieved the keys from lost and found, her mother had to pee again. "I'll pee my pants if I don't go."

Jolene plucked the keys from her mother's fingers, and pointed her forward. "Hurry. Time's ticking."

Her mother sprinted forward, flinging her arms and legs every which way, looking back at Jolene with flushed cheeks. "I'm going as fast as I can."

Her mother craned her neck and offered Jolene a smile as she dashed. Then, out of the corner of Jolene's eye, she saw an oncoming trolley carrying tourists.

"Mom," Jolene yelled. "Stop, Mom!"

The moment her mother faced forward, she smacked right into the trolley and flew straight up in the air, handbag and all. In cruel slow motion, her mother's face contorted into sheer terror as she lifted high, too high, and smacked onto the ground. Then, the wheel of the cart ran over her leg.

Nothing else mattered to Jolene but getting to her mother's side. She leaped, pushing people out of her path as nausea wormed its way up her throat.

Her mother looked up and managed to smile, despite the blood dripping from her cheek. "You're going to kill people leaping around like you did."

Jolene wiped the blood with the back of her hand. "Are you okay?"

She lifted herself and sat up, her face hung in a white cloudy haze of shock. "Yeah, I think so. We should go so you can get back in time. We'll certainly have a good laugh over this on the metro ride back to the station."

Just then, the trolley driver arrived at their side. "Stay calm," he said, glancing with horror at her leg. "I just called 911."

Jolene glanced at her mother's leg. Her bone protruded through her skin, blood soaked and splintered.

Next thing, Jolene woke to the shock of a cold cloth on her forehead. Three strangers stared down into her face, their wrinkles swallowing up their concern.

"You fainted," one of them said.

"She's awake?" her mother asked in a garbled hush.

"Mom?" Jolene tried to sit up, but one of the helpers coaxed her back down.

"Take it easy. Let's wait for the paramedics to arrive."

Jolene ignored the advice. She sat up and crawled to her mother's side.

Someone had covered her mother's leg with a coat. Jolene ran her fingers through her mother's layers, telling her everything was going to be just fine. Her mother smiled. She was obviously in shock and not understanding the extent of her injury. Jolene wrestled with more nausea while waiting on help to arrive.

When the paramedics finally reached her mother, Jolene backed away so they could help her.

"Listen, sweetheart," her mother said after a few minutes, "I want you to go and catch the metro, and get to the airport. I'll call Brad. He'll pick up the car from the airport and come get me."

Jolene leaned back in and cradled her mother's hand. "I'm not going anywhere."

"What about your new dive team?"

"They'll figure it out."

The paramedic placed an oxygen mask over her mother's face. She tore it off, "Maybe you'll be able to go to my party now!"

~ ~

The next day, she brought her mother home from the hospital in a full leg cast. When she got her mother settled, she called her boss, Max, to let him know what happened.

"I'm sorry you're going through this," he said. "How long will you need?"

"At least a few weeks."

"Take all the time you need. For now, I'll hire someone to help get the new dive team up to speed."

"I'll be there as soon as I can."

"Jolene, I don't know how to say this in a way that doesn't sound insensitive, given all you're going through right now. But, seeing as you won't be here on Monday to train the new team, I won't be able to hire you back until the next contract that starts at the end of June."

"End of June?"

27

"We'll be losing Trent and Kito then. They're going to the Maldives once their contracts end here. So, a spot will open back up for you."

Two months. "Max, what about my apartment?"

"Your apartment is safe. Tess and I will hold it for you. It's only two months. You can get everything squared away back home then start nice and fresh."

Once they said their goodbyes, Jolene hung her head between her knees. The room spun, along with concerns on how she would survive the next two months without going insane.

Broken mask, fixed. Broken wall, fixed. Broken leg, almost fixed. So many broken things, fixed. When things broke, she fixed them. When she couldn't fix them, she dodged them.

She needed to fix that about herself. She couldn't dodge the situation at hand.

She needed to fill in those potholes that littered her pathway to peace so she could flow again without taking along the constant nag of guilt for not being the good daughter, the good girlfriend, and the good anything for anyone.

Unlike under the water, she couldn't snorkel her way through the rubble. She could only climb over the debris and hope the weight of her impatience in the terrestrial circuit didn't crush anyone. She had to surrender to the moment at hand, dropping her negativity and drinking up all drops of insight her situation might present. She would seek strength over weakness, freeing herself from any vain attempt at controlling what couldn't be controlled.

"Jolene, honey," her mother called from her bedroom. "Can you fix me some tea, please? The caramel one. Not the caramel spice. The plain caramel," she yelled.

I can fix tea. That I can do.

"Oh, and can you go to the store and buy me a pint of strawberry ice cream? Not the generic one, or the one with chocolate and vanilla. I hate that kind. The good one. The brand name one. I think it starts with a B."

Someone shoot me.

Chapter Three

Sarah loved structure. She loved everything about it, especially the way it kept things aligned with her plans. When someone or something messed with that valuable important asset of life, Sarah contorted into someone she'd love to hate; someone annoying and whiney.

On May twenty-third, she sat in the front seat of her Lexus, staring out the windshield at The Chesapeake House and whined. Chaos stormed into her life that morning and hijacked her plans, slaughtering her sanity with a savagery akin to that of biblical times.

Stupid cicadas.

She wanted to show up, get through the surprise party and renewal of vows, and not piss off her best friend. Of course, life had different plans. It always did. Life loved to screw with her lately, stampeding on her framework and breaking it into little bits of useless sticks.

She wanted to be a good friend, the kind who showed up, paid tribute, and didn't let a silly insect phobia stand in her way. However, the universe wagged its playful little finger at her and said *uh-uh-uh.*

She gripped her steering wheel, and a tantrum bubbled inside, slowly getting ready to erupt. Of all weeks for the once-every-seventeen-years cicada emergence to take place, it had to be the week of the party.

Sarah watched the digital clock on her dashboard gobble up another minute. In another thirty, she would be late for one of the most planned parties of Frenchy's life. Instead of a surprise corporate meeting or a three-hour traffic delay, it had to be an insect infestation to ruin things.

She pressed her head against her steering wheel and a moment later a cicada smacked into her windshield. "Really?" she yelled.

Frenchy let a lot of things slide in life, but she would never accept the fact that Sarah missed the party because of a fear. Frenchy ordered a fondue fountain and an ice sculpture. She ordered cloth napkins instead of the paper kind. She hired a caricature artist. The woman skimped on nothing.

Dodge a cicada attack or a Frenchy silent attack? Neither one appealed to her.

Frenchy didn't understand her fear. Then again, Frenchy grew up with a tarantula for a pet.

When Frenchy first mentioned the party, cicadas never popped into Sarah's mind. As soon as Brad, Frenchy's stepson, mentioned the cicadas to her the day she dropped off the invites, she shuddered. She stood on Frenchy's front stoop and shuddered like a big baby. Brad laughed, and she shuddered even more. Nothing rattled her like cicadas.

No one understood her fear.

"They won't be out until the end of May, so you'll be fine," Brad said, spitting out a wad of bubble gum into the palm of his hand. Then, he chucked it into Frenchy's azalea bush.

Sarah got to work right away on a solid plan to avoid the big-eyed creatures. She'd avoid the outdoors for the five weeks they'd invade. She'd drive straight from her two-car garage to her office's garage. She'd hire a grocery service. All client meetings would take place via Skype. She had to do what she had to do.

If Frenchy would've booked the Marriott, a much more affordable venue, instead of The Chesapeake House, she'd be all set. The Marriott had a parking garage.

Frenchy wanted only the best for Johnny, though.

Sarah shivered as she watched the cicadas continue to land on her windshield and hood.

During the last cicada assault, her mother, not the most patient of women, packed her onto a plane and flew her off to Tampa for the month.

Just last week, as though synchronized to the second, the nymphs had emerged from the ground and hung in their exoskeletons from every branch, weed, and tree trunk throughout the state of Maryland.

That balmy morning, as if ordered by the spirits of every ant and worm she stepped on since childhood, most of the red-eyed buggers broke free of those vile, thin exoskeletons and began their mating frenzy, filling the air with a constant wave of ear-piercing maraca sounds.

She stared at her phone. Frenchy had already called her seventeen times in the past hour, leaving not a single message. If Sarah didn't toughen up in the next thirty minutes, Frenchy would not forgive her.

"Please go away for one minute," she whined. "Just one little minute!"

Soon, guests began to arrive, and dashed towards the entrance, batting their heads, arms, and legs to stop the cicada madness.

Then, a faded and rusted blue Corolla stopped short in front of her car and reversed to pull in beside her. The back of the car crept close to her front bumper, too close. The car's back bumper disappeared, and then came a horrifying crunch and shake.

Sarah sat tall, still gripping her steering wheel. *Unbelievable!*

The car stopped.

A moment later, the car pulled forward then eased backwards into the parking spot next to hers.

The driver's door flew open and out of it popped Jolene. She offered her an apologetic shrug and headed over to Sarah's bumper. She bent over to analyze it, moving from one end of the car to the other.

Then, Maureen, Frenchy's sister-in-law, wearing a flowery dress two sizes too big for her, hobbled to Jolene's side, balancing on a set of crutches. Finally, Brad, wearing a Cuban-style shirt, slid out of the backseat. He swaggered right past his aunt and cousin, saying something over his shoulder, and then he ran towards the front entrance swatting cicadas.

"Well, it's good to know I'm not the only one who screws up," Maureen said.

Jolene shot her an eye roll then disengaged. "Mom, go inside. I'll take care of this."

Maureen didn't argue. She clutched her crutches tighter and hobbled off.

Jolene cradled her waist and sighed. "I don't see any damage. You should come see for yourself."

"I'm not going out there," Sarah said loud enough to be heard through the closed windows. Sarah waved her off. "I believe you. We're fine here."

"You should see this for yourself." Jolene stepped back to look at her bumper from a different angle. Her sleek chestnut-colored hair hung in a low ponytail, and she wore a black tunic under a fitted army green jacket and black dress pants.

"It's okay. I don't need to see."

Jolene rose to the occasion, unaffected by the dozens of cicadas taking up refuge on her sleeves, shoulders, and hair. "Is it the cicadas?"

Sarah settled on a regretful shrug.

"They're harmless," Jolene yelled over the buzz as she headed over to

34

her, frolicking with the cicadas. A moment later, she landed by the driver's side window, plucked a cicada from her sleeve, and placed it in the palm of her hand. "It's cute," she shouted through the window. "Look at those intense red eyes."

Sarah stared in horror as cicadas continued to land on Jolene. "Are you making fun of me?"

Jolene's eyes brightened. "They don't hurt. They tickle."

"Are you crazy?"

"Depends who you ask," Jolene said, shouting over their noise.

They stared at each other.

"I remember you," Jolene said. "You stepped on my toe."

And you winked at me, and I almost orgasmed on the dance floor.

"Yeah, at your uncle's wedding."

"Right," Jolene said, nodding her head. She scanned the lot. "Let me in your car," she said. "We should exchange information in case you want to sue me."

Sarah shook her head. "Absolutely not. You're covered in them."

"I'll brush them off." She glided around to the passenger side, and bent forward. "I won't let any of them near you. I promise."

Sarah weighed her options. Put the car in drive and gun it out of the parking lot, risking her friendship with Frenchy or let Jolene in and risk cicadas hoteling in her hair, the same hair she paid eighty dollars to have whipped up into an informal upsweep a few hours before in her home.

"I'm not leaving. I'll keep standing here until you let me in."

In the seconds between her shallow breaths, Sarah battled her stupid fear, flinging it aside and putting Frenchy above it. She unlocked her passenger door and Jolene slid in while swiping cicadas off her sleeves. They flicked and buzzed.

Sarah squeezed her eyes shut and grabbed her head as if about to crash land from thirty-thousand feet.

"Don't worry. I'm gathering them up." Jolene's arm bumped Sarah's head. "Oops, sorry. Hang on. Let me get this little one here above you, and we'll be all set." She shifted even closer. "Damn. Hang on. Geez, she's a quick one."

Sarah's whimpers filled the car.

"I got her. She's the last. I have them all here in my satchel. If you open your eyes I promise to zipper them in until we get outside."

With her eyes still closed, Sarah asked, "Are you sure?"

"It's just you and me," she whispered.

Sarah inched her eyes open. Waves of cicadas circled the air outside her car. "I'm not a crazy fearful person. I'm not. I'm really not. I'm actually very brave when it comes to other things. Like, I mean, I can do rock climbing. Granted I've never scaled an actual mountain or anything. I wouldn't hesitate to, though. I've also snorkeled and did one of those triathlon things. I'm very brave under different circumstances." She paused. "And, I'm rambling."

"Yes, you are."

A cicada crawled out of Jolene's hair, and Sarah screamed.

"You're making my day," Jolene said, plucking it up and placing it in her satchel.

"I'm glad I can entertain you." Sarah grew annoyed.

Jolene softened into a smile. "I'm not trying to be fresh. I just… I've just never seen this reaction. It is kind of entertaining."

"Troublesome, too," Sarah added. "Don't leave troublesome out."

"I wouldn't have called you that."

"Well, I didn't mean I'm troublesome. Then again, I guess in some ways I am. Anyway, what I meant by troublesome is that I'm in big trouble. I flirted with the idea of behavioral therapy leading up to this attack. I had a therapist all picked out and everything. I kept getting stuck at work, though. Work. Work. Work." Sarah couldn't stop rambling. "That and I didn't want to be this person that I'm being right now, this weird woman sitting in her car and crying about an insect."

"You cried?"

Sarah lowered her visor and noticed her black mascara circles. "I'm not goth." She wiped the mascara, smearing it further. "I just don't like bugs."

"Do you want my help?"

"How?"

"We'll run like hell, and once inside, I'll brush off any clingers. We'll worry about exchanging our information when we're safely inside."

Sarah gripped her steering wheel again. The cicadas kept flicking against the windshield. "I'm not going to sue you. Don't worry."

"Good because I have about two hundred dollars to my name right now." Jolene smiled.

They sat in silence for a few agonizing seconds as Sarah weighed her next move.

"Frenchy's my best friend," Sarah said. "I have to get myself in there."

Jolene placed her hands in her lap. She had a delicate black tattoo of a small fish on the inside of her wrist. "I bet she's pacing and cursing you out right now."

"You don't know Frenchy like I do, if you think that."

"Well, that's true," Jolene said. "I haven't spent much time with her before now."

"She will smile at me and pretend my absence at her party never bothered her. That's how she is. I know her better than that, though. She'll rock that smile, and the guilt will erode what little dignity I have left in me. Soon, I'll be unrecognizable. I'll wander around wearing the shame like a dumpy old woman in a torn and dirty nightgown."

"Well, that would be a shame." Jolene scanned Sarah's fitted red dress. "What you're wearing is a much better choice."

Jolene's penetrating gaze dissolved her fears, for a half second anyway. "Yeah, Frenchy would agree."

They shared a laugh.

"Are you just visiting Maryland?" Sarah asked.

"I am." Jolene dipped her head.

"Okay, from where?"

"Bonaire."

"What's Bonaire?"

"An island in the Caribbean." Jolene fingered her cute fish tattoo. "I'm a diver. I'm sort of stuck here for another month while I wait for my contract to begin again."

"You don't strike me as someone who would get stuck. You're too daring for that."

She laughed. "Daring?"

"Well you did gun it backwards into my car like nobody's business."

Her eyes widened. "Yeah, I'm sorry about that. It's not like me. My mother distracted me." Jolene rolled her eyes. "She turned the radio up instead of down."

"Mothers can do that. My mother used to do the same to me." Sarah sighed, releasing some of her nervous energy. "So scuba, huh?"

"You're stalling."

"Yes," Sarah said, smiling and staring straight ahead. "Yes, I'm stalling. I'm trying to work up the nerve to get out of this car. So, just talk to me about scuba, please."

Jolene leaned back and stretched her arms behind her head, supposedly settling in for the journey. She filled the inside of Sarah's car with the scent of apples and sunshine. "Okay, what do you want to know?"

"Were you scared the first time?"

"I don't get scared."

Sarah slapped her steering wheel. "Everyone has something to fear."

She twisted her mouth. "I do hate being trapped."

"You wear scuba gear! How's that not trapping?"

"I'm talking about in life. I could never sit at a desk or be stuck in a place I don't want to be for too long."

Sarah blew out some residual tension. "You'd hate my life. I'm a desk junkie."

"I'm an open water junkie. Next month I'll be in my glory back in Bonaire."

They stared straight ahead and watched the nature show unfold, as guests arrived and fought their way into the building. "So Maryland is not for you, huh?" Sarah asked.

"Not at all."

Sarah loved Maryland, and couldn't imagine a life not lived with Inner Harbor only a fifteen-minute car ride away or spending time at Frenchy's bakery kneading artisan dough. "I've snorkeled before. Did I mention that?"

"You did. When you were rambling."

"Oh, yes," Sarah said, casting a demure smile.

"You've never tried scuba, have you?" Jolene asked with a chuckle at the end of her question.

"Why the laugh? Am I not cut out for it?"

"Are you?"

"I don't know." Sarah loosened her grip on the steering wheel. "I never considered it before. It can't be that hard. You breathe and float around, right?"

"More or less."

"What else is there?"

Jolene gazed at her. "You can't panic or be fearful."

Something in the way Jolene's lips moved when she spoke those words suddenly challenged Sarah to want to be the sort of person who loved gearing up with an air tank on her back, hooting as she jumped into the middle of the ocean.

Back on Earth, Sarah lowered her visor to take another look at her mascara and hairdo. Pieces of her belabored updo hung from her head, victims to her earlier panic. "So much for all the meticulous attention to detail on this head of hair this morning. Eighty dollars wasted."

Jolene swallowed the beginnings of a laugh. "You've got a—" She twirled her finger at her neck. "—you've got a few pieces that fell out of the twist."

Sarah attempted to stick the ends of one of the fallen tendrils into the disastrous nest. "A sexy look, I know."

"Sexy. Hmm. I'm not sure if sexy is an adequate enough word." That time Jolene let her laughter escape and it filled the car.

Sarah enjoyed listening to it. "By the way, I'm Sarah."

Jolene extended a nod. "I'm Jolene."

"Jolene," Sarah stretched out her name, indulging in its intense flavor on her tongue. "How am I going to get out of this car and into that building without getting pummeled?"

"You're not."

"Well, I have to."

"No, I mean you're not going to escape the pummel."

Sarah shivered. "Then, can you brainstorm a good excuse for me? Tell Frenchy I tripped and bloodied my dress. She's afraid of blood. She faints."

"Your dress is red."

Sarah drew a sharp breath, and it tingled all the way into the deepest part of her brain. "If you help me figure this out, I promise to buy you a drink. I'll even toss one in for your mother. And you know what? I'll even dance with you, and not step on your toes this time."

Jolene gazed at her. "I don't typically dance. I'm not fun like you."

Fun. That's right. She was fun when she wanted to be. Of course, lately she was serious. Very serious. Serious about work, about paying down her mortgage, about finding the best routes to D.C. Serious about everything in general.

"Okay, so you're not fun. But, will you allow me to buy you and your mother a drink if you help me through this?"

"I'm counting on it. As long as there's sangria, you've got yourself a deal."

"Sangria I can do. So, what's the plan?"

Jolene wrapped her hand around Sarah's wrist. "Can you trust me?"

"I don't know you."

"That doesn't matter. Woman to woman, can you trust me?"

The small space began to close in on them. "I can't even catch a full breath." Sarah drew a labored mouthful of air. "See? It's not flowing."

Jolene's eyes softened. "We'll get out of the car and run together."

Sarah laughed.

"Seriously. You'll empower yourself." Jolene's eyes sparkled. "You'll sing happy birthday out of tune with the rest of us then dance the night away."

"You paint it all to be so easy."

"Well, it's not like it's a matter of life and death," she said, grinning.

"Just so you're aware, I'm not weak because I'm afraid of a bug."

Jolene continued to grin. Her absence of words summed up her opinion.

"I'll have you know this isn't some silly phobia. I actually almost died as a kid when a spider bit me. I swear to God. I swung on my gym set in my backyard and it attacked me. I had a huge welt and—"

"—and the spider lost. You're still here."

"Yeah. I won, I suppose."

"Cicadas just want to mate. They don't care about us. We're landing pads," Jolene said. "Now, come on. Let's get this over with."

"I can be brave, you know?"

"Prove it," Jolene said.

"First tell me something. How did you end up in Bonaire?"

Jolene laughed again. "I love the stalling."

Sarah nudged her. "Come on. Tell me."

"I traveled to different resorts and led dive tours then landed in Bonaire and fell in love with it."

"Did you plan this trip so you could see the cicadas?"

"Stop stalling."

"Humor me and just answer my question. Did you come for the cicadas?"

"No. I should have been home long before now. My mother tends to

42

attract personal injury."

"Hence the leg cast and crutches?"

Jolene nodded.

They sat in a contemplative silence for a moment, sharing a knowing glance that spoke of the inevitable. "Promise you'll run with me?" Sarah asked.

"I told you, I'll even swipe them off you once we're inside."

The underlying twinkle that poked itself out from around the toasted warmth of Jolene's eyes told Sarah she could trust her. "Okay. Let me catch a deep breath."

"You're going to feel so empowered after this. So, let's just get it over with." Suddenly, Jolene opened her door and cicadas flew inside.

They clicked and buzzed around Sarah, and she screamed. She had no choice. She had to escape and run. A second later, landing in front of her car, Jolene reached out for her, and Sarah latched onto her hand. Together they sprinted. They dodged the assault, running so fast Sarah's feet barely touched the ground.

They ran too fast. Much too fast.

Jolene tripped and fell to the ground on a whimper, grabbing her ankle.

Sarah squeezed her eyes shut, willing herself to stay focused. Flinging cicadas from her arms and shoulders, she knelt. "You're going to owe me big time for this." She placed her arm around Jolene. "Can you walk on it?"

A cicada flew at her face and Sarah swallowed a cry, afraid to open her mouth and release the full onset of hysterics that piled up in her throat.

Jolene stared at her. "You should go in. They're landing all over you."

Sarah trembled. "I'm okay."

"Yes, you are, aren't you?" Jolene whispered.

Sarah moaned as the cicadas flew around her head. "They're so loud."

"I told you they tickle, right?"

Sarah closed her eyes when one buzzed close to her ear. "Yeah. Sure. Tickle. I'm not sure tickle is an adequate enough word."

"We keep coming up with these inadequate words." Jolene chuckled, and examined her ankle.

Kneeling beside her, covered in cicadas, pride began to build. "I'm doing this. Do you understand how big this is for me?"

"We could sit here for a while longer and enjoy the buzz."

Sarah scrunched her shoulders when they began to swarm near her ears again. "Or, we could *not*."

"Stay still and breathe," she said, her voice unfurling on a melodic beat.

Sarah imagined herself covered and released a soft cry.

"Look at me." Jolene lifted Sarah's chin. "You've lasted at least forty seconds, and you're still okay. They haven't eaten you."

Sarah sighed, comforted by the woman's switch from cocky jokester to nurturer.

"In fact, they're probably discussing what a great landing pad you are." Jolene released her finger from under Sarah's chin then pushed off the ground to her feet. "Your life for the next month just got a whole lot easier. No more clinging to your steering wheel."

Sarah offered her arm as leverage. Jolene leaned into her, bearing little weight on her hurt ankle. "They've probably settled a colony in my hair by now," Sarah said.

Jolene glanced at her hair. "Your hair is glittery."

Sarah groaned.

"Too much?"

Sarah quickened her pace. "Yeah. I'd say. A little bit."

They shuffled to the door, and Sarah yanked it open. Once inside, the cicadas flicked around them. Their buzz echoed against the foyer's cathedral ceilings.

"Well, I'll be damned," Jolene said, living up to her promise and swiping the remaining cicadas from Sarah. "You survived."

"I did. I survived."

"If you can survive this, you can survive anything."

Sarah allowed that fact to infuse in her. "You were right about something."

Jolene cocked her head in wait.

"I'm empowered."

Jolene broke out into a huge smile. "Life's all about capturing those victories. We've got to get you in the water next."

"Let's get these cicadas out of my hair, and then we can chat about future victories."

Jolene put weight on her ankle and moved in closer to examine Sarah's hair. "You could handle scuba."

Sarah shed her helpless, fearless victim attitude. "Of course I could."

Sarah glanced around at the cicadas. Clumsily, they banged into each other and tangled in her hair. In a brave attempt, she unsecured the pins to her updo and let her thick hair fall over her shoulders. She raked her fingers through the curls and freed a few remaining cicadas. One landed in her hand and sat still. Braving even further, Sarah took a deep breath then stroked its back. It remained calm. A sense of giddiness rose in her as she caught its wings and helped it to the ground. A moment later it took flight.

Sarah glanced up at Jolene, flirting with the swelling of pride.

"Now, *that* was sexy," Jolene whispered.

Jolene's whisper sent a series of flutters through Sarah, flutters that sent her spinning way off course.

Chapter Four

Jolene could've escaped the party and run a race at that moment. But, no one needed to know that.

She had twisted her ankle, not sprained it. She could've limped to the entrance on her own. She could've climbed off the bar stool and joined Sarah in stomping her feet and swaying her hips to the beat of Michael Jackson's *Beat It,* had it not been for the fact she didn't like to dance. She avoided the center stage. She preferred observing in such situations, much to the chagrin of exes like Shannon. A person could learn a lot about life by taking a seat and actively watching it unfold.

Sarah had some captivating moves. She claimed the floor, circling around everyone and pulling them into her spontaneous twirls.

She aroused Jolene's interest. On one hand, she feared insignificant things, and on the other, she braved measurable ones. Maybe she gained her bravado by drinking? Uninhibited, the woman stealing partners on the floor did not equal the same woman pecking at ways to stay glued to her steering wheel.

Sarah's fear intrigued Jolene. She wore that fear like an invitation, beckoning someone to open it, analyze it, and smooth over its intensity with a feathery touch. Underneath that masked layer of fear lived someone dying to break free. The way she admired that lone cicada on her palm revealed a curious side and exposed Sarah's earnest desire to live on the edge of comfort.

As Jolene took a sip from her sangria, Frenchy plopped on the stool next to her. "Your mother has eaten the top of her cake by herself. I've turned her into a sugar addict. I bake her way too many treats."

"That's why she's so hyper." Jolene glanced her mother's way. She chatted with Uncle Johnny and Brad.

"Your mother tells me you're heading back soon."

"One more month." Jolene stole another glance at Sarah dancing to *The Twist* with a group of women.

"You remember Sarah?" Frenchy asked.

"I sure do."

"She's a nut." Frenchy squirmed in her dress. "God love her. She braved the cicadas."

"We met in the parking lot." Jolene waved to her ankle. "The result of getting her into this building for you."

Frenchy shook her head. "My God girl, what's it with you and hurt extremities? You're a magnet."

"I got a free night of sangria out of the deal." Jolene lifted her glass and sipped.

They both watched in delight as Sarah spun too fast and landed in the arms of Frenchy's and her mother's neighbor, Jack Hammond. "I think my mother is seeing Jack."

Frenchy put her hand up. "I know nothing other than he fell off the ladder while trying to fix your mother's broken shutter, and your mother made it up to him with large amounts of tea."

"I've seen him dart out of the back door a few times. Why doesn't she tell me about him?"

"Your mother still hasn't gotten over your father's death. I'm sure she's afraid to admit she's got feelings for someone else."

Her mother adored her father. "She quit smoking two weeks ago, so maybe he's going to be good for her," Jolene said.

"I know. Believe me I know. I realize it's best for her. Though, I have to tell you, I'm going to miss my Monday and Wednesday night cigarettes with her."

"You could always buy your own."

"It's not the same. In addition to smoking, I get to help her brainstorm her stories and characters." Frenchy dropped her head then lifted it a moment later. "And also, I always feel youthful when I'm around your mother. I'm the younger one with her, a whole thirteen years younger. I'm more than ten to fifteen years older than most of my other friends. You and Sarah are babies compared to me."

"Your friendships are diverse. That's good. Gives you a nice, wide perspective."

They sat and stared out at the dance floor. Surrounded by a group of teens and little Tony, Sarah demonstrated how to gyrate her hips, swinging her now loose light amber hair around her shoulders. They laughed and goofed the move. Little Tony eventually mastered the sway and stole the show.

"Look at Sarah's smile," Frenchy smirked. "Such a happy façade, just like a beautiful quilt, filled with pretty colors, shapes, and sparkles. And beneath everything, she's got a plushy lining that protects her from her boss every time he blows demands her way."

"I'm glad she's having a good time, then. Sounds like she needs it."

"Sarah needs to have more fun. But don't tell her I said that." Frenchy scooped her lacy dress in her arms and stretched her small frame further on the stool. "I'm fried."

"You need a drink." Jolene waved to the bartender. "What do you want?"

"No." Frenchy unclipped a beaded hair accessory from the back of her bun. "No more for me." She tossed it on the bar. "Dressing up to renew my vows is like gearing up for scuba diving. Twenty million gadgets. Expensive too. This stupid clip cost me one hundred dollars."

Frenchy looked exhausted, like she'd been run over by life. Her wrinkles grew deeper around her eyes and her skin lacked that glow it used to have back before Uncle Johnny married her. "You look gorgeous."

Frenchy sighed. "How's it almost over already? So much planning."

Jolene glanced back over at Sarah. She tore up the dance floor, moving from one person to the next, laughing with each spin. She explored the space, arms open wide, taking in the full sensory effects of the beats, strobe lights, and the smiles of all around. She apparently loved attention, a trait foreign to Jolene. The pressure of always having to be on par to rile up a laugh or admiring glance had to be tiring.

Frenchy tapped Jolene's forearm. "Is she scuba material?"

They both stared out at Sarah. "I've seen her panic."

"She won't panic. We've been snorkeling before."

"It's a little different."

Frenchy nudged her. "Is she your type?"

Jolene placed her drink down. "Did my mother insist that you to ask me that?"

With a twisted smile, Frenchy said, "She's grasping at anything to get you to stay. Humor me with an answer."

"I'm not in the market for a new girlfriend." Though Jolene's curiosity piqued. "Is she?"

She leaned forward. "Sarah doesn't have time. She works like twenty hours a day. I told your mother this, but she asked that I at least inquire." Frenchy played with her beaded hair clip. "Your mother's going to miss you. That's all."

Jolene continued to watch Sarah. "I saw her with a guy at your wedding."

"That was ten years ago." Frenchy rubbed her forehead and yawned. "She's a lesbian if that's what you're trying to ask me."

Jolene turned her head away to show disinterest.

"Let's take your mother and dating life out of this equation for a minute." Jolene arched her eyebrow.

"Sarah needs something," Frenchy said. "And you know the universe sets everything up in our favor. It's no coincidence that you're stuck here with your mother for another month and my best friend needs an outlet other than work."

"She's smiling," Jolene said. "She can't be that miserable with life." Sarah worked her hips to a salsa song. "I mean look at her."

"She needs her window cracked. She needs to let in some fresh air before she suffocates in the breakdown lane. She's stuck and doesn't even know it." Frenchy sighed. "If we could find some way to get her to the shop so she could try scuba like I did, she'll eventually fall in love with the idea of doing something other than looking at reports and dealing with a bunch of old wads sitting around a conference table. I worry about her. She has no life outside of work. I can't even get her to come over for dinner anymore."

"Why would she come try scuba if she can't even accept a dinner invite?"

"Because I'm not as cute as you, nor am I offering a challenge that could excite her."

"This isn't something you can force. She's got to be the one to ask."

"What about a nudge?"

51

Frenchy dangled the idea in front of her. Jolene did love a good challenge. "What did you have in mind?"

"Well, thankfully I know my friend's taste in women." Frenchy arched her eyes, motioning behind her. "Do you see the woman over by the window behind me?"

Jolene looked past her and saw a flirty redhead, twirling a straw in her drink. "This has bad written all over it."

"She's going to be Sarah's ticket to experiencing her first scuba lesson. Once Sarah gets under that water, she'll see the world as it should be seen. It's a win-win for everyone. Sarah gets a little nudge so I can see more of this fun side of her again. You have a little pet project to keep you from strangling your mother. And, I don't have to hear your mother chew me out for not asking. Play along with me?"

Jolene regarded Frenchy, and an odd envy burned through her. Jolene never had such a caring friend. "I don't know how your mind works, but I'm assuming you know what you're doing."

"The redhead is perfect," Frenchy whispered. "She's super boring, and Sarah hates that. She watches the History Channel for the fun of it. She's into data and numbers, something Sarah already has to deal with every single day of her life. She would never want me to set her up with someone like that."

"Then, how will you?"

"I'm not going to. You're not going to let me. She's going to beg for you to save her."

"Is this another one of my mother's ideas?"

"Just play along. You're going to throw Sarah off-balance by reminding her about her scuba lesson. She'll be desperate to get out of the situation I'm going to place her in, so she'll play along."

52

"If she shows up to the invite, she'll get her scuba lesson. Otherwise, I'm not going to talk her into it. Scuba is something that a person wants to experience. It's do or die down there. You know that from the lesson I gave you recently."

"That's why she needs it. She needs something that'll zap her back to this woman in front of us who twirls and colors the room with her rainbow sprinkles." Frenchy wrestled with the tight lace around her waist. "This freaking dress is so itchy."

Jolene eyed the redhead again. "So, what's in it for me?"

"How about twenty bucks?"

Jolene laughed. "Twenty whether she agrees or not?"

"No. She has to say yes."

"Fifty, then."

"Fifty? After everything I've done for your mom?"

Jolene liked Frenchy. She got to know her better during her visit. She'd miss her once she went back to Bonaire. Jolene extended her hand. "Do we have a deal?"

Frenchy accepted her shake. "Fine."

Just then, a flush-faced Sarah approached. "How's the ankle?"

Jolene rubbed it. "I'll be ready to graduate to walking on it without a hobble soon."

Sarah placed her gentle hand on Jolene's arm and squeezed. "Yay. Congrats!" Her smiling eyes lifted her sun-kissed cheeks. Poor woman had no idea what kind of fun they were about to have with her.

Frenchy waved at the redhead. "I want to introduce you to Briana. I'm going to invite her over. Be right back." She slipped off the stool, grabbed her dress, and hurried away.

"She wants to set you up," Jolene whispered to Sarah.

A slight moan, slow and revealing, escaped from Sarah as she considered that news. "She's not my type."

"Are you into men? Is that why?"

Sarah blushed. "I'm not into men."

Jolene couldn't stop the smile from taking over her face. "Frenchy says she's perfect for you."

Sarah twisted her smile. "She can be a little pushy."

"Oh, I know. She's very insistent. She brought over a tray of tarts from her bakery yesterday and made me eat them."

"All in one sitting?"

"Every single last bite."

Sarah stared at her lips, and that stirred something fun and flirty inside of Jolene.

The edges of the unstated furled in on itself and brought them into an intimate mutuality. Then, Sarah glanced over at Frenchy and Briana who sauntered their way. "God help me."

"I'm wondering something," Jolene whispered over Sarah's shoulder.

Sarah turned back to her, pulling her into an intense gaze. "What's that?"

"If you want my help with this or not?"

There went that smile again, stretching clear across Sarah's dewy skin. "I'm not going to argue. I could use the help."

"I've got an idea. Play along with me?"

Sarah nodded then circled her gaze around Jolene's face. "Feel free to avoid injury this time."

Frenchy and Briana approached.

"I told Briana about how you're into marketing, and I learned that she is, too." Frenchy raised an eyebrow. "What're the chances?"

"What're the chances," Sarah said back to Frenchy.

"Do you enjoy digital, print, or strategic marketing?" Briana asked, cocking her head.

Sarah flicked Jolene a desperate look. "Sort of all, I guess."

Jolene leaned in towards Sarah, once again enjoying the opportunity to help her. "So, we're on for tomorrow at the pool?"

"Uh, yes," Sarah moved closer.

Jolene considered the entertaining glow surfacing on Sarah's face, and then she turned to Frenchy. "We've got a date tomorrow. I'm going to teach her how to scuba dive." Jolene reached out to pat Sarah's arm, and a twinkle landed in the green of her eyes.

"A date?" Frenchy cocked her head in the greatest display of theatrics Jolene had ever seen.

"Yes, a date," Sarah played along, linking her arm in Jolene's.

Jolene's pulse quickened against the crook of Sarah's elbow.

"Good thing your ankle is better," Frenchy said.

"It just needed a small rest."

Frenchy eyed them both, pouring on the thick layer of fake surprise. "Well, I certainly didn't see this coming." Frenchy turned to Briana. "Come with me. I need help finding my husband. He might be out back smoking cigars with some of my staff from the bakery."

"I could use a cigarette anyway," Briana said.

Frenchy glanced back at them and rolled her eyes, and then she took off with Briana across the dance floor and towards the back door.

"Thank you." Sarah unlinked her arm from Jolene's.

"The offer's still on the table. Do you want to try out scuba in the pool?"

Sarah fidgeted with her fingers, surveying the safety of the dance floor. "Tomorrow you say?"

"Say yes." The words rushed out before Jolene could stop them.

Sarah twirled a lock of her hair, and gazed at Jolene with playful eyes. "I suppose one little try might be alright."

"You're brave enough to pet a cicada. Scuba's nothing."

"You're right," Sarah said, winking at her.

That wink caused Jolene to blush. "You're on a roll now. Why stop, right?"

"Right." Sarah looked out to the dance floor again, sporting a grin. Finally, she glanced back at Jolene. "Okay," she said, "you've got yourself a date."

A date.

"Looking forward to it."

"Me too." Sarah turned to walk away then stopped. "This is an indoor pool, right? So, no cicadas?"

Jolene laughed. "Oh, this is going to be fun."

"Hey, the parking lot is one thing." Sarah moved closer to her again. "But, scuba equipment in a body of water that could kill me if I freak out is totally different."

Jolene continued to gaze at her. A palpable intensity balled between them, triggering something deep within Jolene to stir, further entertaining her.

"Honey, are you ready to go yet?" Jolene's mother tapped her shoulder.

Her mother's voice cooled the heat pooling between her legs. "Yes," Jolene said, lifting off the stool and landing on her one good ankle.

"So tomorrow?" Sarah asked.

"Absolutely."

"Indoor pool, right?"

"You'll see." Jolene winked.

"Oh, are you taking a scuba lesson?" her mother asked.

"Apparently, I am." Sarah said with a buzz.

"She's a great instructor. You're going to love her."

Jolene cringed. "Mom, why don't you and Brad meet me at the car."

"I'll wait. Pretend I'm not even here. Brad and I aren't speaking."

Oh, for goodness' sake.

"So it's been fun," Jolene continued.

"What about tomorrow? Where and when?" Sarah asked.

"Yeah, I guess you'd need to know those things." She sought out the bartender with a wave. "Can I have a napkin and a pen?"

A moment later, he pushed them towards her. "Here's the address and my cell," she said as she scribbled it. Then, she handed it to Sarah.

"What time?"

"Ten a.m.," Jolene said.

"Ten?" Sarah laughed. "I've just had three martinis. Let's do one?"

"Eleven."

"Twelve?" Sarah asked.

"Eleven-fifteen."

"Eleven-thirty, and I'll bring coffees."

Jolene smiled. She was a sucker for a woman who enjoyed a good challenge. And, hell, she made fifty bucks to boot!

Chapter Five

The sound of cicadas woke Sarah, filling her bedroom with an agitated buzz. She lounged in bed and stared at her swirled plaster ceiling, drawing in an uneasy breath before jumping to her feet.

She reached for her cell and steadied for her escape plan. She'd call Jolene and tell her she had made a mistake in scheduling the scuba session and that she was very sorry. Truly sorry. She'd explain the kind of crazy, warped life she led, and thank her again for her time and help.

She placed her finger on her cell keypad, letting it linger as she replayed the excuse. Maybe texting would be better. Less awkward. She could take her time composing it instead of stumbling over the right words in a real-time phone call. She hated talking on the phone anyway. At least with a text, she could cushion her word choice with cute emoticons.

She needed to think more. So, she opened her stride and headed towards her closet. She tore her T-shirts out of her drawer and began refolding them, an action that helped her think.

She should cancel. She really should.

She folded the sleeves to her Nike shirt inward and over the swoosh symbol.

Canceling would be best. She had that meeting with Nordstrom's scheduled for the following morning. She still needed to prep for it. She reserved Sundays to get ahead on things. She couldn't afford to waste her time on something so frivolous.

Scuba diving of all things.

She placed the folded T-shirt back in the drawer.

If she went, she'd have to get into the pool, which meant she'd need a bathing suit. Did she even have one still? She hadn't been swimming in years.

She probably didn't have one.

So, problem solved.

Clearly the universe knew what strings to pull and what moves to put into play.

Settled, she went back into her bedroom and grabbed her cell.

She needed music. Good, funky music that would get her blood flowing. She opened her Sonos app and turned on Bachata.

She moved to the beat, reflecting back to the night before when she caught Jolene gazing at her on the dance floor. The slight tilt of her head and curious angle of her eyes intoxicated Sarah. She moved her hips in sync with the rhythm, reliving that sensual memory and escaping into its sultry tease. Sarah placed her hands on her hips and moved them with a provocative swing, enjoying the surge of desire for Jolene that began flowing between her legs.

She liked Jolene. She was a prism, simple and pleasing to the eye, yet mesmerizing in her complexity, depending which way the light hit her. Beneath the visible color, radiated a palpable mystery, one that eased her into a subtlety and raised her into boldness by the simple blink of her lashes and the angle of her smile. She wanted to move past the visible, and uncover what brewed underneath all that.

Suddenly, her cell rang.

Frenchy.

"Are you checking up on me?"

"You did drink a few martinis," she said.

"I'm good." *Really good.*

"Maureen told me you're meeting Jolene this afternoon."

"I might cancel."

"What? No. You can't cancel."

"I was drunk when I agreed. I made myself sound like a world-class snorkeler to her, and you and I both know I almost drowned trying."

"She needs this."

"Jolene needs me to learn scuba?"

"Maureen told me she's bored. If she's bored, she'll leave. If she leaves, Maureen will drive me bonkers."

"That's not my problem. My problem is I've got a huge meeting tomorrow and I'm not prepared, yet."

"Do this for me, please?"

Sarah turned the Bachata music down. "You're going to owe me. You're going to owe me a carrot cake, at the very least, and not the skimpy personal size. I want the three layer."

"You got it. I'm good for it. This little scuba date is expensive for me, but well worth it."

"Expensive?"

Faint puffs of air filled in the silence.

"What do you mean by that?"

"Okay, look. I'll be honest with you."

"About?"

"I might've made a teeny tiny bet with Jolene."

Frenchy could never let things evolve on their own. She always had to meddle. "I'm canceling."

"No," she said. "No, you can't. She's looking forward to it. God, I should never have said anything."

"You're always forcing things. Stop forcing."

"It's not forced. Honestly. She's excited."

Sarah stomped over to her kitchen and poured herself some water. "Tell me more about this bet."

"I bet her that if you agreed to try scuba, I'd pay her fifty bucks."

"Why?" Sarah slammed her cup against the counter. "What possessed you to do such a thing?"

"Because you're stressed. You're so stressed. I can't stand to see you this way. You used to be silly. Remember when we were silly together?"

"I'm silly. I laugh. I still joke. I'm fun. Jolene told me I'm fun." Sarah swallowed a bitter hurt. "I'm fun."

"Please promise me you'll go?"

"I'm not promising anything. I'll go if I want to go. I'm not sure I want to go now, though. Maybe I want to be serious today. Maybe I like being serious Sarah. What's wrong with that?"

"I hurt you. Oh God, I hurt you," Frenchy whined.

"I have to go."

Sarah hung up and Frenchy called her right back. She glared at the call without answering it. *I can be fun.*

She scoffed and headed back to her closet to check for that bathing suit.

Sarah yanked her summer storage chest out from under her back shelf. She began flinging shirts, shorts, dresses, sandals, and hats to the side, and then she landed her eyes on her multi-colored tankini at the bottom next to a pair of jean shorts that would not be seeing the light of day ever again.

She picked it up with one finger, staring at its tininess. She would never fit into it. She'd grown at least two sizes since last wearing it. Fun Sarah would've fit into it. *Fun Sarah* no longer existed, though.

With her answer cemented, she picked up her cell and drafted a text. "Hey, it's Sarah. I'm so sorry to have to cancel today but it's been a crazy busy week at work." She paused, rethinking her words.

Crazy could never begin to explain her busy weeks. Lame excuse, anyway. "Work is so much better than spending time doing something new and exciting. I'd rather be boring and serious. So thanks, but no thanks." She reread her words and cringed at their truth then deleted the text.

When had she turned into that woman who got too serious and forgot how to be fun? Her father had worn that hat in the family. *Oh, sorry kids, I have a case to prepare. No time for strolls in the park or whiffle ball today. Maybe in ten years, eh?*

Maybe Frenchy had a point. She was a workaholic. She lived to work.

Without work, who was she?

Could she ever be like Frenchy, running off the beaten path to find unpredictable fun things? Frenchy lived in the land of impulsiveness. She moved her furniture around in her house every month to avoid boredom.

Sarah headed into her living room and glanced at the leg of her couch. It created a permanent groove. She'd never considered moving it or her recliner. Maybe she should? Maybe she should place her recliner near the window then nestle her bookshelf against the dining room wall.

That recliner got on her nerves. It sat like a silent passenger on a tedious and probable journey through the cycle of seasons.

She pushed the recliner, but it wouldn't budge. Its legs remained rooted in their deep grooves, too. She gripped the arm with one hand and lunged her body against it, and it finally shifted. She grunted and pushed some more, enjoying the tickle of empowerment.

Maybe she needed nothing more than that, a quick rearrangement to get the fun vibes flowing again.

She had become pretty stagnant.

When she rose in the mornings, she knew what she'd do with her days. She'd eat her two-egg omelet with melted organic cheddar cheese sided with a glass of kefir milk and her probiotic and vitamin D supplements. She'd shower to her Pandora Jason Mraz channel, humming along as she washed each body part in the exact same order. She'd head out the door by six a.m. to start her hour and a half commute down to D.C. She knew that by the exit for Interstate 495, traffic would snarl, at which point she'd start listening to country songs. She had memorized most every song 93.1 played.

Hell. No wonder she wasn't fun.

She dragged her recliner all the way over to the window and sat in it, taking in the new view. She spotted a pack of cicadas on the trunk of her maple tree. They'd last a month and die. One month. No more than that. Poor little buggers.

What if she only had one month left to live? What would she do with it? Would she sit at work and worry about reports or do something wild and crazy like wear a bathing suit two sizes too small into a pool with Jolene?

Yesterday, she buzzed to life, gliding across the world and viewing it through a new lens. Through that new view, the trees dwarfed, not looking as tall and mighty as they did from her everyday view.

And now, staring out the front window of her house, the sun danced livelier, flickering its rays and creating a surge within her. The spring breeze smelled fresher through her cracked windows, bringing to her the aromas of pine trees and morning dew. Even the high decibel rattle of cicadas rang prettier, creating a distinct pulse that pulled Sarah from a dormancy she clung to without realizing.

She rose, paced over to her mirror and felt a spark ignite in her. She wanted to live out loud. She wanted to grab hold of the opportunity and run with it.

She did need a bathing suit, though. What kind of marketing executive in the world of fashion didn't own a bathing suit? One who worked too hard and forfeited vacations for business dealings. That's who.

She rushed towards her closet again, and grabbed the suit. She examined it and cringed once more. How would she squeeze her thighs into the Lycra? She wouldn't even try. She passed a size six two summers ago. That's what a busy corporate job did to a woman. Made her gain ten pounds and drink five cups of coffee a day to keep up the progress. No time for relaxing, healthy lunches, or for that matter dinners, anymore. Dinner turned into takeout while watching the ten o'clock news.

She was thirty-five, and the wear and tear already set in. So, maybe she could benefit from jumping into a pool with an attractive stranger and breathing out of an air tank.

Who knew, maybe Jolene needed to hit her car. Maybe the cicadas emerged at the right time so she'd end up braving all to help Jolene off the front walk to The Chesapeake House. Maybe her thighs needed to expand as they did so she would have to run out and buy a new suit. Maybe the universe needed her to listen better, and decided to whack her all at once with all those hints to have some fun and to help her overcome certain fears like dodging thumb-sized insects in a single dash, leaping into the deep end of a pool, and spending time with a woman who made her tummy flip.

Before tackling fun, she needed to get a bathing suit.

The mall wouldn't be open until eleven, and by then she'd risk being late. No way could she select a bathing suit in a mall in such a small lot of time. Only Frenchy could do that. Frenchy only had to glance in the window of a store to find her gems. Things came so easy to that woman. She should've been the marketing executive in the fashion industry instead.

Sarah paced her spare bedroom trying to decide her options. Show up without a bathing suit and possibly risk not being able to face another one of her deep fears or bite the bullet, jump in her car and drive to the twenty-four-hour Walmart?

Fifteen minutes later, still in her yoga pants with the hole in the bottom seam and her Ocean City hoodie, she pulled into a parking space at Walmart. They had bathing suits.

They also had cicadas.

Lots of cicadas.

She faced the little buggers, and dashed across the parking lot to the entrance. She had only an hour to find a suit that would hide years of forgoing squats and lunges in lieu of climbing her way up the ladder to a respectable rung at the office.

Sarah searched the signs for the clothing department. She passed the arts and crafts section, the sporting goods aisles, and the furniture. The last time she shopped for a bathing suit, she bought one for her and Frenchy's cruise to the Virgin Islands. On that trip, Sarah almost drowned in waist-deep water when she attempted to snorkel. The mask didn't fit her properly, so she tripped over Frenchy's leg. She was pulled under and became disoriented. The mask ruined that experience, not her.

Sarah trekked down the aisles, and finally came across the clothing section. Sequined shirts dangled from hangers without care. Sweatpants in every color imaginable sat underneath them. She glanced around in search of bathing suits and spotted tan bras with itchy looking seams instead. Everything went against the grain of order.

Sarah hated having no plan.

She had to plan. She had to focus. She needed direction. Without a plan, she wandered. Under the bright lights of the women's section at Walmart, pushing her blue cart around, banging into racks, Sarah lost focus and wandered. She ended up in front of the McDonald's counter and ordered a hash brown.

Minutes later, she came across two racks of bathing suits, strewn together like a community afghan project with no rhyme or reason to size or style. Size sixteens hung near size sixes. One-pieces dangled next to string bikinis.

Overwhelmed, Sarah fingered through the suits.

She'd never find the right suit in time. Maybe the universe didn't want her to. Maybe the universe wanted to lead her away from that rack of ugly cheap bathing suits, back to her car, and into her ergonomic office chair. Maybe those nervous flutters served a purpose, urging her not to flirt with such distractions.

Maybe she was supposed to go on that date with Briana and discuss print versus digital, and not dive into a pool, God only knew if indoor or outdoor, at some scuba shop with some woman who empowered her to do crazy things like play with cicadas in the palm of her hand and agree on a flirt to jump into water while breathing fake air.

Oh hell.

She needed to find a suit, and find one fast.

In one bold, and foolish, move, she picked up a bathing suit in her size and fled to the register, forgoing the typical inner debate and lengthy analyzation process, and taking the damn leap off the tracks of the comfort zone and onto the unpaved road of the unknown.

Watch out world, I'm diving in.

~ ~

After having arranged the tanks, fins, regulators, and BCDs on the poolside, Jolene stood next to Roxie, the shop's Rottweiler, and watched the traffic pass, anxious for Sarah to pull up and get the initial hellos out of their systems.

She kneeled and kissed the top of Roxie's head. "A date. I called it a date. How do I get myself into these silly things?"

Roxie stared up into her eyes.

"It's too late to cancel, I know. Maybe when she arrives I can tell her something's come up and I have to leave town earlier than expected, like on a flight tonight."

Roxie didn't blink.

Jolene sighed. "Fine. A commitment is a commitment." Jolene put her arm around Roxie's shoulder. "I just want to get this over with."

Jolene caught the sound of a car pulling up to the building. Her heart did that stupid thing it always did whenever she contemplated cliff jumping or skydiving. She got up, folded her arms across her chest, and waited for Sarah to enter so they could get the scuba trial lesson started.

~ ~

Sarah sat before the scuba shop. The display window showcased a mannequin wearing scuba gear and right behind it she spotted Jolene. Then, the cicadas began their assault on her windshield, landing on it and mocking her with their big, beady red eyes.

Jolene opened the door and waved her in. "Are we going through this again?"

Sarah paused and watched a whimsical grin take over Jolene's face. She drew a sharp breath. *No. No, we're not going through this again. I'm brave. I'm unstoppable. I'm fun, dammit.*

Sarah reached for the door handle and yanked it, flinging the door open. She would capture another one of those victories, even if it killed her. Sarah grabbed her tote bag with her new ugly bathing suit, and sprinted to the open door. She landed inside the shop on a detained breath.

She took a quick look around. Every square inch presented itself with some piece of equipment, accessory, or clothing. Air tanks, compasses, hoses, and gadgets hung from display racks around the center of the shop. To the far left hung diving vests, wetsuits, masks, fins, and diving boots. To the far right, travel bags and bathing suits draped from hooks against the wall. And where she stood, a wide path opened to the checkout counter. To her immediate right, in front of the large display window, sat an adorable, well-behaved Rottweiler. The dog glanced up at Sarah, sniffed the air then lowered her head against the quilted mat.

"You've got a cicada taking a ride on your back," Jolene said.

Sarah shook herself. Really shook herself. A full out, bent over, shake. She tore out her ponytail and batted her hair, combing through it with terror-induced frenzy.

"I was kidding."

Sarah stopped beating herself up and lifted her head.

Jolene looked at her with wide brown eyes, her long lashes accentuating the smile in them.

She straightened, picking up her tote bag from the floor and slinging it back over her shoulder. "Where did you put the sweet person from last night?"

Jolene smiled and tilted her head, scanning Sarah's face. "You look a little green."

The hash brown from the McDonald's at Walmart crawled up the back of her throat. "That's just the lighting in here." Sarah glanced at the track lighting. "It shouldn't be pointing in that direction. It should be focusing on the merchandise. Like on that mannequin's nose, which is very pointy, by the way. Nobody has a nose like that. It should be more realistic, pudgier. Wouldn't you agree?" She twisted around and looked at Jolene, noticing for the first time the set of small freckles dotting her cheeks.

Jolene stared at her for a long moment, as if considering her question. "I happen to like the color green and pointy noses." Then, she turned and headed over to the shiny black dog. The dog gazed up at Jolene with adoration as she approached.

Sarah followed her. "Is this your dog?"

Jolene shook her head. "No. My friend Gerry's. I'm the babysitter. He's out at the quarry certifying some students this weekend. This is Roxie."

Focusing on Jolene's long dark ponytail, she bent to pet Roxie's scruff. "You have matching hair."

Jolene paused her petting. "I'll take that as a compliment."

"I'll take my green hue as a compliment."

They studied each other, and then Jolene shifted up. "What do you say we get started?"

Sarah stared off into the haze of the late morning sunrays beaming off the hood of her car, and wondered, just for a brief moment, if she should bolt. She shook off the thought. "Okay, let's do this," she whispered.

Jolene relaxed her shoulders, letting her hand fall from the top of Roxie's head. "You don't have to do this if you're uncomfortable."

Sarah's heart shifted, causing her to buckle at the knees as the first hint of unease attempted to spread its oily slick at her feet. "I'm here to do this."

"I want to make sure I didn't veer over the edge too far last night and force you."

"Because you crafted a bet with Frenchy?"

Leaning back on her heels, Jolene pushed herself up from Roxie. "That woman cannot keep anything to herself."

"So just fifty dollars? That's all I'm worth?"

Jolene stooped to pick up a gadget from the floor. She placed it back on a rack. "That's still to be determined." Jolene walked towards the glass counter again, leaving a delightful cottony scent in her wake. "We should get started if we're going to do this. Did you bring a swimsuit?"

Sarah took a quick scan of the rugged bathing suits hanging from the side wall. Suddenly, visions of the flowery, cheap fabric clinging to her belly startled her. Going against the grain of her organized nature, she blurted, "No. I didn't bring one. It's somewhat early in the season still. I haven't even unpacked my summer clothes yet."

Jolene motioned to a door behind them. "No worries. I have some spare wetsuits in the classroom back there. You can suit up and head back to the pool when you're ready."

Sarah's knees weakened as she followed her around the counter and to the door.

Jolene glanced at her tote bag. "I can take that for you and put it behind the counter, if you want."

Sarah clung to it. "No. No, not necessary. It's, uh, it's just my uh, towel." Sarah swallowed hard.

"Towel?"

"Um, yeah. I had plenty of towels ready to go. Not a bathing suit, though."

"Right." Jolene regarded her through playful eyes. Jolene opened the door to a classroom filled with long tables, tanks, hoses, and many other complicated gadgets. "The suits are on that rack over by the dry-erase board."

Sarah entered. A stale aridity hung in the air. "I'll just be a minute."

Alone in the classroom, Sarah reprimanded herself for worming into the situation. She searched the wetsuits for a suitable size. A moment later, she threaded herself into the thick suit, tripping over her feet and falling into a folding chair. *Fuck. Dammit. What the hell?*

"Everything good in there?" Jolene asked.

Sarah composed herself. "Yeah, fine."

A few minutes later, Sarah emerged with a smile. "Let's do this."

Jolene slanted a gaze down Sarah. "You've got it on backwards."

"Excuse me?" Sarah could taste the acridity on her tongue.

Jolene raised her thin eyebrows. "Zipper should be in the back."

"Right." Sarah reached back for the door handle. "Be just a second."

Sarah struggled to climb out of the suit, yanking the thick material inside out. Within a minute she managed to climb back into the grip of it, pulling on the zipper string and closing herself in. She emerged on a deep breath. "I'm ready."

Jolene led her down a long hallway and through a glass door into an indoor pool area.

"Nice," Sarah said on a relaxed breath.

Jolene moved between her and a set of tanks attached to vests. "No cicadas. Just scuba." She lifted one of the vested tanks and placed it into the water.

Bracing for the impact of uncertainty, Sarah dove into rambling mode. "I bet Frenchy can't wait to hear how I did. I still can't believe she put you up to this. You know she's always complaining that I work too hard. I do work hard. In fact, I shouldn't even be here. I have a huge meeting in the morning. I haven't even looked over the material for it. I have no business being here. I'm sure you have better things to do, too. Frenchy doesn't understand this. She's always moving pieces like everyone is part of a jigsaw puzzle, compelling her to put us together."

Sarah watched as Jolene placed the other vested tank in the pool. They floated like drowned victims.

"She cares about you. You're lucky to have someone who watches out for you," Jolene said.

Sarah suddenly wanted to stick her head inside the thick wetsuit and hide from her ugly selfish words. She chose to face them. "You're right. I'm grateful for her. I am. She's a true friend. The best. I mean, she'd run into a burning building for me. She would. She's selfless like that."

"You're stalling again."

Sarah leveled her breaths. The room began to shrink. The salty humidity stung her eyes. Her heart began to race. The wetsuit suddenly tightened, like a giant tourniquet cutting off the oxygen and blood supply to her brain. "We should have Frenchy here with us. She shouldn't miss this. We don't have to do this today."

"She wants you to do this." Jolene approached her and handed her a set of fins and a mask. "It's normal to be nervous. I won't let anything happen to you. I promise," she whispered. "Are you ready to do this?"

73

Sarah giggled.

"Should I take that as a yes?"

Her giggle amplified louder, much to her dismay. She tried to block it, which resulted in a fit of coughing, and then more giggles bubbled up and spilled out. "I'm sorry. I can't help it. I giggle when I get nervous. It comes out of nowhere, like a freak downpour." The ripples grew from deep in her belly and charged through her like a torrential storm, pounding their way up and out of her mouth.

"Are you going to laugh like this underwater?" Jolene asked with a slight serious tone.

Sarah's giggles only intensified then grew into an all-out laugh, the kind that bent her over in stomach cramps. Each time she glanced up at Jolene's serious face, the giggles exploded. "I'm sorry," Sarah swallowed her laughter. "I won't. I promise." Another swell rose and drove through her. *Picture something awful. Picture traffic. Yes, traffic. Terrible snarled traffic and horns honking. Road rage. Middle fingers flying upwards. Mean people cursing at you. Yeah. That's right. Nothing to laugh about with traffic.*

Sarah rose. "I'm good." She pursed her lips together. "Giggles are gone."

Jolene headed to the pool steps. "I've seen people pee themselves, throw up, flee the dock, but never break out into hysterical laughter." She lowered onto the first step. "I've seen it all now."

"I'm not nervous. I'm excited." Sarah headed to the pool, wanting to put an end to the smug look on Jolene's face. She dipped her toes into the pool. "I'm ready," she whispered.

Jolene sank into the pool, pushing her arms backwards and moving away from the steps.

Sarah sat on the top step and placed her fins on. Then, she dipped her finned feet further into the warm, salty pool, clinging to the steamy hot railing for dear life. Every nerve in her body revolted against her impulsive decision to voluntarily sink out of comfort and breathe air from a regulator. *This is fun. So, so fun. Take a breath. Breathe for crying out loud. Open your mouth and draw in the air while you can, you big scared baby. Get in. Get wet. Just whatever you do, stay alive. You have a big meeting in the morning.*

"You're going to need to let go of that railing so I can get you geared up." Jolene stood in the shallow water and lifted a vest, motioning for Sarah to loop her arms through it.

This is fun. Fun people do things like this. They blow off work and free-fall into the arms of impulsivity.

Her heart galloped. She staggered down the three steps and into the shallow end of the pool and towards Jolene.

Sarah clung to her mask, tightening her finger around its rubber straps as she pushed through the water. Her teeth chattered. *I'm going to let Frenchy have it for this. I'm going to march up to her at the bakery and smear dough all over her face. Then, I'm going to smash eggs on top of her head and watch them seep through her hair.*

"Are you ready?"

Sarah swallowed, drawing a shaky breath. She pushed forward and her right fin folded against the bottom of the pool causing her to stumble. She fell and slapped the water for balance. She flailed around like a blubbery whale. Then, her mask fell and floated away from her. She reached out and tried to grab it, but then her darn fin folded again. The more she tried to stand up straight, the more off-balance she became.

Jolene grabbed Sarah's mask and hand then eased her up. "It's easier to walk backwards or sideways with fins."

"I'll remember that." She tried to smile, but her teeth rattled too much.

"Turn your back to me and slip your arm right here in the hole of the vest."

Sarah wheeled around and backed into her. She managed to stick both arms through their respective sleeves without falling face-first into the water again. The vest and tank weighed her down.

"Lower yourself in the water. It'll take the load of the equipment off you."

Jolene squirted gel on her mask lens and rubbed it with her slender finger. Then, she dunked the mask into the water. "Anti-fog." She handed it back to Sarah. "That'll keep everything nice and clear so you can see what's happening in the underwater world."

The underwater world. *Oh hell.*

Jolene caressed her wrists, and spoke slowly. "Are you sure you want to do this?"

Sarah could only nod. If she tried to talk at that moment, she might've chipped a tooth.

"You look terrified."

Sarah shivered. "I'm just cold."

"The water is eighty degrees."

"Weren't you nervous the first time?"

"No."

"No? Really? No? How's that possible?"

Jolene let go of Sarah's wrists and put on her vest. "You have to discover that for yourself."

"I have to do this," Sarah stated. "I'm going to do this. I've got my vest, fins, and mask."

"You're committed."

"I am."

"You also still look very green."

"I feel green," Sarah said.

"We can climb out of the pool, right now. Put one fin behind the other and get back to the landing."

"Back to safety," Sarah stated.

"Back to safety."

"I'm too safe," Sarah declared. "I refuse to be safe another moment. I'm not leaving here until I've taken the plunge and got my blood pumping."

"Let's get your blood pumping then."

Their breaths mingled in the steam. "That's why I'm here. To get my blood pumping."

"To feel alive."

"Yes. I want another chance to feel alive like I did yesterday."

"You buzzed. I could tell."

"My whole body buzzed," Sarah admitted.

"Now, let's expand your mind."

Jolene instructed her on how to breathe using the regulator. She demonstrated, sticking it in her mouth and sucking in the air. Her breath sounded garbled, wrestling to free itself from the constraints of such pressurized force, yet her eyes smiled.

"Okay," Jolene lifted the regulator to Sarah's lips. "You need to put that in your mouth."

She placed it in her mouth and bit down. Drawing a breath, she let it swirl a bit and exhaled.

She did that five times without a problem.

"So, I go under, breathe, and come back up when I'm ready?"

"That's it. Easy as that. Kneel and try."

Jolene secured her mask over her delicate nose, stuck her regulator in between her lips, and sank below the water.

Sarah stood in three feet of water, trembling like a big idiot. *Get your game on.* She stuck the regulator back in her mouth and kneeled. She lowered her head into the water and took a breath. She gulped, and then she panicked while fighting her way back to the surface.

Jolene rose. "Take it slow."

She exhaled and tried to breathe with the regulator again, above the water. "Breathe normal."

Normal? By breathing fake air out of a tank?

On her third normal breath, she submerged and opened her eyes. She could see. Sort of. She could see cloudy water and Jolene watching her. She drew some air then exhaled an even flow as instructed. With each breath, her heart beat faster. Her breath flowed, even underwater. The deeper she drew air, the more her lungs filled. They overinflated. Her chest expanded far too fast and her breaths cut far too short.

The cloudy water closed in around her.

I need real air!

She shot out of the water in a panic, tearing that regulator out of her mouth and gasping.

Jolene surfaced again. "What happened?"

"This is crazy."

Jolene gripped Sarah's arms. "You're in three feet of water. All you have to do is stand and you're safe. You're not going to drown. I swear my life on it."

"Right."

"You're uncomfortable, and that's normal. Stay kneeling and only put your face into the water. When you get comfortable, try to sink your whole body under."

She followed the instruction, and drew her tenth breath without a panic. She braved in deeper, until her whole body descended.

She imagined Jolene watching her, proud and eager for her to get in even deeper. She didn't want to disappoint. She hated to disappoint people. She would do it. She would do it for five minutes. She could do anything for five minutes. People have survived longer than that underwater without air. Haven't they?

She crawled her knees on the gritty pool floor, ignoring that part of her brain that told her to retreat back to the safety of the steps. She'd suffer with disappointment if she let fear take over. She waded in a freaking pool with a seasoned diver not more than two feet from her face. She would not choke on water. She would not die a brutal death. She would thrive and prove to Jolene that she could be fun and brave.

She floated around just under the surface of the water, low enough to be scuba diving. She inhaled and exhaled in steady beats, slow and intended, filling her lungs then emptying them. She spotted Jolene below her, looking up at her with her hands folded at her belly, a relaxed smile resting in her eyes. Her bubbles rose and tickled Sarah's cheeks.

With each exhalation, she sank, drawing closer to Jolene. Then, with each inhalation, she floated higher. Her breaths acted as a pulley system that lowered and raised her. Suddenly, Jolene floated by her side. She took her hand and led her to the deepest end of the pool. A piece of string floated past her, then another. She imagined them to be sea creatures.

She was scuba diving.

No matter what else happened in her life, she could now die with dignity knowing she looked fear in the face and said *no freaking way*. Those words echoed in the far reaches of her water-soaked mind as a small amount of water leaked into her mask, and her eyes fought off the sting of the salty pool water.

~ ~

Jolene hung by Sarah's side during her laps around the pool. She looked calm and in control, very different from the tense woman who walked into the shop just an hour earlier. She loved seeing someone go from panic mode to awe in those first ten minutes of breathing underwater. A magic unfolded under the water that transformed people, opening their eyes to the gift of the moment. A person couldn't multitask in that environment. When life depended on focus, life took front stage. Emails, phone calls, bills, and all of life's responsibilities halted, and the power of the water separated a person from that chaos.

Sarah began to ascend to the top of the deep end of the pool. A relaxed look spread across her face, revealing that her world had opened up to a completely new dimension of time and space.

When they emerged, Sarah stared at the water, shaking her head and blinking. "I didn't want to ascend, but my mask got some water in it."

"It's easy to clear the mask. We go over that and more in certification classes." Jolene swam over to the steps and took off her fins, placing them on the pool's edge.

"So my mask could fill at any time? Like if I'm in the middle of the ocean and one hundred feet down?" Suddenly, Sarah began to tense again. That look of panic sprung on her cheeks, causing them to flinch.

Scuba would be good for Sarah's anxious mind, if she allowed herself to overcome the jitters of death. "Yeah, but it's no big deal. You don't need to see to breathe. It's all about staying relaxed and cool under pressure. Once you are, then you can clear the mask."

"What if the mask is broken?"

Sarah would emerge a new woman if she let herself go and enjoy the freedom that water could provide. "You rely on your dive buddy to get you back. Simple."

Sarah began to shiver again.

Jolene could work with her. She could help transform her fears into empowerment. She had it in her. She saw that much for herself at the party. Sarah glowed after she discovered the beauty of the cicadas. Imagine how she'd glow after realizing the beauty of the sea? "Come on, let's get you out of the pool and dried off," Jolene extended her hand to help her.

Sarah straightened. "I loved it."

The crease in her forehead told a different story. The contradiction intrigued Jolene.

Once out of the water, Sarah dried her hair with a towel she plucked from the tiled floor.

"Oh, I used that to clean the drain this morning," Jolene said, yanking the towel from her hands.

Sarah stared at it, and that green tinge returned to her face. "No big deal."

Jolene enjoyed reading between her contradictions. "Why don't you go get dried off and I'll meet you up front?"

About ten minutes later, Sarah emerged from the dressing room dried and refreshed. She radiated. "I feel amazing." She charged towards the counter and tossed her tote bag on it then bent to pet Roxie.

Jolene noticed a colorful bathing suit spill out of the tote bag along with lip-gloss and a small hand mirror. She smiled, and pushed the items back into the bag before Sarah noticed.

When Sarah rose, her wet hair hung in springy corkscrews around her face. Her lashes appeared long and curvaceous, accentuating her green eyes.

Jolene let her gaze wander around the gentle slope of her nose and to her glossed lips, and delighted in the sudden rise tickling her, a tickle she shouldn't have been entertaining.

"So, what're you going to do with the fifty bucks?" Sarah ran her fingers through her hair, unaware of her sexy appeal.

Caught off guard, Jolene attempted recovery by adjusting Sarah's tote bag. "Likely a dive at the quarry. It'll take a dent out of the price of admission."

Sarah lifted her eyebrow. "Expensive sport, huh?"

"Not if you work in Bonaire as a dive master. Free diving every day. They pay for everything."

Sarah gazed into her eyes, as if trying to figure out the inner workings of her mind. "You really do enjoy living on an island?"

"Life moves at a slower pace on the island. People aren't rushing around or trying to impress others with their fancy cars and houses. It's a laid-back place where people go to have fun and relax."

Sarah studied her. "Sounds like an ideal life for a diver, I suppose."

"It's not for everyone."

"I'd probably go bonkers. I enjoy the hustle and bustle too much for that kind of life."

"It's too fast for me here. My heart races."

Suddenly, Sarah's phone rang. "I have to get this."

Jolene nodded, used to taking a second seat to people and their attachment to technology.

Sarah pressed her cell to her ear, and her forehead creased. "Are you sure?" Pause. "Did you look in the delete folder?" Another dramatic pause. "I'll call you back in a few minutes. We'll straighten this out." She sighed. "I have to go. Work needs me. Big problems. God only knows what's in store."

She cocked her head, looking more like she wanted to pull up a chair and have a long, thoughtful conversation about life and its meaning.

"Did you know the job would be this demanding when you took it?"

She shrugged. "I'm used to it. It pays the bills. Quite well. Sure, it's a tough schedule, but it's alright." The fullness of her dropped eyelids told a different tale.

"What do you do, exactly?"

"I'm in marketing. I work for an advertising agency that manages big retailer conglomerates, and I work a million hours a week. So, I enjoyed this small break. I work a lot. Like every day. Even most Sundays. I'm used to it. It goes with the territory. There's always something popping up that we didn't see coming. Yesterday a wrong headline in a full-page ad in *The New Yorker*, today it appears we've lost an entire month's worth of discovery on a client because we failed to back it up and someone accidentally deleted it."

She glanced at her cell again. "It's all good. Like I said, I'm used to it. I'm grateful. Truly. It's all good. Except for the commute. The commute sucks. I spend anywhere from three to six hours in the car every day, depending on traffic. But, hey," she said, swinging her hair over her shoulder, "I get to practice my singing. Though, I probably should start listening to books. I don't have much time to read anymore."

Sarah twisted her smile.

The woman needed some serious clutter weeded out of her life. With each sentence about work, her face pinched more. Jolene had never seen someone so wound up. And, she'd seen many people come to the island over the years, stressed to the max over their jobs, clinging to their cell phones in the middle of paradise, cursing because they couldn't get a signal. "Do you enjoy the work?"

Sarah looked to the sign behind Jolene, the one advertising the upcoming certification classes and group trips. "That's a good question." She leaned forward and squinted at the sign. "On some level." Sarah zeroed in on the certification class schedule.

"Scuba would be good for you," Jolene said.

"Three full days of training, huh?" Sarah's lips pursed.

"We've got a new class starting Wednesday night."

"I bet Frenchy would love to do this."

"She did. She wanted you to as well."

Sarah pushed her tote bag further up her shoulder. "She's done this?"

Frenchy, a natural, dove right under and found her buoyancy before Jolene could fetch her mask from the pool's edge and descend. "She wanted her and my Uncle Johnny to do something fun together."

"Johnny?" Sarah laughed. "Did he go under?"

"He didn't come."

Sarah furrowed her eyebrows. "Hmm. I'm surprised she didn't ask me."

"Sounds like you would've been too busy anyway."

Sarah's eyes widened.

"I'm sorry. I didn't mean that to sound as judging as it came out." Jolene looked away from her. "I just meant—"

"You're right," Sarah said. "I'm too busy. It's kind of ridiculous." She bit her lip. "Like I said, I shouldn't even be here right now. I have so much to do. But, you intrigued me last night. How could I say no?"

Jolene wouldn't read into that statement. "Frenchy will be pleased you didn't say no. This made her cheerful again."

"Cheerful again? She's always cheerful. Why wouldn't she be cheerful?" Sarah asked, swiping a piece of wet hair from her forehead and pushing it behind her ear.

Jolene blinked. "I suspect my uncle is to blame."

Sarah glanced around the shop, seeming to volley the news around in her head. "I had no idea." A sadness trailed her words. "I'm her best friend. I should know these things."

Jolene offered her a sympathetic nod.

Sarah gazed around the shop in one slow sweep, as if wanting to say something. "I really do have to go."

"Ah, yes. The busy world is waiting."

Sarah nodded and tucked her wet hair behind her ear once again. "When are you going back?"

"In less than a month."

Sarah continued pulling Jolene towards her intense gaze. "That's a shame."

In that sunny storefront, amongst BCDs, regulators, and portable dive computers, that woman took Jolene on an unexpected ride. "How so?"

"I've never been this spontaneous before in my life."

They gazed at each other while Roxie circled her pillow for a more comfortable spot.

"That's a shame."

A pocket of hesitation wedged between them, cradling them in that moment when nothing else in the world mattered but the space they shared. That impulse to cling to the riveting moment underscored the beauty and tragedy of spontaneity.

Sarah readjusted her tote bag, unaware that Jolene had discovered her secret insecurity over a flowery suit. "Well, I guess I should say thank you. You opened my eyes."

"You did great."

She straightened and lifted her cheeks into a big smile. "Yeah, I feel great."

"I can tell. You've got some color back in your cheeks."

Her face glowed. "Yeah, I'm exhilarated."

"Well, that's good. That's a good feeling. We should do it again before I leave, if you want."

Sarah's cell buzzed again. She arched her eyebrow then secured the tote bag strap higher up her shoulder. "I have to go." She sighed.

"Sure. Okay." Jolene reached for a business card. "Oh, hey, take this. You know, in case Frenchy can talk you into getting certified. If it's after I leave, Gerry can hook you up."

Sarah took it and scanned it. "Um." She began to giggle again. "You do realize you misspelled the word diver, right?"

Jolene's face flushed hot. She picked up another card and saw the error. She chuckled. "That's hysterical. And Gerry didn't even notice." She laughed again. "In my defense this is my first card."

Sarah's eyes popped wide. "Oh. You designed them?"

Jolene face grew hotter. "No big deal." She picked up a pen, scribbled out the word and rewrote it. "See," she said, handing her the new one. "All better. Now you'll know you're not calling a divrer shop if you call."

Sarah gripped the card in her two hands and scrunched her shoulders in delight. "This is precious."

Jolene blushed even more.

Sarah placed her hand on Jolene's and squeezed it. "Thank you for being there yesterday and today."

"It's been my pleasure," Jolene whispered.

"A true pleasure," Sarah said, and then she walked towards the exit. Her silhouette disappeared through the door on Jolene's exhale.

She sat on the stool behind the counter and watched as Sarah whacked away a few cicadas before climbing into her car and driving away.

Not wanting to get too attached to the hope of seeing her again, Jolene picked up the latest copy of *Alert Diver* magazine and flipped to the article on fitness training for diving enthusiasts.

Chapter Six

Sarah left the scuba shop and headed to the office. As she drove, she thought of Frenchy. Sarah couldn't remember the last time she had a good heart-to-heart with her best friend. Her focus on work always took over, causing her to do selfish things like push Frenchy's calls to voicemail and choose drinks with her colleagues over visits to her bakery to eat macaroons and indulge in banter about life and love.

That phone call back at the mall garage when the escalator ate Sarah's skirt marked the longest conversation they had in recent times. Even then, Sarah failed to extend the gift of vulnerable exchange, pretending as if everything still fell right into place with them.

Nothing fell into place lately. The world somehow had shifted while she slept and what she woke up to didn't shine quite the same way as it used to. The busyness of life clogged the freeway that used to bring her places that shaped her into someone with purpose, with drive, with ambition.

She could always rely on her friendship with Frenchy. It never failed. Yet, there it sat on the side of the road, rusted and crumbled like a beat-up fender baking in the hot sun.

Sarah drove and kept trying to remember the last time they had a real talk, the kind where they opened up to each other about things that mattered. Sarah knew nothing about Frenchy's life anymore. She could've been living in a new house, been driving a different car, and opened a chain of bakeries for all

Sarah knew.

She missed her best friend.

Friendship happened so mysteriously. At the heart of any good one sat a shared vulnerability. Secrets drew friends together, like freaking out about new strays of gray hair or being traumatized about the ten pounds gained over the holidays.

A friendship thrived only to the point of how deep one went with the embarrassing truths no one else got to see. That's what connected two people. No façade, no makeup, no pretty outfits stood between them. Only a permeable layer existed that allowed for the exchange of truths that bridged the gap between them and the rest of the world.

Friendship required a certain level of openness by placing each other in a position of full disclosure without worry of ridicule or shame. It required the shedding of clever masks and the revealing of intimate details that if the rest of the world had, it could use against a person as ammunition.

Friendship resulted from a valuable exchange, one where the layer of strength was peeled back to expose the authentic layers of a soul, far beneath the surface of perfection.

Frenchy had no clue that Sarah actually cried in the shower every morning because she dreaded the commute ahead of her, the long and stressful drive down a road she never meant to get on. Somehow, things had become rearranged, blocking her exits. Stuck in drive, she accelerated towards a future that lacked silliness and heart-to-heart talks about why Frenchy attempted scuba diving without her and why she failed to mention her love life apparently sucked for her, too.

Sarah pulled off to the side of the freeway and called Frenchy. "What're you doing?"

"I'm up to my elbows in sandwiches for a customer's retirement party in a few hours. Oh, hey, talk to me about your scuba date."

"I loved it," Sarah said, cradling the cell phone, wishing she could lean over to her best friend and hug her.

"How about Jolene? She's pretty awesome, isn't she?"

Sarah chuckled. "Yeah. She was nice to open the shop for me."

"So, you loved it?"

"I did." Sarah struggled to start a real conversation with the only friend who knew her secrets and insecurities.

"I wish you could come by and tell me about it."

"Me, too. But, I've got to get into the office."

"You're going into the office on Sunday?"

"Says the woman in her kitchen making sandwiches for a customer."

"But, this is different," Frenchy said. "It isn't work to me. I'd do this for free."

Sarah would never go into the office for free. "Hmm."

"Is everything okay?" Frenchy asked.

"Yeah. How's everything with you? Everything okay?"

"Yeah. Of course."

"How's Johnny? I didn't get a chance to chat with him last night."

"Oh, yeah, he's great."

Her friend sounded a million miles away. "Frenchy?"

"Yeah, kiddo?"

"Why didn't you tell me about scuba?"

"You were busy and you've been cranky."

She closed her eyes and let the truth swim. "When did I turn into this cranky version of myself?"

"The day you signed on the dotted line for that company."

Sarah could always count on Frenchy to be blunt. "Frenchy, we need to have some fun. We need to carve out time for us again."

"You've got my full attention."

Sarah squeezed her eyes and dove in. "We should get certified in scuba. You know, while Jolene is still here."

"When are you going to have the time?"

That would prove challenging. "I'll figure it out." Another call buzzed in. Work again. "So what do you say?"

"I won't hold my breath."

Sarah's heart twisted, hearing the ugly truth and wanting desperately to break it up and toss it aside. "Good, because holding your breath will kill you."

"Jolene must use that line on everyone," Frenchy laughed.

"It's good to hear that laugh."

"It's good to laugh."

"Frenchy?"

"Yes, kiddo?"

"We'll see each other soon."

"I hope so."

Frenchy hung up first.

Sarah stared ahead at the braking traffic. Stupid weekend drivers. They always caused accidents and slowed travel to barely a crawl.

Sarah wanted so badly to turn around and prep sandwiches with her best friend.

Instead, she listened to her new voice message. Sam spoke frantically, telling her the file had definitely been deleted and they needed to recreate it.

Sarah tossed her cell to the passenger seat and leaned her head against the steering wheel. She was so tired. So tired of always working.

She sat up, straightening her shirt and lowering her visor to get a look at her wet hair.

They did pay her well, at least. Very well. That did help.

Sarah had no clue what she'd be willing to do for free. Walk dogs. She'd definitely walk dogs for free. Oh, and she'd mow grass. She always loved the smell of it when freshly cut. She'd also consider teaching a yoga class.

She'd also help people shop for free, preferably not at Walmart with only an hour to spare. She'd dress most everyone in the office in very different styles than they currently chose. Sam needed to ditch the wick-style polo shirts and replace them with stylish button-downs accessorized with scarfs and maybe some pocket squares. People didn't accessorize enough. The world would be a much bolder and appetizing landscape if people wore fun hats, red flats, and oversized watches.

Yeah, she'd definitely help people shop for free, even though she sucked at shopping for herself. Of course, she had no free time to indulge in anything outside the four walls of that tall window-faced office building. It served as her second home for the past ten years of her life, and cost her potential relationships by forcing her to cancel dates on a moment's notice. The life of a marketing executive at one of the country's busiest advertising firms took great personal sacrifice. Where it lacked peace and tranquility it corrected with bonuses, company cars, and a company credit card to use at her leisure.

She picked up her phone and called Sam back. "I'll be there in about an hour, depending if this stupid traffic jam ever opens."

"I'll be here."

He sure would. He always showed up. Just like her.

~ ~

When she arrived at the office, her hair had dried clumpy. It hung stringy to her shoulders like seaweed. She lowered her visor again and played with it, attempting to part it off to the side. She stared at her eyes. They lacked a sparkle.

Jolene's eyes sparkled. They smiled, in fact.

She had opened the shop for her. Kissed by the drizzle of that fact, her eyes actually began to shine, placing a smile on her face.

I went scuba diving today.

The excitement echoed in her mind.

She stared at Jolene's business card, and traced her finger over the spelling mistake.

She owed it to Frenchy to call and commit to scuba lessons, preferably before Jolene went back to Bonaire. Jolene treated her with patience. She needed someone patient. Someone else would intimidate her. Frenchy needed her to be brave. So, that decided it. She would call Jolene to find out more details. Then, she'd commit to the adventure so she and Frenchy could rebuild what they used to have together, a solid friendship full of risks and no concerns.

Jolene picked up on the second ring. "This is Jolene."

"So, let's say I wanted to get certified as a *divrer*. What would that take?"

Jolene released a soft chuckle. "Well, to become a divrer you need to be able to spell correctly because, you see, if you don't get that right, you'll be liable to giggle a lot. And, you know what happens to people who giggle underwater, right?"

"We make a lot of bubbles?"

"And they tickle."

94

"Well, that sounds lovely." Sarah's voice carried a flirty tone, not at all matching the woman with the stringy hair staring back at her from the visor mirror.

"It would also require you to spend some time with me in the classroom and pool, and then take a quick trip to the quarry when you're ready to get tested."

Sarah exhaled. "Can Frenchy and I start this Wednesday?"

"If you can be here at six, we'll be glad to have you join us."

She typically worked late on Wednesdays because she needed to turn in the weekly Google Analytics reports and analysis to the vice president of client relations by eight a.m. the next morning. "I'll be there. And, this time, I'll be sure to bring a bathing suit."

She hung up, and woke to a new surge, one that took her on a ride somewhat similar to when she showed up for work at Frenchy's bakery back as a high school junior. She needed a new direction, something to kick her off the path of comfort and onto one that forced her to open her eyes and pay attention to the intricacies hiding in places she never considered to look before.

Renewed, she drove to the bagel shop instead of going into the office. What was another half hour going to matter? She needed time to ride out the waves of her newfound bravery first. Her heart drummed a new melody, one that triggered a sense of power and clarity. It beat a feverish tone that steadied her mind on one thing, and one thing only, embracing the temporary rush of life flowing in her again.

Chapter Seven

Jolene's cell rang while she was in the shower, so Maureen answered it.

"Hello, this is Maureen, Jolene's mother. Can I take a message?"

"Hi, Jolene's mother, Maureen. This is Max, from Bonaire. Is Jolene available?"

"She's in the shower. After that, she's heading out to certify some divers. Right up your alley, I suppose," she said with a cheerful edge.

"I hoped to catch her. I've got some good news for her."

Maureen's heart sank. "Oh? Can I get a hint? I love good news," she managed.

"It has to do with her new contract."

"Is it still happening?"

"It sure is. If you could have her call me back?"

"Absolutely."

They said their goodbyes, and then Maureen put Jolene's phone in her backpack.

~ ~

Sarah did something she'd never done in the ten years she worked at Ascension. She used her sick time. She sat in a board meeting listening to Drake from the Seattle office groan on about the lack of support from marketing and how that had negatively affected the quarter's sales. The meeting had already gone over by half an hour, and with the new debate over the sales figures, they'd be there another hour at least. Sarah didn't have an extra hour. She needed to get on the road by three-thirty, at the latest, to avoid gridlock so she could arrive to scuba in time.

When asked a pointed question about Google ads, Sarah grabbed her stomach and flinched, putting on her best acting hat. "I'm sorry. I have to go. It's my stomach," she said, rising from the chair and clenching her fist against her belly. "It might've been something I ate." She scanned the concerned faces of the men and women. "I should go. I'll ask Sam to come in and brief you on the Google ads."

She pushed away from the table, gathering her files. Once clear from the windowed conference room, she headed out to Sam's empty desk.

"Carrie," she called out to her intern. "I'm not feeling well, so I'm heading out. The committee needs Sam to brief them on Google ads for the Seattle store. Can you please tell him to call my cell?"

"Absolutely. I'm on it."

She headed down the elevator to the ground level, and straight into the bathroom where she could get out of her pants suit and into something more casual. Five minutes later she emerged and headed out to the parking garage, swinging her arms to the delightful beat of her quick steps towards a night of freedom. As she approached her car, she ran into Sam sticking his head into the trunk of his car. "Hey Sam."

He popped his head up, and his glasses slid down the bridge of his long nose. "Oh, thank God. I need your help."

Sarah peeked over his shoulder and caught a glimpse of a bag of potting soil. "I left a message with Carrie to ask you to brief the committee on the Google ads."

"I bought some soil to fill the planters in the lobby," he said, sidestepping what she'd just said. "I need to get it out of here and onto the dolly." He cleared his throat and began coughing. "Sorry. I get all choky with dirt." He began swallowing hard.

"Are you alright?"

"Yeah," he struggled. "The dirt squeezes my throat a little, like I'm suffocating. Happens with cotton and wool, too."

He backed away from the trunk and wiped his hands on his dress pants. "I can't stand it."

"What do you need me to do?"

"Help me get the bag on the dolly."

"Of course." She moved to the side of his car and put her pocketbook on the roof. Then, she met him back at the trunk. She reached in and yanked her end of the bag. Sam lifted his end and together they dropped it on the dolly. A cloud of black soil sprayed at their faces, causing Sam to topple backwards and break into a heaving cough. "Thank you," he managed, wiping his dirty hands on his pants again.

Sarah looked at her blue jeans and T-shirt, relieved to see she had gotten away without much more than a dust covering. "I trust you can get it into the building on your own now?"

Sam straightened and flipped her a wary glance. "Do you have a minute?"

"I'm in a hurry."

"I have to tell you something." He coughed again. "Something that can't wait until tomorrow."

"It's going to have to Sam." She walked to the side of his car and reached for her pocketbook, looping its strap around her shoulder. Then, she darted away.

Sam followed her. "I promised you soil. I wanted to deliver it."

She stopped and faced him. "What're you trying to tell me?"

"I'm quitting." His eyes sank. "I can't take it anymore."

A strange echo bounced around her head, knocking her off-balance. He couldn't quit. She needed him. He kept her sane. "You can't leave."

"Yes, I can. I'll be here another two weeks and that's it." He couldn't even look her in the eye. "It's too much. Betsy is ready to divorce me. I'm ready to have a nervous breakdown. I'm tired of spending my nights and weekends in this place. I want to go out to eat on Saturday nights like everyone else does. I want to play golf on Saturday mornings. I want to take dance lessons with Betsy, and I can't." He exhaled sharply. "I want a life again."

"Two weeks? That's it? After everything we've done for you? How am I supposed to hire and train someone in two weeks?"

"With all due respect, that's not my problem, Sarah. You've had every ounce of my soul for the past three years. That's all I have left."

Sarah stared at the lopsided dolly with the potting soil spilling out of its seam onto the cement. He remembered the potting soil he had promised her. He was so thorough; he couldn't leave anything undone. She cradled her face, forgetting about the soil on her hands. Tiny crystals of dirt flew into her eyes. She wiped them with her soiled hands, and that drove in the grit even more. "Dammit."

"You've smeared dirt all over your face."

Sarah blinked and it blurred her vision. "I'm going to be late." She flung her hands in the air. "Just one night. That's all I wanted. One night for myself." The frustrations compressed and lodged in her chest, causing her to pant. "You're so smart Sam. You're so freaking brilliant," she cried. "And lucky. You're very lucky. If I didn't fear losing you, I would tell you I'm happy for you. But, I can't." The tears flowed. "I'm so stressed out; I can't even tell you that."

Sam consoled her by cradling her upper arm with his weak grip. "I'm sorry. I don't know what to say."

"Tell me my makeup isn't completely ruined so I don't have to go back into the office to fix it." She bore her stinging eyes into his. "Please, tell me I don't have to."

He forced a smile, and his eyes pinched the way they did whenever he delivered bad news.

"I envy you." She began to walk backwards towards the entrance of the building, keeping eye contact with him. Finally, she swung her arms in the air in defeat. "I'm happy for you. I am." She pivoted, entered back into the building, and let herself cry.

Within fifteen minutes, she arrived at the entrance of the garage, swatting cicadas with her windshield wipers as she drove forward, trying to focus on the adventure ahead instead of the mess she left behind.

She called Frenchy and told her to be ready to pounce out of her door in an hour.

"We're doing this," Frenchy squealed. "I'm like a kid getting ready to go to Disney."

Sarah hung up and accelerated onto the interstate.

Then, about ten miles into her trek, reality poked her with its mean and vicious spike.

Sarah glared at the long trail of brake lights snaking around the bend at the Interstate 95 split towards Baltimore.

She'd never arrive on time.

The traffic came to a complete stop. She smacked her steering wheel and yelled.

Traffic had a way of stealing that last bit of humanity out of people. It choked the goodness right out of a person's soul, turning them into unrecognizable beasts who punched their steering wheels, flipped people off, flashed dirty looks, and screamed out an obscene amount of fucks, and motherfuckers, and stupid dirt bags, and other things too terrible to recite.

She inched not even twenty feet in ten minutes. Grinding her teeth, she called Frenchy. "I'm never going to get there by six."

"You promised."

"I can't help the illogical workings of stupid people behind the wheel," Sarah said, heaving her words.

"I guess I'll drive myself. Will you show up at all?"

"I'll be there as soon as I can." Sarah flung her phone onto the passenger seat and growled. "I fucking hate you," she yelled at the traffic. "I do! I hate you!"

~ ~

Jolene was prepping paperwork for the class when a few people started to arrive. It would be a full house with ten students seeking certification. As Jolene gathered the paperwork and manuals, her cell dinged with a message.

"I forgot to mention to your mother this is my new cell phone number. Call me. Don't you want to hear the good news? – Max."

Max!

Jolene called him. "Hey you! You talked to my mother?"

"Yeah, when you were in the shower earlier. She didn't tell you?"

Jolene rolled her eyes. "I hurried past her out the door so she probably flaked on that. So what's up?"

"Are you ready to come back?"

"One month and counting. I can't wait."

"We'll need you in about two weeks."

"Two weeks?"

"Why aren't you more excited?"

"I am." Jolene wagged her head. "I'm excited. It's just, well, it's nothing. I'll figure it out."

"Is it your mother's leg?" he asked. "Did it heal?"

"She'll be in a cast for a while, but she's getting around fine."

"So, two weeks works?"

She'd have to have Gerry certify the group at the quarry. Which totally sucked. And her mother. What the hell? She still couldn't deal with the fact that Jolene had a life waiting for her in Bonaire. "I'll work it out."

"We've got a large group coming in on the twenty-first of June, so I'm going to need you maybe a few days before to get you re-acclimated. We have some new procedures we rolled out on the filling stations and lockers, and such. Probably be good for you to know what you're talking about when these people come flying at you like a bunch of excited fish ready to get in the water."

Jolene laughed, but it didn't smooth over the concern.

"It's going to be good to have you back. Things haven't been the same at all."

"It'll be good to be back," Jolene said.

Just then, the door opened, and Frenchy walked in, alone. "Max, I've got to let you go. My class is starting to come in now."

"See you in a couple weeks."

Frenchy waved to her and headed in her direction. "Yeah, see you then."

She greeted Frenchy with a wide smile, despite being upset with her mother and worrying about how she'd break it to Frenchy that she'd be abandoning her and Sarah's certification dive.

~ ~

Sarah stood before the scuba shop an hour and a half late, still fuming. A few cicadas flicked against her, and she brushed them away.

Stupid cicadas.

Before opening the door, she exhaled a few times to flush out the pressure. She did a few neck rolls and shoulder shrugs then eased open the door, tiptoeing into the shop. A gray-headed beefy man sat at the front desk in front of the computer. "You must be Sarah," he said on a smile.

"I sure am."

"They're in the classroom." He pointed to the door.

Sarah began to walk past the counter.

"Oh, wait." He jumped up and handed her a colorful tote bag. "Your books. You'll need them."

She grabbed the handle of the heavy bag. "Wow, lots to learn."

"Your life depends on it." He winked and sat back down to his computer.

If she could survive the traffic jam she just emerged from, she could survive scuba.

She opened the door to the classroom and Jolene stopped talking and nodded at her. "You can sit in that chair." She pointed next to Frenchy. "Okay, anyway, the inflator pump helps with your buoyancy," she continued, demonstrating.

Sarah slid into the chair next to Frenchy. "Hi."

Frenchy put up her hand. "We'll talk after class."

"Right." Sarah opened her tote bag and took out the massive book, *Open Water Diver Certification*, and then she settled in for the lecture.

By the time the class ended at nine p.m., Sarah had decompressed and resumed normal breathing.

"Any questions before we end here tonight?" Jolene asked.

Frenchy leaned over and whispered, "Is it me or does Jolene look pissed?"

Jolene hadn't smiled the entire time. "She's totally pissed."

"Sarah and Frenchy," Jolene raised her voice. "Do you have a question?"

Frenchy cleared her throat. "Permission to speak to you after class, teacher," she said.

Jolene's face softened, and a smile finally surfaced. "If that'll be all, we'll resume back here Saturday morning at nine a.m. We'll get in the pool and start figuring out all these concepts we learned."

Oh, Sarah couldn't do Saturday morning. She had committed to a meeting with the steering committee at eight a.m. to go over edits to the self-study report on their upcoming assessment. Sarah raised her hand. "If we can't come Saturday, is there an alternate?"

"I'm afraid not." Jolene lowered her eyes and closed her training manual. "See anyone who's still interested on Saturday."

Frenchy blew out an exaggerated breath. "Talk about pissing off the teacher. That's what happens when you're late, I guess."

"I can't snap my finger and erase a traffic jam."

"Well, let's help her get in a better mood. I say we get drinks at Apricots."

Sarah had to be up in eight hours to beat the morning rush hour traffic. The work she blew off to be sitting there that night still needed to be done. She couldn't afford to be out having a drink. She glanced up at Jolene still standing at the front desk, now flipping through some paperwork. Her tense jaw took over her face again. "One drink. That's all I can do. Then, I have to get back home. It's a busy time for me."

"I'm tired of hearing that."

"Well, I'm also getting tired of saying it."

"You're cranky again."

"You're not helping."

Frenchy stood and steered towards Jolene. Sarah followed, hoping Jolene didn't turn them down.

~ ~

Jolene did not turn them down. Within half an hour, they all sat at a table at Apricots with cosmopolitans in front of them.

"We all look like we've been run over." Frenchy sipped her drink. "What's up with your mood tonight, Jolene?"

Jolene fingered the tip of her glass. "My mother."

"What has she done now?"

"She's laying on the guilt extra thick. She'll do anything to keep me here. That's my excuse." She pointed her eyes to Sarah. "Yours?"

"Traffic." Sarah pushed past fingering her glass and took a mighty swig, and then she angled towards Frenchy. "What about you?"

"Johnny didn't eat my stew today. He came home with it still in his lunch tote, room temperature and ruined." She gulped her drink.

"We're going to need another round or two," Jolene said.

None of them argued.

They each drank another two rounds, while listening to a one-man guitarist sing covers of James Taylor.

"We're all looking pretty pathetic right now," Frenchy said, taking another sip. "Let's have some fun." She rubbed her palms together.

Sarah leaned her head back on a laugh and startled herself. The room spun.

"Let's talk about our deepest fears," Frenchy said. "You first, Sarah."

Sarah came right out with it. "That's easy. Dying."

"No way," Jolene said. "That's way too easy."

Sarah traced her finger around the rim of her glass. "Okay, I've got another one."

The two women arched their eyebrows.

"Giggling underwater."

Jolene tilted her head. "Still not enough." She stretched the syllable out so it hung between them, long and sexy.

"Well, hang on, Ms. Perfect Fear Admitter," Sarah said. "Why don't you set the example for us?"

Jolene sat back and viewed her with a sidelong glance. "Living with regrets."

Sarah and Frenchy nodded.

"Mm, yeah, good one," Frenchy said.

"Yeah, good one, for sure," Sarah agreed. "Do you have any regrets?" she asked Jolene.

Jolene regarded her question with a narrowing of the eyes, zeroing in on the ketchup bottle. "Don't we all?"

Sarah wrinkled her nose. "You can't do that. You can't answer my question with a new question."

"Sarah's a rule player," Frenchy interjected. "Fair warning." She raised her hands in surrender mode.

Jolene's voice sank a few decibels. "Okay, fine. I'll answer your question. I no longer have any regrets."

"None?" Sarah asked.

"None. I packaged up my last regret by visiting my mother. I've got a good three years before they'll pile up again and I'll find myself back on an airplane here to correct everything."

Sarah's phone, sitting on the table next to her silverware, buzzed. She swiped the message away to silence it. "So, it's a good thing we caught you for these lessons when we did."

"Does anyone want to know my fear?" Frenchy tapped the table.

Jolene and Sarah shared a smile.

"I have this recurring nightmare that I wake up and my entire head of hair has turned gray. I keep having it. It's not that I'm vain or anything. I just fear looking like I'm Johnny's mother."

Frenchy already had a gray streak highlighting the front of her hairline. Sarah loved that beautiful feature. "First of all, you're thirteen years younger than him."

"Women age differently than men," Frenchy said. "You know this."

"If my hair would come in as shiny and white as your streak, I'd never turn to the bottle."

"Well, highlights would look nice on you," Frenchy said. "You should put some right through your front pieces. It would bring out your green eyes."

Suddenly, Sarah loathed her faded amber hair. Her phone buzzed again with a new message. It buzzed vigorously, screaming at her to stop ignoring it. She glared at it then back at Frenchy. "I like my hair the way it is."

Her phone buzzed again. "Oh, for goodness' sake." Sarah cupped her hand over it, as though that would stop the tyrannical pinging from her constant, annoying companion. "This is why you should never accept a company phone. They can contact you whenever they want."

"Ah, to be owned by a company," Frenchy said. "No, thank you." She took a long sip of her Cosmo.

Jolene glanced at the cell. "That's another one of your fears right there."

"I'm not afraid of it," Sarah said. "Annoyed, yes. Afraid, no. That's ridiculous."

"You never grip something like that unless you're afraid of letting it go."

"I don't fear my phone." Sarah's defenses rose.

"Sorry, I don't believe you." Jolene smirked. "You enjoy being needed, and fear the consequences if you're not."

She didn't fear such a thing. Fear oozed an ugliness. It snuck in like a ninja, and doused everything in its tracks with soot. She had no room for that blackness. None. Zilch. Fear had no place in her life. No more. Especially not from a stupid phone.

"I'll prove it to you." Sarah put her phone away. "See? No fear."

Jolene squirmed on her stool. "Now, that's freedom." She tilted her head, and her eyes took on a smoldering sheen. "Freedom looks really good on you."

Sarah blushed. In between the pulse of that blush came the annoying buzz of her cell phone again. She needed to check on it. Work expected her to pick up anything before ten p.m.

"It's driving her crazy not to check it," Frenchy said. "Look at her lips." She pointed to them as though Jolene would have a difficult time finding them on her own. "Do you see how they get all stretchy and tense? Happens every time work comes calling her."

"Maybe it's important?" Jolene asked.

It always was, but she refused to cave.

"Seriously, you should get it." Jolene twisted her mouth. "Anything that comes out of my lips right now can't be trusted. These drinks are going straight to my head."

Frenchy dug it out of her pocketbook and handed it to her. "Go ahead before you have a coronary."

Relief opened and spilled through Sarah. "Fine, but only because you're forcing me."

This was her life. She chose it. At some point along the way she had decided to sign on the dotted line and sacrifice her life to the company so they could provide her with a good salary, car, clothing allowance, credit card, master's degree, and all of the finest perks so she'd stay frozen in the foundation they laid for her. She picked up her cell and read the last message in a string of texts from Sam. "We've got a BIG issue! Where are you???"

She hesitated then texted back. "What now?"

He responded in a snap. "Peter wrote his part of the annual report around the wrong set of stats. His entire piece is wrong. And, he's not answering his phone, either."

She pounded her fingers against the cell. "Then, we rewrite it."

"How? It's due in the morning."

"I'll text you in an hour when I get home. We'll figure something out." Together, they always figured it out. That's why they always called her.

She rolled her eyes. "Ladies. I'm sorry, but I'm going to have to cut this short."

"Another big problem?" Jolene asked.

Sarah rubbed her eyes, already fried from the long day. "Yeah."

"Why do you do it?"

She contemplated her answer over a long sip. She got caught in a groove and couldn't get out. She had no way out unless she let go of it all and tried something new. That would require too much sacrifice. She'd have to forfeit everything she worked so hard to achieve, her house, her car, her retirement account, her stock options, her expensive tastes in style, and her organic vegetables for smoothies. "Because I love my job."

"That's all that matters, then." Jolene crossed her arms over her chest and took in the room.

They sat staring out at the sea of busyness, entertained by the chaotic medley of chatter.

"Being here has put things into perspective," Jolene said.

"How so?" Sarah asked, curious.

"It's shown me what I value, and can never take for granted."

"What do you value?" Sarah asked.

"Peace." A billowy sigh escaped her full lips. "It's so rushed here. Everyone is so irritable." She paused, reflecting on Sarah. "People don't even smile at each other. In fact, when I smile at someone, they look at me as if I'm about to rob them. They start securing their pocketbook straps over their shoulder or look away and rush past." Her voice rose, likely the product of a fourth Cosmo. "My heart," she tapped it. "It pounds too hard when I'm here. It's like everyone is so caught up and fixated on getting bigger and better, that they forget to take a glass of lemonade out to the back patio and enjoy the fresh air."

"Hey, it's not my fault your mother doesn't smoke anymore," Frenchy said, crossing her arms over her chest. "She says sitting out on the patio is too difficult right now. So I can't sip lemonade with her."

"I'm not blaming you." Jolene's eyes started to sink. "I'm talking in general terms. Most people don't take the time to do what you have done with my mother. Friends don't get together anymore, and if they do," she looked at Sarah, "no offense, they're on their cell phones sitting across from each other. Just look around."

They did. Everywhere Sarah turned people clung to their cell phones. She was a fool, too. A silly fool clinging to a piece of technology. "That's reality."

"It doesn't have to be." Jolene's eyes opened wider. "It's a matter of getting off the wrong track and getting on a better one. Just like my ex did. She didn't like her life with me, so she leaped off the path and got onto a new one. At least she went against the grain. I can't fault her for that."

Sarah and Frenchy shared a concerned look. Jolene morphed from sweet, calm, and assured to someone polluted by the dirty stress of a clogged life.

Frenchy reached for Jolene's wrist. "Maybe it's time to switch to water for us all. What do you say?"

Jolene shifted, pulling her hand back. "Why's it the only track that's acceptable is the one everyone else runs on?"

Sarah didn't like that new side of Jolene. "People don't just step off tracks they've been on for ten years," Sarah said. "Especially if the track is good to them." Her defenses rose again. "Life requires that a person works hard, and when she does, she gets rewarded, justifiably so. There's nothing wrong with working hard."

"I didn't say that. Though, maybe you can agree that people choose to work hard doing the wrong things sometimes and end up fighting their way through life instead of enjoying it and letting it flow."

"That's not realistic." Sarah crossed her arms over her chest. She glared at the empty Cosmo glass in front of Jolene, no longer enjoying its effects. "That's very idealistic. Not everyone can leave it all behind and go live on an island. Life isn't a vacation. It's about putting forth effort, bringing value to the world, and...and..."

"Listen," Jolene said, slurring and reaching across the table for Sarah's wrist. "I'm not trying to sound elite. That's not me, right Frenchy?"

"It's not." Frenchy shook her head.

"You asked me about my perspective." Jolene paused. "I offered you my opinion."

Sarah gritted her teeth through a forced smile.

"I'm not meant to live in a busy society," Jolene said. "I'm meant for simple things like the sun, the sand, and a small humble apartment. I can't stand materialism."

Sarah challenged Jolene's stare. "You need material to live in this world. You need things. We're not living in the days of hunting and gathering. People nest. It's what we do to survive as civilizations. We build houses, fill them with comfortable items, and live a safe life. Why suffer when you don't have to?"

Sarah breathed in and out. The three sat and waited out the moment. Everything Jolene had said rang true, even in her drunken state. Sarah didn't want to take it in and let it marinate for too long, though. That kind of soul-searching reeked of emotional and mental danger for anyone already established and invested in her life. Her roots had grown too deep to pull out now. To entertain anything opposite of that would cause irreparable damage to the foundation she worked so hard to set.

"What I'm advocating is the complete opposite of suffering." Jolene wobbled on her stool.

"I don't disagree with anything you've said." Sarah relaxed her arms and dropped them into her lap. "I'm sure I look like a raving lunatic stuck to my cell phone, but I'm okay with it." Much better than losing everything she gained.

"I'm sorry. I've had too much to drink, and I need to stop talking." Jolene's voice sank. "I'm going to have some regrets tomorrow."

Sarah fell silent.

They differed. They differed a lot. Like miles apart.

Jolene cocked her head, and offered an apologetic smile. "Will you be back on Saturday or did I ruin that chance?"

In a flash, her smile reeled Sarah back. "I'll do my best."

~ ~

Later that night, after fixing the work issue by rewriting Pete's part, Sarah soaked in a bubble bath, contemplating her life. Her life satisfied her. Didn't it? Maybe she compared herself too much to people who didn't have to work as hard for happiness, people like the Jolenes and Frenchys of the world.

Sarah started working for The Ascension Group seven months after graduating college. Before that, in addition to working at Frenchy's bakery, she worked as an assistant in a dead-end position while she job-searched for something better.

The task of job searching for seven long months killed her with its grueling demands, not to mention, humiliating results. No one wanted to hire an inexperienced recent college graduate who dipped strawberries into chocolate and baked croissants in her best friend's bakery to pay for college. They wanted solid experience, and during college, Sarah couldn't afford to take time out for an internship. So, Sarah did the next best thing. She volunteered as a writer for a high-end, franchised boutique company who needed someone to write their newsletters. What started out as a chance to get published clips to get a solid job in marketing turned into one of the greatest pleasures of Sarah's early professional life.

She started off writing segments about jewelry making and fashion trends, and then eventually the owner asked her to write something more compelling, something with more of an edge, something that would get people seeking out their weekly digests. That's when Sarah came up with the brilliant idea of a continual short story, like a sitcom only in writing, of a team of fashion experts, their clients and their stories, and all the drama and trials that resulted when they entered or exited the boutique's doors.

It became an instant hit. Subscriber rates quadrupled after the fifth story published, and online retail sales took off on a whole new level, even allowing the franchise to add more fashion stylists to cater to their growing list of clients.

That franchised group of boutiques not only had offered her a chance to build her skills, but they also inadvertently introduced her to their advertising firm, The Ascension Group. Her seven months of job searching ended when The Ascension Group swooped in and took her right into their marketing department where she got her own cubicle with tall walls, a printer, and a coffee percolator.

She landed a job in the company where every communications major wanted to work. Prestigious for their top-end clients, The Ascension Group only hired the best of the best, at least that's what they told Sarah in the breakroom one day after she received a bonus check for her help with bringing their prized franchised boutique client to a new level.

"It will be a conflict of interest if you continue writing for them outside of this firm though," Tom, the marketing vice president, said to her a month after her hiring. "We're going to need you to cut that tie unless they're willing to pay us for that service."

"Would I get that pay through you, then?"

Tom folded the smile back into a serious tone. "I'm afraid not. That would be part of your job as Marketing Specialist."

"Marketing Specialist?"

"That's right. We're so pleased with your work, that we're reclassing your position to a specialist. So, even though you would get a raise for that, it would be considered payment for your new responsibilities and not payment of any special projects a client requests on the firm's behalf."

"What if they don't agree to pay for the service? Do I still get my reclass and raise?"

"Absolutely. One is not contingent on the other."

Her first of many concessions, Sarah continued to agree to their demands. She didn't see those as settling on her dream. She lived her dream. She had a job at a prestigious firm, and they treated her well, with many perks to smooth over the rough patches of time when she entered and exited the building in complete darkness without seeing the sun.

Her father would've been proud of her. He worked his butt off until the day he dropped dead of a heart attack at forty-two. Her mother, had she gotten to see her graduate high school, would've told her to do something fun with her life, something like becoming a manicurist. Of course, her three siblings wouldn't have cared. They barely called her for Christmas, let alone subjected themselves to random phone calls about life and business. They all blamed the miles of separation between them, but Sarah surmised they didn't nurture their sibling bonds because it hurt too much to pretend they didn't notice the big, huge void where their mother's laughter and father's advice used to dance.

So, Sarah traversed life on her own, figuring out the angles, roadblocks, and hidden surprises along the way. She learned early on that she would need tough skin to survive the business world. In business, she didn't worry. She wore her father's hat, and never let them see her sweat. She liked to imagine he guided her steps and decisions still.

The business world, even with all its rewards and security, was a place a person learned to either love or hate.

The special perk of the job in the beginning, working alongside other creatives, turned into an eating frenzy where everyone championed for one thing, and one thing only, success. Sarah learned pretty early on about its vicious environment, full of competitive professionals all trying to reach their career comfort zones at the top. Grateful for just a seat at the table, Sarah focused on getting things done.

Her colleagues, who at first offered her muffins and flavored coffees, began to show their true colors right about the time Sarah earned her reclass. Apparently, they didn't enjoy sharing the rungs on the ladder leading to greater views and even greater padding to the wallet. However, some of her colleagues, creative elves as they referred to themselves, praised her climb.

One day she walked out an assistant, the next a specialist, and before long, she shared corporate lunches off-site brushing around ideas with the people who pulled the strings on projects, the same projects she used to originate. The days of brainstorming on whiteboards while eating popcorn and Skittles disappeared.

She missed being one of the creative elves who kept Ascension powering some of the most dynamic displays of marketing finesse in the country. Endless hours of analyzing charts and reports to calculate assumptions and guesses on the predictability of future forecasts replaced those moments. Most days, she sat with her jaw dropped, scratching her head with the tip of her pencil as she tried to keep up with the lingo, the acronyms, the jeers, the snide remarks about the creative elves, as they drank premium coffee, not the crap the elves drank in the cubicle dungeon.

Ten years into the company, and Sarah grew into a part of its foundation, able to make decisions on her own and embed herself into its success. On those days when she sifted through gobs of problems, they'd toss another benefit her way to ease the stress.

Those benefits piled up and buried her, though, buried her in an unforgiving sludge of obligations where she had to put them before anyone else, even herself.

She'd sometimes let the anxiety seep out before she could wipe away its ooze.

"Why don't you leave?" Frenchy would argue.

"I'm venting."

She had to vent or else risk a stroke brought on by the constant bombardment of pressure of her twelve-hour workday.

"You should try something new. That job is killing you."

"What doesn't challenge me will create a weak point in me," Sarah would say.

She refused to go in reverse. She had worked too hard. To go backwards meant trashing things that pleased her like a well-structured bank account and a comfortable house and car.

"At least you're a success. Most people your age are still struggling to buy a house."

She was successful, whatever that meant.

Success didn't taste good, though. It lingered in the back of her throat at the end of the day, spilling its yucky aftertaste all through her as she tossed and turned in her big, empty bed. "I do love my house, at least."

"As long as you've got everything you need, that's all that I care about."

"I do." Too many unknowns existed outside the door of her life.

What if on the other side of that door she opened every day sat total failure? What if she lacked resources? How would she pay her mortgage? What if she got stuck in an even worse groove and death became the only way out? What if it turned out that the pain of what existed on the other side of that door hurt more than the daily pain of trudging down the interstate at all hours of the day and night? At least at the office, she knew what to expect. She understood that sometimes in life, a person just had to get it done.

She had no right to complain or vent.

What put her on a pedestal above a man working the vegetable fields in California, bent over at the hip for ten hours a day to earn enough money to put hot soup and clean water on his family's dinner table?

Was she that spoiled? Everyone suffered a little death inside from time to time. Why not her?

Of course, what if on the other side of that door lived a greater destiny? A brighter version of all she envisioned. A life where she actually wanted to wake up and work?

She sank beneath the bubbles and blew out. That kind of unrealistic thinking got people into trouble.

Chapter Eight

To deal with her hangover, Jolene traveled out to Centennial Lake and sat on a bench overlooking the part of the water that grew lily pads. It was no Bonaire ocean, but water nonetheless. Water nourished her soul and helped her to find peace in the folds of the hectic space that surrounded her.

She brought one of her father's books with her and read for a little while, taking in the lessons and meditating on them. The words brought her to a place where she could relax, create some space in her mind, and reclaim that part of her soul the busy world soiled.

Surrounded by only the song of the birds, Jolene sat still and observed. She would continue to learn to be the quiet ambassador to chaos, trying her best not to let anything derail the peaceful classroom of the moment.

The night before kept creeping into her mind, vying for a spot, though. Total failure. She never should've drank. But, within each ripple of indecision, indifference, and judgement sat a teachable moment that offered guidance. That's what the book she held said.

She also knew from previous experience that those moments traced the fabric of reality with a delicate touch. If she listened carefully, she would be able to detect its song echoing through the wind, a companion to both her joys and disappointments. In that wind, the gems of knowledge blossomed from its verses, reminding her that she never had to fear being alone without answers to life's tough questions.

Each lesson built upon past ones and created the foundation for truth, compassion, and love. Presented as hardships, she was learning to recognize each lesson's power as a gift further enhanced by the bliss of curiosity. When curiosity circled, she had faith that her heart would open and allow for expansion. She refused to be a victim of circumstance. She wanted to become a carrier of knowledge, eager to learn and share what the world offered her.

That morning's meditation by the lakefront worked for a while. But, her mind continued to wander back to her drunken judgments from the night before. She cringed at her terrible behavior.

~ ~

Later that afternoon, Jolene begged her mother to join her on the back patio, wanting to air out the negative undertow before she left again. Jolene leaned back in her chair and pondered the past day's fallout.

"Want to play Scrabble?" her mother asked.

Scrabble helped them bond. It filled the silence in between them. "Sure."

Her mother set up the game board. "You look like you're facing the end of the world. Care to tell me what's going on?"

Jolene sat taller. "Why didn't you tell me Max called yesterday?"

"I'm sorry. It must have slipped my mind, honey." She motioned to Jolene's tiles. "You can go first."

Instead of agonizing over the choice, Jolene tossed down a simple word, *life*. "I like being a diver, Mom."

Her mother's eyes opened wider. "I know."

"Then, why wouldn't you want me to go back?"

Her mother looked at her tiles, and her bottom lip started to quiver. "It's lonely here without you."

"What're you so afraid of, Mom?"

Her mother studied her tiles and played the word *feverish*. "Who said I'm afraid?"

"You're clinging. You only cling when you fear losing something."

Her mother stared at her. "I guess I fear losing you."

Jolene laid down the word *vessel*. "You'll never lose me."

Her mother studied the Scrabble board. "I'll be alright."

Wanting to shift the conversation to something weighing on her mind, Jolene said, "I know about Jack."

Her mother flinched. "Jack? Jack's just a good neighbor."

Jolene reached out for her mother's wrist. "It's okay, Mom."

"What's okay?"

"To let go."

She shifted in her chair, wrestling with a sigh. "He's good at fixing things."

Jolene's lips trembled upwards into a small grin, fighting against the trickle of sadness that she might not be needed in her role as the fixer anymore. "That's good news, Mom."

They sat in silence, and then her mother asked, "So, when are you leaving?"

"Max wants me there in two weeks. I'm supposed to certify Frenchy and her friend Sarah, though. I'm going to tell him I need to wait out the month."

"Will you lose your contract?"

"I don't know. It's the right thing to do."

"You're not one to veer away from a responsibility. Just like your dad."

"Once I'm committed, I stay there." Jolene reflected on her mother's sad eyes. "I hate leaving you. I wish things could be different."

"I want you to be happy, dear." She squeezed the bridge of her nose. "I'll be fine."

"Why don't you fly out there with me, Mom? I have a pullout couch I can sleep on. You can take my bed. You can spend some time writing from there. Maybe it'll help if you get to know why I love that place so much."

"I'm not flying."

Jolene leaned back in her chair. "You've got to attempt it, too. It can't all be me."

"You know I'm deathly afraid to fly," she snapped. "If you want to go back, go. I should never have piled on the guilt."

Jolene sat up. "We need to talk about this fear of yours."

"We have nothing to talk about. I won't fly. It freaks me out how a big hunk of metal can hang in the air. End of story." She stood and hobbled towards the sliding door. "I'm tired." She limped forward, and then just before the step into the kitchen, her foot got caught and she lost her balance. She fell backwards into a planter then rolled over onto her healing leg.

Jolene jumped up.

"I'm good." Her mother flung her hands in the air. "All is good."

~ ~

"My daughter is about to make a huge mistake," Maureen said to Frenchy.

Frenchy cradled the phone in the crook of her neck as she kneaded dough. "How so?"

"She's about to put herself into a tight spot, and I'm afraid she's going to kick herself later for it."

Frenchy pressed into the dough, flattening it. Then, she sprinkled flour on it. "She hates regrets."

"Yeah, I know." Maureen's voice faded.

"What did she do?"

"Jolene got the call to go back to Bonaire early, and she's going to turn it down."

"I'm confused," Frenchy said. "Why would she do that?"

"She's obligated to certify you and your friend."

Frenchy stopped kneading and gripped the phone with her floured hands. "Well, that's not good. I can't have that on my conscience."

"What do we do?"

"I'll take care of this."

"You know I hate to see my little girl leave, but I've come to realize that this isn't home for her anymore. She's like a piece of driftwood when in Maryland. She is getting more hardened by the day. She belongs elsewhere, and it's finally sinking in to this old heart of mine."

"How did you come to understand this?"

"The twinkle in her eye disappeared yesterday when we talked. I've become a burden. Frenchy, I don't want to be a burden."

~ ~

Frenchy called Sarah and explained things to her, about how Jolene might risk her contract because of their certification.

"We should back out," Sarah said.

"It's best. As much as I want to do this, I don't want to keep her from something valuable out of some sense of obligation."

Without Jolene, Sarah's motivation to jump into a dark, algae-filled lake died. "I agree. I'll take care of it."

Jolene understood her purpose. She understood that her purpose extended far beyond just paying bills and dying. She had an important role, one that touched others.

125

Unlike her, Jolene had a purpose to bring people joy. She knew what she wanted and why she wanted it. She lived to help people explore their deepest desires and open their eyes to the beauty of life beyond the terrestrial landscape that littered most people's lives with ridiculously long and monotonous to-do lists. She found ways to create meaning and joy for others through her actions. She understood she'd never find purpose by sitting at a desk and pushing numbers all day.

Sarah would not crush Jolene's dreams because she wanted to learn how to scuba dive.

~ ~

After talking with her mother the day before, Jolene had called Max to let him know she'd be unable to get to Bonaire in time for the new divers. A reluctant Max agreed to allow her the extra two weeks she'd need to tie her loose ends. Of course, that meant asking one of the divers to stay on until she could arrive. The diver had agreed because, like everyone who worked for Max, he didn't want to let him down.

Jolene finished putting the new three-millimeter wetsuits on display when the front door bell chimed and in waded Sarah, carrying a weak smile.

Roxie looked up from her pad near the window and wagged her tail. Sarah walked over to her and petted the top of her head, and then she looked up at Jolene. "Can we talk?"

The heavy delivery of her question didn't sit right. It pressed against Jolene's chest, blocking any chance to catch a full breath. "Of course." Jolene rounded the counter. "Listen, I'm sorry about the other night. I don't know what got into me. My mother had upset me, so I drank more than I would normally. That didn't turn into a good idea. I should know better."

Sarah stood and pulled the strap to her pocketbook higher on her shoulder.

"What you said rang true. All of it. Honesty is a nice feature. It looks good on you."

Jolene moved closer, narrowing the space between them. "I suck at taking compliments."

Sarah regarded her for a long moment. "I love them." She took a step closer and her lips curved into a grin. "Just saying."

The weight of the air lifted. "So what brings you by?"

Sarah dug into her pocketbook. "Well, two things." She pulled out a long and narrow box. "New generic business cards for the shop." She handed the box to Jolene. "I can create individual ones for whomever wants them, if you like the design that is."

Jolene opened the box and pulled out a card. "Nice and simple. I like it."

"Always best to go simple when you can."

"Does that mean, despite being drunk, I won the debate on simplicity from the other night?"

Sarah drew a breath. "Well, like with scuba, simple isn't for everyone."

Jolene caught sight of the sudden downturn of her lips and crease in her forehead. "I get that."

"There's a lot about me you'll never get."

A sadness drizzled from Sarah's words, a sadness layered in truth that their worlds would never complement each other. "I suppose that's true of us both."

"I need to confess something." Sarah continued to stare deep into her eyes.

Jolene swallowed, taking in the fullness of that moment. "Go on," she said, breathlessly.

"It's about this whole scuba thing."

Jolene braced for the inevitable. "What about it?"

"I'm really sorry, but scuba just isn't for me, and Frenchy isn't into it if I don't do it." Her words tumbled out like shattered pieces of glass, sharp and splintered. "I'm sorry, but it's hard with my life."

Jolene remained grounded, crossing her arms over her chest. "I thought you'd say that."

"You did?"

"It's okay. I get it. We determined that simplicity and scuba aren't for everyone."

Jolene saw a visible shiver go through Sarah. "I'm busy, you know?"

She nodded and backed a few steps away then saw Sarah's clutched hand around her cell phone. "You are. If it's what you want, then, that's a good thing."

"Yeah. I, um," Sarah looked around the shop then fixed her gaze on the display of dive computers. "I have a good job, and it's taken me a long time to get here," she said, talking to the computers. "I don't see this fitting into that schedule. As it is, Saturday is impossible for me to get to class." She looked back at Jolene with a firmness that didn't match the affection in her voice. "I've got reports and meetings with steering committee members."

Jolene studied the pain surfacing in Sarah's light eyes. "You don't have to explain."

"I hope we can still stay in touch," Sarah said, wrestling with her pocketbook strap again.

"Sure. Send me a message from time to time and let me know how things are going."

The volume of silence reverberated an uncomfortable pitch.

"So when are you going back?"

"Very soon." Jolene's answer fled up her throat and launched itself with surprising confidence.

Sarah blinked.

Not sure what else to say, Jolene circled away and adjusted the wetsuits she'd just organized. As she picked up one from the rack, Sarah placed her hand on her shoulder. "Thank you for everything."

Jolene reached up and cradled her warm hand, pressing her eyes closed as the heat swirled in her. "You're most welcome."

Sarah's hand slipped away. "I should let you get back to work."

Jolene spun towards her. "It's been a pleasure."

"A true pleasure," Sarah whispered before she turned and walked out of the shop.

Jolene once again watched her silhouette disappear on a graceful sweep, like the closing act of a sad play that left the audience with constricted throats.

She wanted Sarah to like scuba. She wanted her to become certified and take a trip to Bonaire. She wanted to be able to show off her world to someone who mattered. She wanted to open Sarah's eyes to what the majority of the world would never see, which was that life bloomed into so much more beneath everything material and replicable.

Jolene was lonely, and craved to share that with someone other than strangers. For one brief and careless moment in time, she had entertained that idea in her head and let it take up a prominent seat, blinding her to the reality that she was indeed a loner, a rare specimen who would spend her lifetime outside the bubble of where ninety-nine percent of the world's population existed. To enter that bubble would cause it to burst, because she didn't have what it took to travel inside its limiting walls. She'd suffocate and need to find a way to breathe. She'd have to break out and emerge on the outside where few found comfort.

She couldn't force what didn't fit.

That desperate woman hiding inside of her wanted Sarah to fall in love with the quiet beat of the sea. But, did she actually crave Sarah or did she just want to fix someone who needed fixing?

Her heart ached. Regretfully, she had to stop blowing such idealistic bubbles.

A customer entering the shop brought her back to the present moment, to a new improved moment that she could course-correct.

She rose out of the wreckage. "How can I help you?"

The woman looked around confused. "I'm sorry, this isn't Charm City Running."

Jolene pointed to the right. "It's one street over on the same side."

The woman left without as much as a thank you. Just another rushed person trying to get somewhere else fast.

She walked behind the counter and got her cell. She texted Max. "I can get there on time. See you very soon."

Chapter Nine

After leaving Jolene, Sarah drove to the office intent on burying herself in a project. Focusing on something important always kept her in check. She needed to get herself into check. The uncertainties taking space in her mind grew too loud on the ride down the interstate. If she could enter into the building, log into her computer, and bury herself in an important project, she'd be fine. Just fine. Absolutely freaking fine.

Work always stole her away from her personal life, and at that point, she viewed it as a full advantage.

Bring it on.

When Sarah focused, she got things done. She succeeded in her job. She succeeded like a champion, like a boxer in the ring. She stood above her opponent, bloodied and sweaty, victory streaming through every vessel. When she focused, no distraction got in her way.

Her days didn't allow for distractions. She didn't have what others did, a life, so to speak. She didn't have to get up and surprise a spouse with a quickie before jumping in the shower. She didn't have to scream at kids to wake up. She didn't have to cook pancakes in a skillet far too small to get them all cooked on time for her family. She didn't have to leave work in the middle of the day to run her kids to doctor appointments, ballet lessons, or baseball practice. She didn't have to worry about sitting at the dining room table with them, trying to figure out how to solve their arithmetic homework using the new modern-day method of computation.

She didn't have to deal with anyone but herself.

That lonely thought seeped through her like sludge.

Corporate America loved people like Sarah.

They could count on her to stay late, come in early, work weekends, and in a snap, travel to locations to solve communication hang-ups. Sarah was a team player with perks for the company; perks that included an obscene amount of selfless energy channeled where they asked her to direct it.

That particular morning, they needed her to put on her best analytical hat and figure out how to get more sales with fewer incentives. Typically, Sarah would wrack her brain, nurturing a solid answer that solved the issue.

Not that morning.

No way.

Not even possible.

Her brain stopped in the breakdown lane and failed to kick back into working gear. It stayed idle, revving on the curiosity of Jolene's touch and cottony clean scent.

She didn't want to focus on numbers. She would have a lifetime to devote to numbers once she could put aside the restless desires growing in her. Once Jolene left, she could focus again. She could get back into her groove and push out forecasts and brilliant ideas. She could maintain her reputation as the one who could produce without interruption. She could return to her position on the ladder to her goals as soon as that woman boarded her plane and took off, back to her life and her passion. Until then, Sarah wondered how she'd get any work done.

She wanted to nurture the memory of Jolene's soft lips curling upwards and causing her cheeks to blush and eyes to sparkle.

She wanted the chance to kiss and cuddle with her, and breathe in her charm.

She sat and stared at her computer disinterested in what it disclosed, problem after problem that required her full attention; attention she couldn't drum up even if someone handed her a million dollars.

She wanted the chance to see her one last time. One more time. What would be the harm? Why should she tame the desire to stand in her presence one last time? Soon the chance would be gone and she'd falter against a thick slush of anguish, wishing she could've acted with more impulse, more like the woman Jolene brought out in her twice since their meeting at the party.

Sarah had spent her entire adult life trying to sell that desire and zest for life to consumers. To capture even a sliver of that zest, they had to risk something important to taste it and tumble into its warm embrace. As a marketing executive, she painted a familiar picture for the sake of fulfilling the basic need of comfort. And, it worked. Too busy with everyday life to deal with turbulence, people feasted on the bait of indulgence. Sarah wanted to feast, too.

Unable to stop the avalanche of her craving, she called Frenchy, wanting to put an idea into play. "It's done. I told her scuba isn't for me, and you're not interested in doing it without me. This way, she wouldn't be obligated to stay."

"I know. Her mother called me to thank me for helping. She's leaving on Saturday."

Saturday. She let that sink in for a moment before launching into her idea. "Let's throw her a party." Jolene needed a party. Sarah needed a party. They all needed one. She wanted some fun before life turned back into a series of problems and solutions. "A going away party. Something simple because you know how she likes that. We could decorate your back patio, throw some music on, and grill. We could do a Caribbean style menu. Nothing too fancy. Just pineapples and chicken on skewers and maybe piña coladas with those little umbrellas."

"You and I think so much alike. It's freaky."

"We should thank her in some way, you know, for everything she's done for us. It's the right thing to do. A person leaves for a venture and you throw her a party to let her know she'll be missed."

"Oh, I'm so excited. You know you fired up the party-planning engine in me, right? Once you crank the key, you can't turn back. Say the word, and I'll put the pedal to the metal and make this happen."

"Make it happen," Sarah said breathlessly. "She needs a party."

"A party it is."

"Great. Friday night maybe?"

"I'll be sure to drag her across the street if I have to," Frenchy said. "Oh, can you create one of those banner thingies that I can hang from the patio? You know, something along the lines of *good luck, we're going to miss you, blah, blah, blah*?"

Sarah swayed in her chair, powered by a gust of something refreshing and bold. "Of course."

"I'll bake her a cake shaped like an air tank."

"Try to figure out a way to add bubbles. She likes bubbles."

"Bubbles. Of course!"

"Bubble. Bubble," Sarah said, rising from her chair and staring out the window at the bright blue sky.

"I love throwing a good party," Frenchy said. "Though, I hate goodbyes."

"Yeah, me too," Sarah said, tripping over the sudden chill that accompanied the words.

"See you Friday."

Sarah opened back up to a smile. That little smile carried her through the pile of problems on her desk. By the time she closed her door at eighty-thirty that evening, long after her colleagues went home, cooked dinner, took their kids to baseball, did their homework, and tucked them into bed, she headed out the door, ready to go home.

Instead of listening to country music, she drove in silence, entertained by the growing desire to take another bubble bath and indulge herself in something more exciting and dangerous than marketing strategies for once.

~ ~

On Friday evening, after Jolene fastened the buckle on her suitcase and placed it near the front door, she followed her mother across the street to Frenchy and her uncle's house for a backyard barbecue. The cicadas had quieted for the day, and now only a few trickled around, finding their last hoorah under the setting sun.

When they rounded the side of the house, Jolene could hear the crackling of a fire in the pit and water splashing from swimmers. The air had a feeling of nostalgia to it. It reminded Jolene of those childhood moments when she'd huddle around a makeshift fireplace in her backyard with her parents and goofy cousin, roasting marshmallows then later running into the fields behind their fenced yard to catch fireflies.

Long tables covered with elegant white lacy tablecloths and sky blue runners created an intimate setting. Cocktail tables, draped in the same fashion, set a festive mood with their exotic-flowered centerpieces. The delicious scent of herbs and lemons, and charbroiled meats floated in the air.

Suddenly, the crowd came to a halt. Then, in one guttural voice, they yelled out congratulations and began clapping.

Frenchy cupped her hands and yelled. "Speech! Speech!"

Jolene turned to her mother. "Did you know about this?"

"You bet. I kept it a secret. Imagine that?"

Jolene gazed at her mother and saw that glittering pride in her eyes, the same one she saw the day she had arrived a few months earlier. "I feel very embarrassed right now," she whispered to her.

"I know you hate parties, but we all love you too much to not send you off into the sunset knowing you will be missed."

Jolene glanced around, scanning the crowd of friends from the dive shop and from her neighborhood. No Sarah. A wave of disappointment washed over her.

Frenchy came up beside her and handed her a shot glass. "This is from Uncle Johnny. He's sorry he had to miss the party, but something came up and he couldn't be here. He sends his best."

Poor Frenchy, always providing a fresh excuse for him. Jolene grabbed the glass and emptied it in one quick swallow. The crowd cheered and the music restarted. "Let's have a party."

~ ~

Sarah sat in her car, steadying her breaths. She stared at the night sky, feeling the sadness of having to say goodbye. She wanted to see Jolene's smile one last time, take it in and place it in her memory where she'd be able to go back and see it whenever she needed to feel better. She needed one last dose of Jolene Aster.

Out she climbed, carrying her bottle of expensive wine she had kept in her office, something that now reeked of pretentious rot. Jolene was simple.

136

She'd take one look at that bottle and know that Sarah wanted to impress one last flattering image. Did she want Jolene to remember her as a wine snob? No. She wanted her to remember her as a kind, thoughtful person who had her act together, who didn't hate her life and wish she could wake up from the nightmare that took it over.

Sarah was a lot of things, but not a person who liked others to see her weaknesses. She placed the wine bottle on her front seat, closed the door, and advanced with purpose towards Frenchy's backyard, ignoring the dead cicadas blanketing the street.

~ ~

Sarah entered the backyard and all the faces blurred, except for Jolene's. She stood talking with her mother and a few other people, laughing and tilting her head backwards. She wore a candied smile, ready to move forward and leave it all behind.

An energy radiated from Jolene that spread outward, infusing Sarah with the fresh vibe of being alive, of breathing, of taking in the simplistic moments and getting high off their sweetness. Jolene differed from anyone she'd known. She moved through the air with grace and powered the space with her vitality for all that flowed above the looping roadways that trapped most people.

That vitality had the power to remind people that living life on one's own terms rejuvenated and kept things from the drag of complacency. In each turn, each new direction, each stride forward, she left no regrets. When she took a step, she did so with confidence. No doubt, Jolene realized if she didn't take that step, she'd succumb to the root of all death, the dreaded comfort zone where people went to kill their dreams.

Sarah decided to text her as she watched from the opposite end of the yard. "I'm going to miss you."

Alerted to the buzz, Jolene dug her cell out of her front pocket. She glanced at it and a smile grew.

"I see you blushing." Sarah texted again. "Why are you blushing?"

A larger smile rose on Jolene's face as she scanned the crowd. Then, she found her, and that smile transformed into a surrendered shrug. Jolene's smile radiated brighter with each step towards her. She landed in front of her carrying a glow. "I'm so glad you came," Jolene said. "I wanted the chance to say goodbye."

"Goodbye? Who's saying goodbye right now?" Sarah grabbed a flute glass from one of Frenchy's bakery staff. "I'm not saying goodbye right now. We have a party to enjoy." She grabbed a plate from the table. "And crepes. We have lots of crepes."

Jolene grabbed a plate too, and together they filled them with crepes, lentil salad and barbequed pork chops seasoned with a tart and tangy marinade.

After they gorged on food, Sarah pulled Jolene towards the patio area that served as a makeshift dance floor. "I'm getting at least one dance before we say goodbye."

Jolene pulled backwards. "No. I don't dance. I'm clumsy and people end up stepping on my toes. It's very embarrassing."

A beautiful crimson hue rose on her face.

Sarah led her into a small space in the corner of the dance floor, and pulled her in close. "Looks like I've found another fear."

Jolene began to move her hips, and soon fell right into place in Sarah's arms. "You see what I just did with that fear?" Jolene asked.

Sarah moaned and led her into a turn. She watched with deep pleasure as Jolene opened to the melody with stylized grace, flicking her long hair in tandem with her sultry sway.

When the song ended, Jolene led her towards the bar.

Under the subtle glow of stringed golden lights and the spicy scent of the barbeque, they shared silly stories of childhood mishaps and family debacles. Sarah wanted the night to last, but of course, it disappeared as fast as a covert wink.

"I have a confession," Sarah said, as the night grew closer to midnight.

Jolene tilted her head in the way Sarah already grew fond of. "I'm listening."

"I'm seriously going to miss you."

"I'm going to miss you too," Jolene said with a wary face.

"I have another thing to confess."

Jolene arched her eyebrow.

"I lied the other day. I did. I flat out lied." Sarah paused then dove into the delivery of her truth. "Scuba actually is for me. It is. I want to do it. I want to jump into a big body of water and breathe air out of a tank."

"Why did you lie?"

"Frenchy and I didn't want you to miss out on your contract."

"Aw, really?"

"And your mother, too."

"My mother?"

"I promised I wouldn't say anything, but it's kind of cool that your mom loves you enough to let you go." Sarah gazed over at Maureen who was chatting with Jack. "She wants you to be happy. We all do."

Jolene followed her gaze and grinned. "Thanks for telling me about my mom." She bit her lip. "That means a great deal."

They shared a comfortable slice of silence before Sarah had to get going. She had a long day ahead of her in a few short hours, and a series of never-ending days after that. The fun had to end at some point. "Care to walk me to my car?"

Jolene released a murmur. "Of course."

They strolled out to the side yard, close enough that their hands brushed together.

Sarah stopped before the driveway, before the harshness of the streetlights. She gazed at Jolene, taking in her beauty and wanting to gather the courage to kiss her.

"I hope you'll get certified and come visit me one day. I'd love to show you my world."

Sarah wanted to see her world. She wanted off her own world and onto Jolene's, at least once in her lifetime. She wanted to escape into it and take a ride, hugging Jolene as she led the way off the loop and onto paths that flipped her upside down and offered her a new perspective on those things in life that always bored her when right side up. She wanted to feel the breeze as they flew away and left the problems aside, both indulging on the freshness that entered as they rounded the curves. She wanted to latch onto that momentum and keep pursuing the adventure that could never happen on the tried and true paths of Sarah's reality. Even if just once.

"Maybe one day I'll surprise you."

Jolene fidgeted with her fingers as she stood before her. "Promise me one thing."

Sarah stood tall in front of her. "What's that?"

"Promise me you'll do something every day to feel alive. You know, shake things up so they don't get all rusty and stagnant. Face those cicadas and underwater giggles whenever you can."

Jolene pulled on her heart, and Sarah wanted to wrap herself in her arms. Instead, she nodded. "Yeah, I promise you I will."

"Good."

Sarah caught the finality in her voice. "I should go."

Jolene nodded.

"I want you to know I'm grateful for all you did. You helped me," she said, veering to move in closer, "and, well, thank you."

Jolene paused, as if reluctant to share her thoughts. "No problem. Thanks for coming."

They gazed at each other for a solid, uninterrupted moment. Then, Jolene splayed her ivory fingers on Sarah's cheek, cradling them there for a long, beautiful pause.

"Jolene," her mother yelled. "You've got to see this."

Jolene dropped her hand and laughed. "Her timing is impeccable."

"You should go."

"Yeah."

One of them had to walk away. They couldn't stand there forever in question, wondering what pain they would feel once they saw each other for the last time. They had to turn and walk away, rip the Band-Aid off and move forward with their different lives.

Jolene opened her arms. "Can I get a hug?"

"Of course." Sarah fell into her embrace. "Thanks for everything," she whispered.

After a moment, Jolene backed away from the hug. "Always a pleasure."

"Okay then, safe travels." Sarah's throat tightened. She relieved it by turning and rushing away, out of the darkness of the pine trees and into the light where nothing could hide. She hurried towards her car, parked under a bright, glaring yellow streetlight, sniffing back a sadness she'd yet to feel for anyone in her life.

If Sarah traipsed away like that, like some cold executive shaking a customer's hand and wishing her well, she'd never be able to forgive herself. She may never see that woman again, never have the chance to take her in her arms and feel what her lips would do to her once they connected with hers. Would she be always shameful of that moment in her life when she chickened out and went back to her safety zone, on the field where grass only grew one way, allowing not even a clover in to color it with diversity? She couldn't bear to stand in a green field of grass and wonder what that clover could've done to the landscape had she been brave enough to let it enter and bloom.

She didn't want that moment to go undiscovered.

She whirled about and rushed back towards the side yard, wanting to shake something up in her life that offered no promise, no future, nothing but the glory of that one moment. As she passed the circular driveway and entered the path towards the backyard, Sarah saw Jolene standing still and facing her, like a glowing silhouette.

Without a word, Sarah approached her and let her guard down, destroying that what-if question before it could overpower her. She cradled Jolene's face in her hands and looked deep into her eyes.

Under the glow of the moon, Sarah kissed Jolene's velvety lips. They warmed against hers, comforting and soothing the tinged edges of the void from moments ago.

"I hate regrets, too," Sarah said, her voice a mere whisper.

"I'm glad to hear that."

Jolene's breath teased Sarah with its tangy flirt.

Sarah slid her hands down to Jolene's waist, pulling her closer. The moon responded by shadowing them in privacy to explore the beauty in the softness of their kiss. Sarah pressed herself against Jolene, seeking out her breath, wanting to stay connected with her pulse, her sweet taste, her undivided attention.

Jolene pulled away, and then she kissed Sarah's eyelids with slow, deliberate, endearing tenderness. Then, she traveled back to her lips. When Jolene brushed her lips again, Sarah could taste the salt that her own tears had created. They tasted real and raw, and of a new truth, one that, no doubt, would eventually lead her straight into the arms of a ballsy move somewhere around the bend.

Sarah pulled back and gazed into Jolene's eyes for a long, sensually charged moment. "That's going to stay with me for a very long time."

"I hope so." Jolene smiled, and caressed Sarah's cheek. "Get certified, and come visit me." Then, she walked away, glancing back over her shoulder one last time before going back to her party, to the party that would send her off into a world Sarah wanted to get to know a whole lot better.

Chapter Ten

On her first morning back in Bonaire, Jolene invited a fellow lead from her team, Will, out for a dive. As Jolene finned along, she focused on the creatures and their wondrous world. She swam along at a melodic pace, buoyant and one with the water.

Diving was her therapy. She entered into its oxygen-rich office and listened to what it had to tell her. It always warned her to slow down and take life in with the respect it deserved. Jolene would relax and follow its wise instruction. It would remind her to stay alert to the subtle nuisances glistening in her peripheral, challenging her to wait with patience on her next fancy, so as to enjoy the space that opened and allowed for the recharge of her mind. Cleared of clutter, free from the bombardment of self-talk, Jolene learned to embrace the moment at hand as a time for replenishing what the world above eroded. Diving taught her that clarity was her biggest ally, and through that clarity she could love life abundantly.

Jolene finned towards the coral, hovering above a patch of white sand and some blue parrotfish. She landed back in her element, in that peaceful ravine that challenged her mind, body, and spirit to focus on that one precious moment where nothing else in the world mattered but the breaths she drew and the respect she shared with the world around her.

As she eventually began her ascent, she thought of Sarah. She hoped one day soon Sarah would visit and she'd be able to share that Zen experience with her.

~ ~

When she returned to her apartment a few hours later, sand-covered and wet still, she delighted at a new text message from Sarah.

"I hope you arrived back safely, and I hope that island appreciates your return. Maryland doesn't feel quite right without you. I hope that didn't sound too weird. It did. Didn't it? I don't care. I'll say it again. Maryland misses you. Okay, maybe it's me more than the state. Yes, I miss you. So there you have it. I miss you."

Jolene enjoyed Sarah's rambling. "You need to come to Bonaire," Jolene responded. "Let Maryland groan a bit more in your absence."

Jolene showered as she waited on her reply, taking extra time to enjoy the rich lather of the suds as they tickled her scalp and traveled down her shoulders and across her tender nipples. She smoothed the suds down her belly and into her now pulsing area of desire, hungry and very much awake.

Alone in her vanilla scented, steamy haven, Jolene tiptoed into the moment, exciting the parts of her that had been asleep far too long. She closed her eyes, and allowed the warm water to bring her into a sweet embrace with imaginings of Sarah sharing the droplets as they explored their entwined bodies. The fantasy of Sarah's delicate lips brought her into a blissful high with their eager journey down her neck, past the curvature of one of her swollen breasts, and onto her erect nipple hungry for release.

Jolene traced her navel with the tip of her wet finger then traveled down to her clit, intensifying the pulse that demanded attention. While imagining Sarah taking pleasure with the heat of her tender breast, Jolene sought to relieve the pressure building between her legs. As her fingers flicked, her body bucked, and within seconds, her body trembled as she came in a fit of ecstasy.

~ ~

"Can I ask you something personal?" Sarah had texted her back.

Jolene's stomach fluttered. "Sure."

"Have you ever had your heart broken?"

Jolene leaned back in her recliner. "Briefly."

"Briefly? How's briefly possible? You couldn't have loved her then. You can't love someone and only be briefly heartbroken."

Jolene chuckled. She adored the way Sarah's mind worked as if it was overrun with sugar, and then it spun its wheels to chase out the pent-up energy. "I thought I loved her. Then, she left Bonaire, and I never missed her."

"Why did she leave?"

"She missed her family too much to be away from them. It's kind of typical."

Ten minutes passed with no reply.

Had she come across as insensitive?

Ugh, she hated the sudden feeling of insecurity that coated her.

If Jolene kept flirting with those curiosities over Sarah, she would land in dangerous territory.

She put her phone on the table near her recliner and entered back into the moment at hand with some deep breathing.

~ ~

Several days had passed before Sarah called her again.

Jolene stared at the phone and steadied her hand over her gently thumping heart. She picked it up and Sarah's voice caused her heart to buck at a new level.

"Why did you move to Bonaire? I mean I know it's paradise and all that hoopla. But, what possessed you to pack your bags for good and leave home in the first place?"

Jolene remembered that day with vivid detail. The rain poured down. Her mother's tense eyes blanched her. The car stunk like mildew and despair. "My mother drove me to take my driver's test when I turned sixteen. When I passed, she let me drive her old clunker home. As we passed by the library near our neighborhood, she said to me, 'Now I can finally stop taking the bus to get groceries and go to the bank. I have you now.'"

"Your mother wanted you to be her driver?"

"She hated driving, and still does. When I turned eighteen, I got away. She needed to get brave, and as long as I remained her taxi driver and her mediator in tricky conversations, she would never be able to stand on her own and survive."

"She trapped you," Sarah stated. "That's why you fear being trapped. You moved away to avoid any regrets that staying would've caused."

"You have me all figured out," Jolene teased.

"I'm still working on that," Sarah said. "So, Maryland doesn't stand a chance, does it?"

"I get these anxious pings in my heart when I'm there. I feel like I'm always looking over my shoulder. All the work I did to find peace through the years gets unraveled the minute I step off the plane. It's too busy, too fast."

"It sure is. My life is a constant blur," Sarah said. "I don't know what my mind would reveal if I learned to sit quiet and listen to it. I would be afraid to find out. My mind is always plagued with a constant stream of background static. All the time. It's as if someone is shoveling coal into my engine and stoking it. It never sputters, only goes at everything with blazing speeds. It's exhausting. I should do something about that. I should do something about a lot of things, but," she took a breath, "I don't have the time." She sighed. "It's my job. It's all I have. I feel a sense of obligation to the place. They paid for my master's degree. They pad my account with stock options. They pay me well. I mean really well. I lack for nothing. I even have a house cleaner and a gardener. Of course, no one actually gets to see their work because—"

"—because you're too busy."

"Because I'm too busy. And, that brings me to another fear I'd like to reveal."

"I'm listening."

"I fear that I will die forgetting the spicy thrill of food. Everything tastes bland, even though I douse it in red-hot peppers. Does that ever happen to you?"

"Italian dressing causes me to sweat, dear."

"Can I be honest with you?" Sarah asked.

"Go on."

"My tummy just did a little flip when you called me dear."

Jolene's tummy reciprocated. "Then, dear, I shall refer to you by that more often."

"I'd like that."

Another week passed by when Sarah contacted her again. That time by text. "Do you ever have stressful days?"

"No one's immune." The day before, two entitled divers ignored Jolene's instructions and stayed below a whole twenty minutes past the group's planned dive. They could've been lost or in distress, for all Jolene knew. Just as she was about to dive back in to search for them, they surfaced and told her they had paid for a scuba trip and they would spend it any way they pleased.

The second dive of the morning had to be cut short, thanks to their selfishness. "I live in paradise, but I still have to face some of the headaches of dealing with people that you do."

"It's so unsettling, isn't it?" Sarah texted back.

"Nothing's perfect. Life takes patience."

"Patience for what?"

"Dreams."

"Aren't you already where you want to be in life?" Sarah asked her.

"Of course, but it's important to have new dreams on the horizon."

"What about living right now, in the present? Don't dreams get in the way of that?"

"We need dreams," Jolene said. "The issue comes in when we focus only on the end result and ignore the space in between now and then."

"What're your dreams?" Sarah asked.

"I want to open a scuba shop on the island with a gift boutique attached. I'll sell dive gear and the artisans on Bonaire can sell their work through consignment. Win-win for everyone."

"How do you stay focused on the goal and still remain so focused on the now?"

"Well, I plot points, so I have a faint idea of where I'm going. Then, I head towards them. The trick is to stay present in each step. That's where the magic of life resides. It resides in now, not some future date. If I never arrive at the date, that's okay because I enjoyed the moments in between."

"You're so lucky that you know your purpose."

"It's taken me time," Jolene said. "I used to never want to be comfortable. I never wanted to put a lot of leverage into something that might disappoint, because I feared that if I relied too much on those roots to keep me grounded,

I could end up in a disastrous situation one day where those roots would upend when the wind blew too hard."

"What changed?"

"I read some books. My father's books in his den. They reminded me that a person can't grow without roots."

"That's very profound."

"Books are full of life lessons."

"Can I tell you a secret?" Sarah asked.

Jolene loved the word secret. It hinted of intimacy, and she craved that right then. "I'd love to hear your secret."

A long pause ensued, one that comforted and aroused Jolene's desire for more of Sarah.

"I don't love my job. I don't. This didn't fully dawn on me until lately. One day I woke up and realized maybe there's more to life than clocking in and clocking out. I miss the climb. Now I'm coasting. I know my job inside and out, and even though I'm tossed problems all day long, I only have to dig into my trashcan of past issues and I solve them. I know where to find them. The routine kind of sucks the life out of it now. I need to find a way to love it again."

"What specifically would help you love it again?"

"I need more than numbers. All I do is deal with numbers now. I've forfeited creativity for number crunching. Without an outlet for my creativity, I've turned into an old bitter lady chucking strangers the bird along the Beltway."

"You wouldn't chuck the bird, would you?"

"Oh, I would. I do. I do it most every day. Strangers look over at me, and I chuck the bird. With good reason. They cut me off. They ride my ass.

They're texting. So, I chuck the bird often. I'll probably be shot one of these days. I'm becoming more addicted to my imaginary button every day."

"Imaginary button?"

"Yes. When I press it down, I erase all the angry, rude people who like to cut me off and tailgate me and I get to turn them into pixie dust. Poof. Gone. Just like that. It keeps me sane. I should be sane."

"Sane would never look as good on you."

"So you're agreeing I'm a little insane?"

"You're quirky." Jolene braved on, "And, I like it."

"You've transformed quirky into a cool thing. I'll take the compliment."

Jolene could spend the rest of her life distracted by their chat, never tiring of the digression. "I enjoy your rambles, you know."

"I'm a rambling fool, huh?" Sarah asked.

"A fool? No. You're too curious and determined to be a fool. Not to mention, a little fun."

"Just a little?"

~ ~

Jolene enjoyed talking with Sarah. They'd have those philosophical discussions and never settle on an actual answer to their questions. They'd leave each other hanging in curious denouement, clinging to the excitement of their next chat.

Jolene found herself being further drawn into Sarah's complex view, where her search for meaning evolved into a journey of her own self-discovery, poking the critical question of why she existed. Jolene began to ask herself what her purpose was. Bringing a lifetime experience capable of changing the way people interacted with the world? Did it go deeper? Did it need to go deeper? Would it grow to be more than diving by day, sleeping alone by night, and falling for a woman who had no real grasp on what she wanted, either?

Jolene had to be careful. Sarah couldn't live on an island any more than she could live so far away from the sea.

Text messaging and static-riddled phone calls would eventually turn into frustration, brought on by both the cruelty and beauty of the big looming ocean that lay between them.

~ ~

Jolene needed to get her heart and head back into balance. She needed a therapeutic escape. So, she asked Neil to join her for an early morning dive.

Under the water, Jolene set out to free herself from the complexities of concern, of the internal clock that suddenly began to inhibit her flow. The past and the future had no place underwater. Only that one singular moment mattered, when time dissolved and the present unfolded like a delicate flower, one precious petal at a time, each owning the space as it extended its affection outward to all in the fortunate position to witness it give birth to new vibrant shades of the rainbow and elaborate textures.

Within a few minutes, Jolene simmered in the peace of the sea, the only place that accepted her without expectation, opening its spirited arms to her in a symbiotic hug that calmed and centered.

By the time she and Neil reached their maximum depth of sixty feet, her consciousness shifted from overthinking, overanalyzing, and second-guessing to dancing with the eternal grace of being one with the feverish and dizzying beat of life. Swaddled in a buoyant embrace, the water guided Jolene to shift from dwelling on things she couldn't control to being immersed in the presence of majesty.

Free of time and the problems it carried in its wake, she flowed along the steady path of peace, a peace that trickled through her with delicious tease and lifted her out of the depths of worry and into the light of healing energy. Each breath hugged the next in one beautiful sonnet that caressed her soul, bringing about a profound sense of belonging to something greater than herself.

Connected to the boundless source of inspiration, Jolene drank from the savory cup of life, taking in all she could embrace.

That dive started out as any other, and turned into a spiritual revival, bringing her heart back to its finest beat where it joined with the beauty of the kelp, swaying to its earthy song. Her appetite for the underwater wilderness increased with each stroke, bringing her to exclusive destinations only accessible to those willing to let go of time and escape into the passion of the current.

~ ~

Jolene's words did something to Sarah. She wanted to be a better version of herself. Jolene opened her eyes to the trail of dissatisfaction she left behind her, piling up like brick walls to her ill-crafted plans at a good life. As a kid, Sarah had dreamed up a life filled with love, laughter, and fun. She saw herself on top, respected by her peers and subordinates, eager to be a part of something important, something purposeful, and something rewarding.

Sarah failed in all three parts. She had no obvious love life to speak of, and never had. All her past relationships hinged on lies and deceit brought on by self-defeating fears of not being able to materialize her desires. She barely laughed, unless she hung out with Frenchy and her grandson. And, fun. She didn't have time for fun. For the sake of comfort, she structured her life without regard to leeway to avoid the very thing she ended up creating, chaos.

No matter how much Sarah clung to the comfort zone, the thorns of circumstance found a way to rise through the ground and prick her anyway. With the constant flow of unknowns seeping in beneath everything, nothing stayed solid.

No surprise, when a person built anything on shaky ground, things tended to crumble. Standing in the rubble of those grainy plans, one would start to see the fallacies everywhere. They first showed up as little sticks, poking their splintery presences through the fallen chaos that once formed a symbol of strength. Then, those splinters rose and before long, a person would find herself tripping over them and failing to find any piece of solid ground to act as a lift out of the tumultuous field of disorder that once disguised itself as a solid plan.

Perhaps, like Jolene, she could find a way to enjoy her career again. She had created a false sense of expectations based on the ridiculous notion that a person could work twelve- to fifteen-hour days and not burn out, at least in the short-term. She created a major problem with those short-term bursts of focus. They turned into nonstop short-term projects because everyone assumed Sarah had what it took to get the job done. Who cared that she didn't get to eat dinner around a dining room table anymore? Who cared that she hadn't spoken with her best friend since Jolene's going away party a month before? Who cared that she missed Frenchy's grandson's birthday party because a client needed his reports immediately?

The company executives didn't care.

By jumping whenever they said jump, Sarah only communicated that she didn't care either. She created her own problem and only she could solve it. But how? Start working like a normal person, and set new standards? Maybe if she worked ten-hour days, she might enjoy the clients more. She wouldn't be irritated at every turn of the page because she'd be refreshed from having a balanced life where if she wanted to have dinner with her best friend at a normal dinner hour, she actually could.

Jolene set a fire in her, and Sarah wanted to keep feeding it. For the first time since graduating college, she didn't fear asking the question *what if*.

What if she got scuba certified? What if she went with Frenchy on a trip to Bonaire? What if she and Jolene enjoyed a long-distance friendship that could result in something even more meaningful than shared text messages in the middle of the night?

The question caused her to toss all night long in her lonely bed. In the shadows of the night, she decided to call Frenchy the next morning.

As usual, though, Sarah had to rush to get out the door on time. When she remembered to call Frenchy that afternoon she didn't answer. Then, she got sidetracked on another stupid work project.

Chapter Eleven

Frenchy opened her front door with five grocery bags hanging from each arm. She nudged the door shut with her heel before looking up and noticing the cable wires dangling from where her flat-screen television should've been hanging.

She dropped her bags of eggs, tomatoes, and other dinner fixings. Cans of white beans and tomato soup rolled across the wooden floor where her area rug from France should've been.

She scanned the room, taking inventory. Johnny's electric piano and Gibson guitar were gone, and the grungy recliner that still stunk of antiquated times when people smoked pipes and watched *The Three Stooges*, gone. Someone also stole the picture that Johnny's grandfather had painted for them of the lake house in Banner Elk.

She circled towards her dining room. "The wine rack and vintage wines. Oh my God, and the camera?"

Panic swam fast, drowning her in a swift and furious rampage of vulnerability. She dashed up the stairs to her bedroom. Her beloved Sleep Number bed. Gone. Yet the television still sat on top of the nightstand, cables secured.

She heard a noise. She stood still and the hum of silence that followed deafened her.

Click.

She glanced at the open window and saw the string from her mini-blinds hitting the frame.

She sighed. Then, something dreadful planted itself.

The robbers could still be in the house.

She dashed down the stairs and back into the foyer, tripping over her grocery bags and cracking the eggs as she pulled open the door. The muggy summer air suffocated her. She stood alone in her front yard panting like an overheated dog.

She peeked into the garage window. Everything was gone.

A knot sat in her stomach, pushing all senses south. She reasoned out that maybe the robbers collected junk the same way Johnny did. Surely, they could use all those rusty wrenches and gaudy stolen street signs for something better than dust collectors in a double bay garage. Right?

A troublesome question trampled through her mind, one that pushed her to the edge of reason in search for logic. Who would steal the stained coffee mug with Johnny's name on it other than someone with that identical name and thirst for grime?

The unsettling answer crawled into her heart like a tiger on the hunt for weak prey, slow, assertive and focused on one thing—to eat the beating heart right out of her.

They fought the night of Jolene's party when Frenchy begged Johnny not to go on that vacation with a group of strangers he started to call friends.

They had settled it.

Right?

Frenchy trusted her gut as one would trust an umbilical cord to provide life-sustaining nutrients. The guitar, the piano, the flat screen, the bed, all of it Johnny wanted.

A sickening buzz short-circuited its way up her throat and into her head where it zapped her with horrific intensity. Maybe he had a logical explanation. Maybe he hired people to paint the house. Maybe he orchestrated that as a prank, teaching her one of his many life lessons.

She reached into her pocket for her cell, and called her husband. It rang five times before he picked up.

"Hey," he said in a strange echo of a voice.

She tested him. "We've been robbed."

"We weren't robbed."

"We *were* robbed. Don't tell me we weren't." Her voice hinged on hysteria.

"You didn't see my note in the foyer?"

"What note? What did it say?"

"You should go read it and call me back."

"Don't be stupid. Tell me what it says. Are we renovating? Are we painting?" She couldn't form a swallow.

"Read the note."

"Tell me. I'm right here on the phone." Her throat dried as if sprayed with varnish.

"I'm going to hang up. Read it and call me back."

She surveyed the neighborhood and noticed Maureen gardening. She wore her cheery sun hat with the red flower Frenchy adored.

Did she see him moving his things out?

Frenchy waved, and Maureen stood and offered her a hearty wave back.

Does she know?

She marched towards her front door and entered. She glanced at the table in the foyer and saw her name handwritten on an envelope. She ripped it open.

"Frenchy, I'm sorry to leave this way, but I saw no other option. I've contemplated this move for some time now, but never knew quite how to bring it up. Bottom line is that I'm miserable. I have been for a while. I've tried to tell you this countless times, but you never listen to me. I talk and you ignore me. I'm in prison, like I have no way of escaping and enjoying my life. I want to be free. I want to live life. I turned sixty. What do I have to show for living my life? A big house with no experiences? I can't do this anymore. I told you we never should've gotten married. The marriage messed us up. Then, the whole redoing our vows thing did me in. I told you not to do that. I wish you would've listened to me in the first place. Call me when you get this."

~ ~

Frenchy walked. She walked for five hours straight without taking a break. She walked through her neighborhood, down Route 1, into Arbutus, around the UMBC campus, up Frederick Road in Catonsville, and circled back to the place she used to call home up until Johnny destroyed it with his selfish need to be free.

She just wanted to bring that man joy by serving him homemade chicken soups and French biscuits on cold winter days. She wanted to snuggle with him on the couch, watch old movies, and eat pie. She just wanted a partner who relished in the smell of freshly baked bread on Sunday mornings as they curled up to steaming mugs of hot cocoa. What she got instead was someone as cold as the marble stoop outside her front door. She cooked him breakfast, lunch and dinner, and he had the nerve to come home from his automotive shop with his tote still full. "The guys wanted to eat out," he'd say.

She tried to cook healthy for him, and he ate hot dogs and baked beans instead. He was sixty and verging on a major heart attack. Frenchy just wanted to protect him. She sat through his stupid sitcoms each night, pretending to find them as funny as he did. She slept in flannels every night, even in the middle of the blazing heat of summer, so he could be comfortable with a fan blowing on high speed. She sacrificed her craft room so he could have a music room full of dusty sheet music and a piano with missing keys.

How embarrassing. What would she ever tell Sarah? How could she tell her employees? Would Maureen still favor her as a sister-in-law?

She managed to get through an entire two weeks without telling a soul. If she didn't talk about it, it would die out eventually, shrivel up like a piece of dead sunburned skin and fall off. Maybe the result would be better.

It had to be better.

Sarah called several times, but she couldn't talk to her. Not yet.

She walked for hours each evening, emptying her mind on the pavement so she could get through the night without crying.

On a Tuesday, two weeks later, she turned another year older and treated herself to half a box of wine. A little drunk and blurry eyed, she opened her refrigerator and stared at a sea of vegetables she had purchased the day Johnny stole her sense of place in the world. She pulled out two tomatoes, a head of broccoli and some snap peas. She could toss in some chicken and call it a decent lunch for the next day.

For dinner, she'd open a can of tuna fish and toss in a few celery bits.

She began her dash around the kitchen, prepping for no one but herself.

She cut half the celery stalk and stared at the other end. "How wasteful and pointless for you," she whispered.

She picked up the unused half and smoothed her fingers over its grainy texture. "You worked all season long to grow to become an important part of the food chain. Dreadful how I waste you like this."

She chomped into it and wrestled to break its stringy grip with her teeth. "I know how you feel." She chewed it. "If I discard you in the trash can, your purpose will be taken away from you. You were meant for greater things, more than sitting idle on top of junk waiting on trash day. You were supposed to be absorbed and used as rich fuel to produce energy and potential. You could've been a catalyst to greatness. You know," Frenchy said, staring at its dull green, "I'm not very different than you right now. The least I could do is start composting. At least one of us would have purpose."

She wrapped the celery stalk in foil, taking care to tuck it in and preserve its life. She twirled it around with her finger.

"He was my purpose. He's the reason I bought you. I'm sorry, but I don't like you," she spoke to the celery stalk. "You taste like dishwater." Tears began to roll down her cheeks. "Everything I did, I did for him. What am I supposed to do with the rest of my life now?"

She tore off the foil. "No reason two of us should rot." She bit into the celery, attacking it with her indifference, forcing purpose back into the room by allowing at least one of them to exist for a reason.

As she swallowed the last of the stringy blandness, her cell rang.

Sarah.

She collected herself then decided to answer. "Hey."

"Happy Birthday to you. Happy Birthday to you. Happy Birthday, my young friend. Happy Birthday to you!"

Frenchy picked up a towel from the counter and covered her mouth with it, forcing the cry back down her throat. She faked a giggle to bring her back to the surface.

"Are you crying?"

She cleared her throat, composing herself for the sake of salvaging a morsel of her dignity. No one would understand. Not even Sarah. "No."

"Are you sure?"

"Yes."

A long pause ensued. "Did I interrupt you, then?"

Frenchy swallowed the lump in her throat. "I'm fixing a salad."

"Salad? For your birthday?"

"I'm getting older. I need to be healthy."

"I have an idea of how we can celebrate this new year of yours. Let's continue with our scuba training and get certified. Then, let's go to Bonaire! Let's do it. Let's just do it! What do you say? Best birthday gift ever?"

Frenchy could barely breathe. The empty room swallowed her and chewed her into stringy pieces of useless nothingness. She couldn't handle Sarah's happiness. Not now. "I've got to work on some things right now," Frenchy said. "It's not a good time."

"Is everything alright?"

"I'm busy with the bakery right now. You know how that is?"

"Yeah. I do. Let's change that."

"I said not right now," Frenchy snapped. "You're not the only one with things going on in life."

"What's with the attitude?"

"I'm overwhelmed. It'll pass. It always does."

Sarah sighed her irritation. Then, in her usual scattered way, asked, "What kind of cake are you having after your salad?"

Frenchy dropped her shoulders. "Not sure, yet."

"Ah, Johnny isn't home with it, yet."

Emotion swelled in her throat. "Listen, I have to go."

"Yeah, okay. I'll call soon."

How long could she keep up the charade? Even gone, Johnny casted the upper hand with his silence, picking off layers and leaving Frenchy naked. Anger began to cork its way up her spine, powered by the notion that Johnny put her in that position to wither and assume that she failed at the one thing she rocked at, love.

Two weeks later, Frenchy heard a knock at the front door. It was Maureen.

She didn't answer.

She couldn't.

She hadn't even talked to her best friend about it, how could she talk to her ex-sister-in-law?

~ ~

For Sarah, time marched on like a soldier in the heat of battle. It stopped for no one, and before long, another span of weeks had passed since she spoke with Frenchy.

Sarah snuck into an empty office once the facilities management guy carried the last of Sam's belongings out of it. Thankfully, he stayed on additional time until she could secure his replacement. Not one shred of Sam's existence remained, aside from the nail holes where he hung collages of his family in Nags Head. If all went well in the coming week, Sarah's new assistant, Sally, would fill the walls with her personal belongings and become the newest member of The Ascension Group.

Sarah would spoil her with a new stand-up desk and bookshelf, and if Sally didn't object, she'd even decorate the walls with the new success pictures she bought at Milton's Gallery on her trip to New York City in early spring. She would treat Sally well, and in return she hoped Sally would reciprocate.

Of course other members of leadership wanted their assistants to have the office, too.

Her director, Tom, had hinted to Sarah that the tides would begin to change. "With the new owners, we'll even get that new gym we've been pitching for."

A gym would be perfect. The stupid gym around the corner from her house opened at five a.m. Due to rush hour traffic, that didn't leave her enough time to exercise, shower and get to work on time for her nine a.m. staff meeting. With a gym on-site, Sarah could leave her house at five a.m., before rush hour traffic. Then, she could exercise and shower right at work.

"Between us," Tom, said, "I'm marking the room as taken so accounting doesn't sneak in and claim it for themselves. Good things are in store. Be patient, keep your head low, and don't cause waves."

Tom always had her back.

Sarah noticed a small crack in the wall above the footer molding in the corner of the room. She'd get Henry from maintenance to fix it right away, as soon as she got word Sally could move in.

Just then, Calvin, the marketing student intern from USG, rushed past the door. Sarah froze, not wanting to be seen drooling over the empty space. Then, her cell rang.

Frenchy.

She picked up on the end of the first ring. "Hello," she whispered, kneeling in the hidden corner. "It's about time you returned my call."

"Do you have plans tonight?" Frenchy asked.

Calvin passed by again, that time with excruciating slowness as he read a report.

"Well?" Frenchy asked.

"I'll be at the office," she continued to whisper. "You know this."

"We need to talk. I'm sorry I haven't called you back. I've been so—"

"—yeah. Yeah. I know. Busy." Hurt curled around the edges of Sarah's words. Frenchy hadn't returned any of Sarah's calls. Sarah hadn't been in the mood to be snapped at either. "So, is everything okay?"

"Long story. Best over wine. Do you have time for dinner tonight or not?"

She couldn't drop work projects to get drunk on cheap wine like she used to back in their early days. "I'm going to be here until at least seven."

"Well, I eat dinner at five," Frenchy said. "But, I can do seven."

"It won't be seven. It'll be more like eight-thirty. And, I can't stay long. I've got a huge meeting in the morning." Sarah exhaled the last of her energy.

"You're killing yourself for them. You know they'd spit you out and kick you to the side if they needed to, right? That's what assholes do. They use you to get what they want then toss you out like a greasy bag from a fast food joint. Would they visit your gravesite if you died on them right now?"

"I'm sure they'd send flowers. They'd fill the funeral home with lots and lots of daisies. They know I love them. They know a lot about me here. They know when I need to pee, when I get hungry, when I'm on my period. We're close. Really close. Like a pseudo family."

"They're all a bunch of junkies, and quite frankly you're turning into one yourself. Everyone puts work before people, and I'm sick of it." Frenchy verged on hysterics.

"What's wrong with you?"

"People are nothing but selfish idiots," she cried.

"You're freaking me out, Frenchy. Is something wrong?"

"I need you."

"Of course," Sarah softened. "I'm here for you. What's happening?"

"I'll be okay. I just need to chat."

Sarah rose and tiptoed to the door, glancing both ways to ensure a clean exit. Once in the hallway, she picked up her pace, heading back to her corner office. "Okay. I'll try to leave here earlier. Should I bring the bread Johnny likes?"

"No," she said with a firm stop. "Bring that wine I like."

"I'm not bringing boxed wine to dinner. I'll get a bottle."

"Just bring the damn box," Frenchy snapped and hung up.

~ ~

Best friends were supposed to be there for each other to wipe the spills when life got messy. Frenchy maintained their friendship much better than she did. Frenchy always said the right thing. She always had an appropriate card to mark an occasion. She never failed to call and sing her Christmas carols each year.

Frenchy was Sarah's reliable jacket. She could wear her for weeks on end and never tire. Then, when the sun rose a little higher in the sky and remained a bit longer, Sarah draped her over the side of her chaise lounge for the season. When cooler, less-friendly conditions rushed in, she only had to reach for her trusted jacket and be comforted. The cold, miserable barrenness of winter couldn't destroy what that jacket protected.

Frenchy was always the one nurturing and protecting. But, Frenchy sounded like she needed Sarah to stand up and be her jacket now.

Sarah first met Frenchy in high school when she needed a job to pay for her car. She entered into Frenchy's Parisian bakery shop and applied to be counter help. "You're perfect," Frenchy said, spinning her around to face the kitchen. "You see that counter there?" Frenchy pointed to the stainless steel work area behind the serving counter.

"Sure, yeah."

"That's where the magic happens. That's where we create happiness. We take dough and we knead it until it becomes soft and pliable, flexible to the rigidity of the box it came to us in. It comes to us as powder, and we turn it into something people can sink their teeth into, something that waters their mouths and keeps them coming back for more. We're in the business of baking love."

Frenchy impressed Sarah as a woman who had a few broken synapses brought on by a few too many psychedelic mushrooms in her high school days. "Yeah, that's great. Listen, I just need a job."

"Oh, honey, this isn't just a job. You're going to learn so much from everyone here. That's Big Mike in the back room."

Big Mike walked by a small round window in the door, showcasing his chef hat and angular jawline.

"He makes the best truffles. What's your favorite baked good?"

Sarah wanted to run. She wanted to bolt out the door and get away from the freak woman who spoke with way too much excitement for nine in the morning. "I wouldn't know. I'm sorry."

Concern took over her smile. "Oh, don't worry. I'll fix that. Here," she said, pulling out the stool. "You sit right here and I'll get you something that you'll never be able to forget."

Two minutes later, a creamy, chocolaty ball of heaven sat before Sarah alongside a steaming oversized mug of hot chocolate. From the first moment her tongue met with the flavorful truffle, Sarah's life would never be the same again.

Almost thirteen years her senior, Frenchy became her best friend. Many conversations took place while getting high off the sweet aromas of éclairs and cream puffs at the back counter of her colorful, toasty bakery shop.

They got through dating mishaps, car accidents, deaths, and health crises together. Frenchy helped her discover the therapeutic effects of coffee. Sarah loved the bold, aromatic flavor of the roasted beans. She loved how that richness lingered long after that last delicious sip. Sarah couldn't get through a morning without at least three cups since.

Frenchy stood in line next to her at the community college as she enrolled. Frenchy knocked sense into her when she announced she'd be quitting community college two classes from graduation because she received her first B. Frenchy threw her a graduation party, and she wiped away her tears when her siblings, sprawled all across the country, failed to show up and celebrate. Frenchy jumped up and down in her living room with her when she got the job offer at Ascension. When Sarah landed in her current role as a marketing executive, the youngest in the company, Frenchy stopped by with balloons and chocolate-covered strawberries.

So when Frenchy begged her to bring cheap wine, she obeyed.

Sarah could've used some extra fine-tuning in the friendship department. She didn't have the eloquent words at her disposal. She didn't know how to comfort. She had no clue what to do with all the silence that engulfed Frenchy's living room as they sat stiffly, staring ahead at the unlit fireplace.

"I don't know what to say," Sarah finally came out with it.

"You don't have to say anything. Sit here and get drunk with me."

"Why didn't you tell me you were having issues?"

"Two reasons. One, I'm embarrassed. So, I wanted to see if I could fix it before anyone realized it broke. Why worry you if I didn't have to?"

"And two?"

"I didn't want to bring you down."

Sarah took another sip of the bitter, stale merlot. Wires stuck out of the hole Johnny left behind when he stole the flat-screen television. "Was he cheating?"

"He says no."

Johnny wouldn't cheat. The two of them fit together, at least on the surface. Frenchy waited until her late thirties to get married. She refused to settle on the idiots who treated her to the occasional dinner or night out to country line dancing at the Dixie Exchange. When Johnny walked into her life, Frenchy smiled from her soul. Sarah had never seen her friend's face light up as it did for him. "I don't get it."

"I reasoned that maybe he was sick." Frenchy laughed and a tear rolled down her cheek. "But he's not sick. He's selfish. He told me I stopped being fun for him after I went through my early bout with menopause."

"What an asshole." The words lingered like a visitor on her tongue.

"He said I forced him into this marriage. He said the ultimatum ruined it for him."

"An ultimatum?"

"We'd been dating for years, Sarah. The man had been taking milk from the cow long enough. I wanted a firm commitment. I wanted to get married and have a big party. I wanted to wear a wedding dress and have my hair done and dance in front of a room of people."

Nothing good ever came from being forced.

"He suggests that we should be amicable about this. As if I'm going to step off to the side as he dictates what he gets and what I get. He said this can be easy or hard. I told him to bring it and marched out. He thinks I'm going to move into some rancid, overcrowded apartment building? He's got another thing coming."

"You better get this house."

Frenchy swallowed hard. "It stinks of him. I don't even want it. I figure we'll just sell the damn thing."

"So what's next?"

"I've had plenty of time to pity myself, and I'm sick of doing that. He's out gallivanting with who knows who, while I'm sulking over him? I don't want to be pathetic anymore. I hope I can stop."

Sarah hesitated on the end of a nod. "You've already stopped."

Frenchy stared at her as if waiting on more.

"I totally suck at this life advice stuff," Sarah said.

"You do kind of suck sometimes," Frenchy softened. "You're here when it counts, though."

Sarah opened her arms, and her best friend eased into them on a sniffle. "I have an idea."

"I already know what's coming out of your mouth," Frenchy said.

Of course she did. "It's a revived suggestion."

"You're going to fall in love with Jolene then leave me too."

"I would never leave you."

Frenchy lifted up. "Promise."

"Double promise."

"I'm not ready for a vacation to paradise just yet."

"It's okay," Sarah said. "I understand."

Her friend slipped back into the crook of her arm again, and the two emptied their glasses. Frenchy likely wondered what she'd do with the rest of her life, while Sarah mulled over whether she'd get another chance to meet up with the woman she'd been unable to get off her mind since Frenchy's party for her ungrateful, selfish jerk of an ex-husband.

~ ~

A few weeks later, when Frenchy called her and begged her to come to her bakery so they could chat, Sarah didn't refuse. Sarah showed up at four a.m., before the bakery opened, to be the friend Frenchy needed.

"He's in Italy right now." Frenchy slammed the spatula into the ciabatta flat bread. "While I'm packing up the house, the same house we built together from the ground up, he's strolling the streets of Milan with that stupid crooked grin of his, probably wearing those awful sandals with the stained straps. He's disgusting." She slammed the ciabatta again, that time sending it spinning off the counter and across the floor.

They both stared at it.

"You know how I found out about Italy?"

Sarah put a wad of dough in front of Frenchy. "Let's focus on something better."

She pounded the dough with her fist. "No. I'm done being quiet about this and pretending it doesn't bother me that he stole my life and splattered it all over the place. He promised me it wasn't about someone else. He looked right at me and promised me."

She raised her fist for another punch, but Sarah stopped her. "You need your knuckles."

"And he needed me." She began to sob. "He needed me, and he doesn't anymore. Now he has some bimbo named Tamara following him around like a loyal puppy." She began pulling at the dough. "I found revenge in imagining him stuffing his face with tasteless, frozen dinners on a folding chair. Now I lost that. I lost that, Sarah," she yelled and started throwing little balls of dough at the counter. "He stole my revenge!"

Sarah attempted to grab her wrist, but she wrestled back.

"You know how I found out about Tamara the bimbo?" The tears rolled

172

down her cheeks with a vengeance. "Tony told me. Little Tony," she wailed.

Tony, her precious grandson. Sarah surmised Frenchy mourned the loss of her in-law family more than the loss of Johnny. She lived for those Thursday nights when she and Johnny grilled bread and cheese for Tony and played with Legos in the middle of the living room floor.

"I'm sorry," Sarah said, placing her hands on a wad of dough. "You shouldn't have to suffer through any of this."

Frenchy's chin quivered. "It's not fair what he did to us."

"No. It's not."

"How dare he toss me out like a bag of garbage after all I've done for him? How dare he?" Frenchy cried.

The gravity of her despair scorched its way to the surface, burning a hole right through Frenchy's broken lid that disguised itself as protection.

"Life is so broken." Frenchy pressed her palm into the stretchy dough ball. It spread and the edges cracked. "Look, I can't even make sticky buns anymore."

Before Sarah could blink, Frenchy's body went into self-driving mode and she lost all control. Soon, dough found its way to the palm of her hands and she launched it, ball after ball, against the backsplash. "Fuck him."

Splatter.

Splatter.

Splatter.

Sarah joined in.

"Little Tony says Tamara the bimbo is awesome." Frenchy wound up her hands. "He says she's awesome. How the hell am I supposed to compete with that?"

They launched balls of dough like rockets. The release amazed Sarah.

With every throw, a little bit of tension subsided and left Sarah spinning with a sense of power. "You know, I used to like my job back before it got all serious. Why do people have to mess with things when they're not broken?"

"Because they're idiots. Complete idiots," Frenchy yelled as she launched into another assault against the backsplash. "I like that word. From now on, that's going to be my new name for him, The Idiot."

"I thought I hit the big leagues when I became an Ascension employee," Sarah said, joining in the war against their unhappiness. "I molded my own niche, and knew what they expected of me each day. Now, I have no idea why I'm even there. I sit in meetings all day that I don't care about, and am forced to report my notes to a president who wants to demote anyone who requires an hour off for a doctor appointment. It's despicable."

They tossed more dough and screamed as if someone had ripped their hearts right out from under their chests until finally they landed on the powdered floor in a heap of laughter.

"You know what we need?" Frenchy asked after they finally caught their breaths.

"Our sanity?"

"Sanity is overrated."

"True. Sometimes I wonder if it's better to live in ignorant bliss like The Idiot does," Sarah said, rubbing her chalky hands on her apron.

"We need to do something crazy, something that'll put that spark back in our hearts like we had, way back when we were still innocent enough to love life."

The void in Frenchy's eyes scared Sarah.

"You love life still. You have to. You're Frenchy. You're the one who always knocks sense into everyone. You can't not love life." Sarah reached out for Frenchy's hand. "Please tell me you still love life. I couldn't handle it if you didn't."

She broke out into a half smile. "You always know what to say, don't you?" Frenchy squeezed her hand, and then she wiped her face, smearing the dough further into her graying hair.

They stared at each other. Then, Sarah asked, "What do you suggest?"

"We take that trip using The Idiot's money. He owed it to me, so I snatched it back."

Excitement bubbled in Sarah. "Yeah?"

Frenchy climbed to her feet. "Hell yeah. I need to shake things up. So do you. We deserve this. I'll call Gerry and get us started back on our scuba lessons. You call Jolene and tell her the good news. Then, tell that stupid company of yours you need two weeks off because you've got a ticket to paradise."

Nothing would stop Sarah from going. Now that Frenchy was game, Sarah would figure out a way to get the time off from work. She had to. She could barely contain herself. She wanted to leap and squeal, and within seconds she did. "We're really going?"

"We are," Frenchy said. "Gosh, I feel so alive right now. I'm excited about something for the first time since planning the party for The Idiot. Even Maureen says her brother's an idiot."

Frenchy began to clear the mess from the counter. "I've got something to look forward to other than nasty emails from him and seeing little Tony light up every time he talks about the bimbo." Frenchy spun around and flung more dough in the air. "We're going to have such a good time. This is what we need. No drama. Just fun in the sun."

Frenchy's face beamed.

A big goofy smile landed on Sarah's face, thrilled by the spontaneous ride ahead, but a little apprehensive about pulling off the scuba diving in the middle of the ocean part. "We can do this."

"We can do this? We're not taking an exam or facing a lion in its den." Frenchy's face flinched.

Sarah reached out for her friend's hands. "Relax. I'm extremely excited. I'm just going over the logistics in my head."

"That's your problem. You're too far in your head. Here's your chance to drain your brain of all that nonsense, let go, and do something fun for a change." She handed her the broom. "Now, help me clean this mess."

Chapter Twelve

Jolene looked forward to her playful banter with Sarah. Their chats and messages became flirtier over time. What was the harm? They both suffered from loneliness. They both enjoyed the flirting. "Someone new started here this week," Jolene teased. "She asked me on a date."

"Are you going?"

"Should I?"

"Sounds like a potential dream come true for you. Someone who lives right there on the island. You can't get any better than that. Good for you. Really, it's good for you. You should be happy. You should definitely be happy."

Jolene pictured Sarah typing, her fingers a blur as she sported a maniacal face. Even in a text, she could hear her rushed commentary fighting its way free. "What would that be like for us, you know, if I started dating someone else?"

"I guess it might be strange for us to chat as often as we do."

"Would that bother you?" Jolene asked.

"Do you like her?"

"You didn't answer my question."

"It would irritate me."

Jolene sealed her eyes and took in the warmth of Sarah's jealousy. It comforted her. Sarah desired her. "Does this mean you're jealous?"

"I am. I can't help it. I don't like imagining you feeding someone appetizers and gazing into her eyes as the sun sets over the tropical waters that I'm sure will be the backdrop to every romantic dinner you enjoy together. I don't like it."

The texting paused.

"I should let my words marinate before sending," Sarah wrote. "I sound like a jealous lunatic. We shared one kiss and suddenly I don't want your lips brushing against another woman's. How childish am I? I'm very childish. You should know this about me."

"It's hot."

"The temperature is hot?"

"That, too."

"Too?" Sarah asked.

"I like that you're jealous."

"That's very cruel," Sarah wrote.

Testing Sarah's jealousy level like that was somewhat cruel. Fun, but slightly cruel. "Can I tell you something and you promise not to scold me?"

"Scolding can be fun under the right circumstances."

"Everything is fun with you," Jolene wrote, attracted to that side of her. "Dying of thirst in a desert would be fun with you, dear."

"It would be," Sarah wrote. "You're right. I'd turn it into a game. And, I'd win. I always win. Except when it comes to preventing that date from happening."

"Okay, promise not to scold."

"Fine," Sarah wrote.

"I was just playing you."

Not even a blink later, Sarah answered. "So, no date?"

"No to the date. There's not even a new person. This was just my lame attempt at being playful. I obviously have a lot to learn."

"No, I think you've got it down. I like this playful side."

"I'll take note of that," Jolene wrote.

"So how I interpreted this whole fabricated stunt matters to you?" Sarah asked.

"It does."

"Well good. That's very good because what I'm about to say would be awkward had you not answered that way."

"What would that be?" Jolene asked.

"Frenchy and I are coming to Bonaire."

Prickly heat rose on her arms. A wave of joy formed and rushed towards her. "You better not be joking."

"We've already lined up certification training with Gerry. We'll be heading to the quarry for our certification dive in two weeks."

Jolene paced her apartment living room. "You're actually coming to Bonaire?"

Sarah paused. "I am. I'm ready to wake up and have some fun."

After they ended their text, Jolene went for a run. She ran very fast, too fast for the ninety plus degrees of the island that day. Sweat poured down her face, stinging her eyes and spilling between her lips.

After the initial wave dissipated and slipped back into the dream from where it originated, Jolene freaked out, which freaked her out even more because not much sent her into a tailspin.

They'd end up having sex, which then meant they'd end up falling harder for each other, which then meant they'd part on a tearful goodbye and be left with an even deeper void than they had now.

Or worse, Sarah, in full-vacation mode, would do something rash like quit her job and move to Bonaire. And just like with Shannon, she would realize she missed her life too much, missed the convenience of having a Walmart Supercenter and Lowe's down the street, and missed having a skyscraper office building with premiere parking and a corner windowed office to venture into each day. She'd miss her car and the logic of traffic lights, and the ability to hop a plane at any time of the day to be in NYC or Florida or California within an hour or five.

She'd face a similar destiny to her life with Shannon, only that time, when things turned sour and the honeymoon phase ended, and the reality of being surrounded by the deep blue ocean settled in for Sarah, it would hurt. It would hurt like hell because unlike with Shannon, Sarah mattered to her.

~ ~

Sarah learned early on in her climb up the corporate ladder that knowledge didn't matter. Getting things done did. Sarah learned to be resourceful. She got to know many of the interns, ones Sam had overseen. They impressed her with their ability to adapt and react to the stressful demands of the job. They did so better than she did, actually.

Sarah caught on to the benefits of building a team of people hungry for success. She figured out that she didn't need to have her hand in every last detail for things to shine. She had to let go and trust that what she delegated to those interns, would be returned to her in respectable shape.

They spoiled her. When her new assistant, Sally, arrived fresh out of college, she showed up wearing a shiny gloss on her face that begged for recognition and knowledge. She had that new engine purr where she could keep going at a nice steady pace from sunrise to sunset and leave still showcasing a glow.

Sarah sat in a great position, suddenly, and the timing couldn't be better. She and Frenchy had begun their scuba classroom and pool work in anticipation for their quarry dive. Sally and the interns had things so under control; Sarah even got to sneak out of the office early on the day of their last certification class and exam. She decided to surprise Frenchy at the bakery.

Frenchy handed her an apron. "You look radiant."

"I feel radiant."

"Well, at least that makes one of us." Frenchy added white beans to a pot of boiling water. "The Idiot accused me of stealing my own money. What an ass, right?"

Sarah put on the apron and began washing the pile of dishes. "Forget about him for now. Let him whine. That money belongs to you. Right?"

"Are you questioning my integrity?"

"No, I'm making a point."

"That point being?" The beans bubbled up and over the side of the pan, spewing on the burner and creating a haze of smoke. "Shit," Frenchy said, reaching for the handle. "He's driving me so crazy I can't even cook cassoulet."

Sarah shut off the water and faced her friend. "Why are you letting him get the best of you?"

"I'm angry, and I have every right to be."

Sarah stuttered over the words resting on her tongue. "You're bitter. Stop being bitter. You're smiley. You're supposed to smile and brighten the world. He shouldn't bitter you. Screw him."

Frenchy wiped the burner with a dishrag, venting a fiery rage. Finally, she tossed the dishrag down and put her hands to her hips. "You're right," she screamed. "You're right, and I can't do anything about it." Tears squirted from her eyes. Her entire face swelled under their power. "I'm bitter and angry and I hate that man. I hate everything he's done. I hate his pigheaded, selfish ways. I hate the way he slouches. I hate the way he pulls on the edge of his stupid moustache. I hate the way he steps up and tries to control me after everything he's done. He owes me," she yelled. "So, you know what I'm going to do to get over this bitterness everyone can't handle?"

Her eyes raged. Sarah backed away.

"I'm going to buy scuba equipment." Her eyes began to dance wild like a mad scientist. "That's right, I'm going to stride in there and tell Gerry to hook me up with the best of the best. I want everything from the mask to the fins to a fancy dive computer, right down to those vented earplugs that help with equalizing my ears. If I'm going to do this, you bet I'm going to do this in style. Screw him."

She picked up her dishrag and circled it around the burner again. "You should too. You have the money. If you don't, stick it on your damn credit card. I need you to commit to this. I need this dammit, and nothing or no one is going to interfere. Got that?"

Sarah needed no help committing. She would board that plane no matter what. "Got it," she whispered.

"You better not come to me and tell me you've got a meeting next weekend. So help you. We're going to that quarry and we're going to dive to a depth of sixty feet and show that butthole of an idiot that he's not the only one who's going to start living life in the danger zone. That's right," she said on a screech. "Are you game?"

"I'm game," Sarah said on a fearful whisper.

Frenchy exhaled, gathered herself with a good shrug, and focused on her beans again. "I hope we see turtles in Bonaire," she said calmly as if she'd spent the last five minutes relaxing in a bubble bath and sipping a smooth glass of chardonnay. "Paradise puts The Idiot way out of my mind."

Sarah began sweeping the tiled floor. "This trip is going to be good for us."

"We're going to spend our days on a boat in the middle of turquoise water and not take any guilt along when we pig out at the all-you-can-eat buffets." Frenchy turned to her. "We need this."

"We do."

"We need to go out there and be two free women on the loose. We'll leave our fears and my rotten luck behind, and be different women for two whole weeks. Hell, I may even decide to kiss a woman." She spooned some beans to her lips for a taste.

"Oh, by the way," she continued, "I'm also splurging on a truck for us. I want to rent one of those cute little pickups I saw on the resort's website so we can see the island. I'm not flying to a foreign country and sitting my behind on just one five-acre parcel of land. I want to see the donkeys and flamingos. They run free there. They have a donkey sanctuary. I wonder if I can ride a donkey?"

Frenchy needed that distraction. For the first time in her life, Sarah could be there for her. That filled her with purpose, a purpose she had been dead to for some time.

Frenchy pushed a pile of brochures in her hands. "Study these. I got them from Gerry. They're more extensive guides on how to hand signal under the water. If we're going to do this, we're going to do this the right way. I don't want to be sixty feet under and not be able to communicate with you."

"I will."

"Promise."

"Promise," Sarah said.

~ ~

That night, they walked out of Bubbles Dive Shop with six bags of scuba equipment and luggage to hold said equipment. "I'm not about to trust a resort's rental equipment with my life," Frenchy said like a scuba pro. "The Idiot should know better than to mess with this woman."

Sarah tossed one of the bags over her shoulder. "You don't have to justify anything to me, but you're not paying for mine."

"The Idiot paid for it as far as I'm concerned. Give me that pleasure, at least. I earned it."

Thousands of dollars and a hell of a lot of *absolutely nots* later, Sarah accepted Frenchy's generous gift, courtesy, she informed Sarah, of the fool otherwise known to her for eternity as The Idiot.

"You didn't have to purchase it for me," Sarah said for the umpteenth time on the drive home.

"Listen, you gave me a gift today by letting me buy it for you. I thank you for that. I'm happy, and right now, I need happy."

~ ~

The week leading up to her certification dive, Sarah marveled at the video Jolene had sent to her of a dive she went on. A fellow diver filmed her with his GoPro. She looked so peaceful and radiant under the water, moving through it with graceful strokes.

Sarah refused to let on how nervous she started becoming as the certification weekend loomed. The night before, she had dreamed the regulator had fallen out of her mouth and she swallowed a lungful of water. Then, she fell to the bottom of a murky pile of mush.

What if she didn't pass? Or worse. What if she died trying?

On the morning of the certification dive trip, Jolene texted her. "I wanted to wish you great luck today. Be safe. Stay focused. I'll chat with you on the other side of certification!"

Sarah read her message five times, and with each sweep over the words, she failed to steady her rapid pulse any. In four short hours, she would embark on the first of the five dives it would take to become a certified open water diver.

Chapter Thirteen

They arrived at the quarry cottage and checked in for the weekend. The cottage slept eight people. Sarah and Frenchy claimed two of the bottom bunks while six of their other fellow students laid out their sleeping bags on the remaining ones. Gerry, his assistant, Clive, and the last two students would stay in an adjacent smaller cottage.

"Now that's a man who knows how to part the air and live life," Frenchy said while setting up her folding chair and watching as Gerry pulled tanks out of the back of his pickup truck. Frenchy plopped in her chair. "I hope he doesn't have to save our asses out there."

Sarah's nerves escalated.

Who did she suddenly think she was being all brave and reckless while her team worked their asses off in the office? She should've been at her desk with them ironing out the details to a new account instead of pretending to enjoy the thrill of diving into an algae slick lake with rusted school busses and airplanes to serve as attractions.

Not long after everyone settled in, Gerry took them to the quarry to begin their first three dives of the two-day weekend. "This first one will be easy. We'll snorkel around the top of the lake and get our bearings. Though, I want to see you change to your regulators once you're comfortable and out in the middle of the lake. It's a good way to get used to breathing and finning in an open environment."

Piece of cake. Sarah and Frenchy passed that first journey like they'd both grown up with swimming pools in their backyards.

The second dive proved a bit more challenging. They descended as a group to a ten-foot landing and performed a series of their tests. At one point, Frenchy should've handed Sarah her alternate regulator to ascend to the surface together. Well, Sarah had taken out her regulator and continued exhaling as instructed, waiting for Frenchy to hand her the second regulator. Frenchy couldn't get it unlatched. In a panic, Sarah bolted to the surface and gulped a lungful of fresh air.

A moment later, Gerry and Frenchy surfaced too. "If this happens under deeper water, you can't rush to the top," Gerry said. "You can kill yourself. You have to stop, focus, and work with each other. What else could you've done down there assuming, Sarah, that your apparatus broke?"

In the clear-minded natural air, Sarah's mind opened. "We could've buddy breathed off her main regulator."

Despite that minor incident, they passed the second dive as well. On it, they dove to a depth of twenty-five feet for ten minutes and circled a helicopter that the quarry staff had planted on the murky bottom.

"Okay, for our final dive of the day, let's set out to a depth of thirty feet. Anything below this, we'll need to remember we can't rush to the surface. We'll need to hover for three minutes at that depth then ascend.

They all nodded, understanding from their studies. Sarah maintained control, and settled into the dive, enjoying the deep resonating hum of her breaths.

By the time they surfaced, Sarah wanted to toss her hands up and cheer. She had spent the entire afternoon breathing underwater, something she never would've dreamed of doing had she not first scaled the fear of the cicadas.

"Two more dives to go tomorrow and you'll be certified divers," Gerry said to the group.

That night, Sarah didn't sleep. She lay on the bottom bunk distracted by the ear-piercing chirps of crickets.

The next morning, she rose to a cheerful Frenchy who cooked eggs over a skillet on the open fire.

She couldn't eat. She played with the eggs, pushing them from one side of the plastic plate to the other. She just wanted to get into the water and get certified.

The next two dives would be deeper and more intense, requiring her to summon the courage to go beyond the safe zone and into a depth that required more critical thinking and patience.

On the fourth dive of their test, they dove to a depth of forty feet. The water was colder and darker. Gerry led them with a flashlight, rounding them up like cattle, as Clive monitored the back. Sarah followed Gerry's flashlight, careful not to let it out of her sight. She peeked to her right, to where Frenchy should've been, and she couldn't find her. She scanned off to her left, and still no Frenchy. She looked below her, and still she couldn't find her. She circled around and only saw Clive's flashlight. She began to panic, turning her head every which way to find her friend. She had committed the worst act as a diver; she lost her dive buddy.

Clive finned to her side and pointed up. Frenchy hovered at least ten feet above them, clueless to the panic she had caused. Frenchy descended to her level and Sarah began gesturing her anger, which of course turned Frenchy into a raving lunatic, waving her hands. Their first underwater fight and neither one could figure out what the hell the other said.

Frenchy kept floating above her, causing Sarah to exert herself too much to rise to her level and stay buoyant.

She wanted the dive to end.

Exhausted, she still had to circle back to the docks. The end point hung out in the distance, too far away. Way too far.

Then, they came across a basketball hoop underwater. They descended to a depth of forty-five feet. Everyone started landing and picking up weighted balls to shoot hoops. Sarah considered the dark and ominous water. Trapped, she wanted to flee, to head back, and to be safe dammit. They all played, forgetting they hung submerged in a huge body of water. They shared the balls as if on the courts under a cloudless summer day, as if they had no fear that at any moment a mask could fill, a regulator could stop working, or an air tank could drain out. She had too much time to think.

She glanced at Gerry and he flashed her the *are-you-okay* hand signal. She signaled back a hesitant yes, but should've said no.

No freaking way.

Her lungs couldn't fill with enough air. Maybe her tank had malfunctioned? She needed more oxygen. The more air she breathed, the quicker it would run out. So, she tried to slow her inhalations and extend her exhalations.

As she exhaled, she kept dropping closer to the ground, a depth far too deep. Every time she'd breathe in, she'd rise too fast. So she'd breathe out again and drop. She dizzied herself. She looked to the surface and saw the light from the sun. Could she survive the trek back?

She still couldn't get enough air.

They played while death banged on her door, pulling her into its merciless hole. Gerry kept on finning as if he didn't have a care in the world, especially

190

about her dying on his watch.

She didn't want to die. Not yet. She hadn't even drafted a will. She hadn't cleared her email inbox. She never got to say goodbye to Jolene. My God, she needed to get out of the water. She needed air. Real air. She pressed her inflator and finned, trying to get a little higher. She couldn't rise fast enough. She saw her death play out before her, drowning on the bottom of an army green stagnant lake.

She dropped her weights and flew to the surface. As she rose, the distance to the top seemed to stretch on forever. Everything in her told her to fin faster and get the hell out of danger.

When she broke through the surface, she tore the regulator out of her mouth and inhaled. She still couldn't get a full breath. She sputtered until finally it caught and her mind started to clear and focus on the bright blue sky above.

No way in hell would she be able to dive in the middle of the ocean. No way in hell.

A few minutes later, the rest of the divers emerged, and Gerry swam over to her. "What happened?"

She didn't want to admit defeat. Embarrassed now that she didn't die, she lied. "My ears. They began to hurt. I assumed if I got to the surface, they'd get better."

Gerry lowered his mask and stared at her. "Are you okay?"

"Yeah, sure." Though her chest did rattle a little when she drew a breath.

"Okay, let's shake it off. We'll go in, take a rest and we'll make our last dive an easy one."

How would she go back under?

But, if she didn't dive that last one, she'd never dive again. Never see

Jolene again. Never take a trip to Bonaire.

Gerry waved to the team. "Let's go back to our blankets and get refreshed."

She followed the group back to shore, remaining silent.

When they got to land, Sarah peeled off her wetsuit and lowered her head between her legs. Frenchy sat beside her and placed her hand on her back. "Your ears, huh?"

Even admitting her defeat to Frenchy would cement her into a position she couldn't afford to be in. She would do the last dive, even if it killed her. She would not walk away without getting certified. "They ached in the cold water, that's all."

Frenchy stared at her with an arched eyebrow.

"Fine. I almost killed myself out there." She caved and unloaded her fear. "What will I do in the middle of the ocean?"

"You'll have a boat in sight when we get to Bonaire. Besides, Jolene will be there to help out. She's not going to let you drown out there. She saves everything. Even squirrels who run out in the middle of the road. Do you know she once blocked traffic for ten minutes on the interstate saving a raccoon from becoming roadkill?"

"What if I have gas bubbles in my veins right now? It's possible. I ascended like a rocket from forty something feet."

Frenchy creased her forehead and scanned her face. "Well, at least you can die saying you've done what only one percent of two and a half percent of the world's population has done." She shrugged. "That's something, isn't it?"

Sarah leaned her head back and glanced at a passing fluffy cloud. What had she gotten herself into?

"You know you don't have to do this, right? We can go back to the cabin, pack, and drive home."

Go back to what she'd always known. Life commuting up and down Interstate 95 like a stupid hamster going round and round on a wheel, never even contemplating life outside that wheel. "We're doing this."

Frenchy tapped her back, "That's the spirit."

A few minutes later, they started to get back in the wetsuits. That time, she couldn't fit her legs into it. She pulled the wetsuit over her ankle and struggled like hell to get it over her calf and thigh. "Why's this so hard?" Sarah asked, breathless after just one leg.

Frenchy already had hers zippered. "It's hot out here. So hurry."

Sarah managed to place her other ankle in the suit. It tightened, pulling at her skin. "I need your help, Frenchy."

Frenchy stood in front of her. "Put your foot on my stomach and pull on the damn thing. They're all waiting for us."

Sarah did just that. She pushed and Frenchy grunted. They must've looked like a couple of winners in the blazing sun. A bunch of divers sat at adjacent picnic tables talking and glancing over with laughter curling at the edges of their faces.

Sarah pushed harder and Frenchy tumbled backwards. "Oh, gosh I'm sorry." Sarah stood and helped her up. Frenchy reassumed her position.

Sarah once again pushed and pulled and finally her leg entered. She exhaled, exhausted. She stood to fish the rest of her body into the wetsuit, only something weird happened. "Something isn't right."

Frenchy stood back and examined her, and then she broke out into hysterics. "That's because you put your legs in your armholes!" Frenchy slapped her thighs, leaping around and pointing. "Your armholes!"

She flashed Frenchy a warning. With sweat dripping down her face, and extreme exhaustion peeling back the last remaining remnants of clarity, Sarah set up to right her wrong, struggling against the attack of Frenchy's cackles. At one point, she looked over at the table of divers and they pretended not to notice her corking herself backwards into a wetsuit. Frenchy cast them in for a good laugh at her expense. "She put her legs in her armholes. Her armholes!"

They all broke out into hysterics, everyone except for Sarah. She felt like a fool. "In my defense, I'm anxious and it's hot out here. Not to mention, everything looks the same with these wetsuits. They're a never-ending piece of black foam neoprene."

Frenchy tossed her arm around Sarah. "I'm sorry. I shouldn't have mocked you. But you stuck your legs in the armholes. That's pretty funny."

Sarah eased. "I'm sure one day I'll be able to laugh about it. Right now, I just want to get this over with."

By the time they geared up with their equipment and entered the quarry, Sarah was exhausted.

Death would be kind. Do you hear me, universe? Death would be really kind.

"Ready divers?" Gerry asked, lowering himself into the water.

Frenchy leaned into her. "I'm letting go."

Sarah snapped her head towards her. "What?"

"I'm letting go of the anger I've carried with me. Right now. I'm leaving it on the shore. It's not coming in here with me."

Frenchy smiled and tiptoed into the water, and Sarah followed behind, suddenly forgetting her malfunction and anger. Inspired by Frenchy's lightness, Sarah decided to descend and let go, too.

Something appealing happened to a person when she stripped herself of fear and let go. The world opened its doors of opportunity, allowing her to see it in a whole new light.

If her fate had death written on it, then so be it. At least they could say she tried.

She descended on a long exhale to a comfortable depth of a planned thirty feet. At that depth, she could race to the top if she needed without the threat of her lungs exploding at the top. So, in the negation of fear, she rode out the dive and focused on Gerry's flashlight as if it was a star in the universe. She trailed after it, breathing in and out in restful beats, admiring how her body could rise and fall in direct relation to her own mechanics.

They ventured out farther into the lake, and eventually began to circle back around. They moved faster and pushed harder, and Sarah's lungs started to burn. Her chest rattled, but she stayed calm, understanding the safety of the surface hung only a short distance away.

By the time they returned to the dock, she wheezed and coughed. She blamed it on allergies.

"I did the same thing as you on my certification dive," Gerry said as they waded through the knee-deep water to the pebbled shore.

Sarah found comfort in that.

"This isn't normal, what we do," he said. "It's not normal."

Something in that statement empowered Sarah. She had done something that required bravery. She did it. For once, she didn't follow the paved road. She chose one that required boldness and courage. She liked the grit in that.

When she looked over at Frenchy and saw her wide smile, she realized she enjoyed the grit in it, too.

"If you start to feel sick, you need to let me know," Gerry said.

"I'm good," she said. "In fact, I'm better than good. I'm great."

I freakin' did it!

~ ~

Jolene couldn't wait to hear from Sarah. Gerry said her breathing rattled and eyes glazed after her final dive. "Are you okay?"

"Of course I am. I passed."

"No, I mean are you really okay?"

"He told you about my ears, didn't he?"

Jolene knew Sarah's ears had nothing to do with her rapid ascent. "Most every diver has at least one panic attack in her life. It happens."

"Panic attack? Did Gerry say that?"

"We both have well over two thousand dives logged. You don't have to be embarrassed. This happens. If your ears had hurt, your instinct would have been to avoid the pain, and the faster you rise, the harder the pain. So, you panicked? Big deal."

"Oh," Sarah typed. "Well, I feel a little foolish now."

"Can we talk? Can I call you?"

"I'd like that," Sarah typed.

A moment later, she said hello.

"It's nice to hear your voice," Jolene said, enjoying its tickle.

"It's better to hear yours," Sarah said. "Truly. I had a moment where I worried that I'd never get to ramble and chuckle in between my words with you again."

Jolene released one in response. "You know," she began, "I suffered a panic attack while leading a tour."

"You panicked, too?"

"Yup. I dove with a group of seasoned divers. One of them hovered above

196

some coral with his camera. He got in real low to snap a picture of a lionfish. He didn't see the green moray eel hiding under the coral. The eel reached up and snapped his hand right in that tender area between your thumb and pointer. Blood everywhere. I started banging on my tank to alert all the divers in our group to head back to the boat. I finned beside the diver and his blood colored the water red. Everything blurred out of control. Logic trashed itself by the wayside. Everything started to spin, and I just needed to get out of that water. I didn't want to die with that man."

"That sounds terrifying."

"When we got to thirty feet, we had to hover for three minutes and do our safety stop. I wanted to flee to the surface, but he controlled the situation, offering me a peaceful nod. He started to signal slow, relaxed breaths with his uninjured hand. I followed his hand like a cellist would follow a conductor, relying on him to keep me calm under his distress."

"What happened to his hand?"

"The next day, he came back on my boat and dove again. The doctors had stitched it and placed a full-length plastic protectant on it. He told me he'd waited all year long for that trip. So, he would dive."

"Were you afraid to go back in the water?" Sarah asked.

"Terrified. But, if I didn't, I'd regret it. You already know how I dislike regrets."

"That's why I went back in for the last dive at the quarry. If I didn't, I'd hate myself for it. I didn't want to die, but I also didn't want to cling to the safety zone. It's so lonely and boring, and I don't want to be lonely or boring anymore. I'm tired of being safe."

"Safety is a basic need," Jolene said. "That's why most people prefer safety over discomfort. But, safety is dangerous. It keeps us stiff and immobile."

"Can I ask you something?"

"Sure," Jolene said after a hesitation.

"If I cave like this in Bonaire will you get me through it?"

"You have all the power within you to push yourself."

"I like it when you push me instead."

"Have I pushed you?"

"Unknowingly, yes," Sarah whispered. "That's a good thing. I've been stuck in a rut, bored and tired. I didn't realize it until I started digging at the ground and seeing that my entire life is built on quicksand. Every day I drive the same road, park in the same spot, eat the same breakfast and lunch, see the same people, sit at the same desk, and fight the same fight. Since meeting you, I've come back alive. I'm totally alive. I'm doing things I never imagined, and my whole body has awoken. Even in the quarry, when I panicked and then came to the surface, gratitude sank in, a gratitude for the pain in my lungs and the blaring sun in my eyes. I don't like discomfort, but I came out of it a new person, a stronger person. When I went back in and enjoyed the next dive, I tossed out the idea of surviving, and replaced it with thriving."

Jolene closed her eyes in a silent retreat, and the miles between them filled with a palpable heat, the kind that comforted like a fluffy blanket on a rainy winter night. She wanted to escape with her under it and cuddle, erasing all hesitation with the calm and steady force that her affinity offered. She wanted to stay protected in that moment before the cruel eyes of reality tore that blanket away, and all that potential intimacy evaporated in a flash.

She opened her eyes anyway, and decided to get uncomfortable and speak her truth. "I can't wait to see you."

Sarah released a soft sigh. "You have no idea how nice it is to hear you say that."

"You have a way of bringing out my honesty."

"Well that makes two of us."

Chapter Fourteen

Sarah enjoyed being needed. It offered her a sense of purpose. The Ascension Group needed her. Requesting the time off resulted in an immediate meeting to see who would do what in her absence.

The night before the trip, Jolene texted Sarah. "You should get some rest. It's going to be a long day for you tomorrow."

Sarah glanced at her watch. It was ten o'clock and she still needed to pack her toiletries, recheck her list, and check on a voicemail from Tom. "Tomorrow, then," she wrote.

"Are you sure I can't pick you both up? I can beg Neil to take the afternoon shift."

"We're good. Frenchy rented a truck. Work your day as usual and we'll meet up like we planned at five-ish."

A few minutes later, as she rechecked her list, she remembered Tom.

She hesitated over her keypad, understanding the repercussions of listening to his voicemail. She listened anyway. "It's Tom. I hate to call you right now, but I need to ask you something before you take off. Please call anytime. My phone is on."

Of course it is.

Sarah called him back.

"I need your help," he said with a desperate tone.

"Tom," she stretched out his name in warning.

"Ashley quit."

Fuck.

Ashley managed the larger of the accounts at Ascension. They'd climbed the ranks together until Ashley's last promotion put her a rung above.

"Why?"

"She screwed up big time, and left."

"Left?"

"Done. She no longer wanted to deal with the entitled people at Zak's Department Store. She left a huge mess in her wake. We're all freaking out."

They were one of Ascension's top clients. If they pulled out, Ascension would be in serious trouble. "I'm leaving in seven hours. I still need to finish packing. I need to brush my teeth. Also, my head is pounding, like it's going to explode. I can't have my head explode, Tom. I'm going diving. I need my head clear. I can't do this right now. You're going to have to figure this out."

"They won't take my call."

"Why would they take mine?"

"They asked for you."

Sarah tossed her head in her hands. "I'm tired, Tom. I mean really tired. Not just blurry eyed, but full-out zombie type exhausted."

"I need your help with this. I wouldn't ask if I didn't. They're willing to talk tomorrow."

"Tomorrow I'll be out of the country."

"They're willing to Skype."

So there it went, as it always did, Sarah falling in like a good soldier to clean someone else's mess.

~ ~

The next morning, Sarah sat back in her airplane seat and opened her laptop.

Frenchy sighed.

"Zip it," Sarah warned.

Frenchy stuffed buds into her ears. "I'm sorry for you. I am."

"Sorry for me?"

"Attached to that metal hunk of technology."

"It's the way the world works."

Sarah tapped the laptop keys harder.

Frenchy curled her hand around Sarah's wrist. "You know I'm playing with you because I hate flying and it's taking my focus off this, right?"

"You love fucking with me. You do. You really do. I need to review these stupid notes so I can articulate something worthwhile later on. If I don't correct this problem, a lot of people will suffer."

"You're all-important, aren't you?" Frenchy closed her eyes and inhaled.

"Yes, Frenchy. To them I am."

Frenchy opened her eyes and chuckled. "You're so easy to get riled up. You should've eaten one of my special brownies. That would've calmed you down."

Sarah glared at her, and they locked eyes. "You're crazy."

"And you love that about me."

Sarah looked away, and then she trudged back into the info Tom had sent her about Ashley's mess.

Frenchy patted her wrist and closed her eyes again, settling her head back against the seat. "Thanks for doing this with me."

~ ~

Six hours later, they landed in Bonaire and received the keys to their blue, four-door pickup truck.

"So many palm trees," Frenchy said, gripping the dashboard as Sarah drove around a tight curve.

"And cacti," Sarah said. "And shrubs. So many shrubs."

As they headed down a long stretch of road, Sarah peeked to the left and caught the glistening sun on the turquoise water. "Wow."

"Watch where you're going," Frenchy screamed. "And slow down."

"You have no right to complain. You're the one who had to eat a special brownie."

"That wore off as soon as the wheels lifted off the ground."

"We're in a foreign country. I won't take any chances." She gunned it.

"You drive like a maniac. I'd like to enjoy at least one dive if you don't mind. Just slow down."

"You're the one who wanted to rent a truck."

"Well, you're the one who turned into a goody two-shoes," Frenchy said. "You know how I get about flying. So you zip it."

"I'm not a goody two-shoes. I'll have you know—"

"Zip it."

Zip it she did.

A few miles later, they arrived at the resort, irritated with each other.

Jolene had arranged for an upgrade for them from a junior suite to a grand master, which did help to squelch the irritation. Frenchy still grumbled as she struggled to push the luggage cart towards their suite.

They entered the large space, decorated in luxurious creams and shades of aqua and equipped with a breathtaking view of the ocean.

Frenchy flung off her shoes and slid across the walnut-colored floorboards as if riding a massive wave to shore. "Yeah, baby, this is what I'm talking about."

Frenchy knelt and brushed her hand against the floor. "This can't be wood." Her words flew out as if part of an argument. "Imagine people coming back to their room with salt water and sand all over their feet? Would the wood even last? These have to be something else. But, they look like wood."

"They're ceramic," Sarah growled. "Who cares anyway?"

"You're right," Frenchy said. "Who cares?"

Sarah collected herself. Poor Frenchy needed her to. They were in paradise, and once she did her part with Zak's, she'd put work behind her and indulge in their deserved vacation.

She placed her laptop case on the desk and began to unzip it. "Just think, while you're basking in the sun, The Idiot is likely stuck in Maryland in his dirty old garage tinkering with someone's car troubles. And you, my friend," Sarah scanned her case for her external hard drive, "you will be steeping in paradise, soothed by the water lapping against the shore and entertained by the delightful sounds of birds singing to you every day."

"You don't have to worry that I'm even considering him. I'm absolutely fine."

Sarah knew her best friend better than that. They were twin souls after all, each mirroring the other in the most curious of ways. Although born to different parents and raised in different decades, they were convinced to be twins in a former life. They knew each other's thoughts before the other one spoke. They favored the same style of bohemian clothes. Most remarkable, they both shared a distinct matching history of coincidences like seeing eagles in their trees on the same day and losing their grandfathers on the same date, two years apart.

Sarah watched Frenchy unfold a smile onto her face like spreading a fine linen napkin across her lap, smooth and refined, anything to prove her strength, even though she had died a little inside. Frenchy never pretended anything. She wore her emotions on her face.

Something had changed. Something dramatic. She seemed fragile, like if the wrong word hit her at the wrong time, she might crack into a bunch of little pieces.

As Sarah changed into her business attire, Frenchy reached for the curtain rod. She yanked the sheer fabric open, dragging its lightness with her heavy, determined steps until the entire room sat in the glow of the glorious Bonaire sunshine.

"Who cares about anything other than this?" Frenchy stood facing outward. "Who cares that we're in paradise and you're cranky? Who cares that my best friend is more concerned with a stupid client than what's out in front of her right now?"

Zippering her skirt, Sarah joined Frenchy by the window. "I promise, once this meeting is done, I'll let go of the cranky attitude."

Frenchy crossed her arms over her chest. "I'm cranky too."

"I couldn't tell."

They chuckled then stared out in silence.

"What a view," Sarah said.

"Sure is." Frenchy folded her hands in front of her, looking so vulnerable and small against the expansive forefront of the open water. "I can't wait to see what these two weeks have in store for us." Frenchy shot her a mischievous grin. "We'll discuss it all over drinks."

"Sounds like a plan." Sarah headed back to the laptop.

Frenchy swiveled around and arched her eyebrow. "Seriously, I feel sorry for you. You may as well be speeding down a hot metal slide straight into the flames of hell."

"My laptop will be closed in less than an hour." She rustled the bottom layers of her hair and spread them over her suit-lined shoulders. "Now how do I look? Presentable?"

"Out of place in paradise."

"I promise to get out of this suit and into a cute sundress in no time."

"Okay, I'm going to that colorful little bar on the beach, the one in the brochure, and I'm going to drink frozen mudslides." Frenchy passed by Sarah. "Meet me and Jolene there at five p.m."

Jolene's name rolled around in her belly like tumbleweed. It tickled and brushed against every tender nerve, sending ripples of delight through her.

"Sure, I'll meet you there."

She logged into her email and read one from Tom. "Hi Sara, the folks from Zak's are running a little late. Sit tight, they'll be on as soon as possible."

She hated that Tom still forgot she had an H at the end of her name.

She rose from her chair and went to shut the curtain. Then, she noticed the silhouette of a woman walking the beach. She neared closer, swinging her arms and once in a while flipping her long hair over her bare shoulders. With each gentle stride, her skirt flowed behind.

Sarah narrowed her eyes to get a better look. The woman bore a striking resemblance to Jolene.

The Jolene look-alike strolled by, unaware of Sarah's gaze. Sarah watched as she disappeared around the bend in the beach, heading in the same direction as that cute little bar where Frenchy had gone to indulge in a spirited cocktail while Sarah whored herself off to a company who couldn't even spell her name correctly.

By two-thirty, Tom emailed her back. "The rep from Zak's is stuck in some mean traffic. A trailer flipped on I-95 and dumped a truckload of dog kibble over four lanes. It's more than likely going to be another hour instead. We owe you big time. We'll make this up to you. Just standby, okay?"

What choice did she have?

So she sat in a hotel room wearing a business suit in paradise. Meanwhile her best friend got buzzed at a beach bar called Coconuts.

She decided to take a stroll.

She strolled down a pathway that led to the back of the suites and over a footbridge. From there she saw boats lined up at a dock. She continued to stroll and came upon a cute shop with diving gear, postcards and T-shirts. She decided to pop in and have a look around. When she opened the door, she saw a group of people standing before a counter. A twenty-something-year-old blond guy with tanned skin stood behind that counter, and Jolene, looking radiant and sun-kissed, stood right beside him.

~ ~

As Jolene handed a guest the schedule, she spotted Sarah leaning against the seafoam green wall, wearing a sexy smile and a business suit.

She turned back to the guest. "I'll meet you down at the dock in about ten minutes and we'll get the skills test started."

On that, the man and his group turned and shuffled away, leaving Jolene a wide-angle view of Sarah and her smile.

Will plucked up the tool kit from under the counter. "I'm going to test some of the Nitrox tanks in the back. I'll send Tara up here while you test the group."

She nodded, not breaking her gaze with Sarah who bit her lower lip and winked.

Jolene rounded the corner and headed over to her, opening her arms. Sarah slid right into them, wrapping herself into a hug. "It's so good to see you," Sarah whispered.

Jolene cuddled her for a long moment, drinking up her fresh scent and warmth. Then, she found her lips and sank into her sweetness. She continued to enjoy the tender kiss until she heard the squeak of the door alerting her that Tara had arrived. Jolene backed away and scanned Sarah's business suit.

"I have a last-minute meeting on Skype in about twenty minutes. I needed to kill some time. I thought this was just a gift shop."

"A meeting? You've got to be kidding!"

Sarah inhaled. "I'm serious." She glanced at her watch. "I guess I should get back to my room so I'm not late."

Jolene cocked her head. "When do I get to see you, you know, for more than thirty seconds?"

"In an hour at Coconuts?"

"I'll be there, still wet from getting in the water and testing these divers."

"It's a beach bar. I'm the one in a suit." Sarah smiled and bounced away, looking back over her shoulder. "See you soon."

~ ~

An hour later, after the team from Zak's canceled their meeting due to the dog kibble spill, Sarah arrived at Coconuts.

Colorful umbrellas adorned gray finished tables with faux wood tops, and comfy rattan chairs with blue and tan striped cushions added to the casual effect of the seaside bar. People sipped tropical drinks and munched on fried appetizers as they laughed and swayed along to the reggae vibes filling the late-afternoon air.

Sarah spotted Frenchy and Jolene at a table close to the water's edge. As promised, Jolene was still wet, her hair hanging in long sexy tangles. Sarah's stomach flipped as she approached and slid onto an empty stool.

"How did the meeting go?" Jolene asked.

"They canceled it," Sarah said, scanning the cocktail menu. "What're you ladies drinking?"

"Rum swizzles." Frenchy sucked on her straw. "Much more tropical than a mudslide."

Sarah's cell buzzed.

"Office is closed," Frenchy said. "Put that thing away. Please."

"Of course, yes. It's likely just Tom returning my call." Sarah glanced at her phone then caught the sigh from Frenchy. "Forget it. You're right. Office is closed." She tossed it in her pocketbook. She'd sneak a peek of it later. "See, all gone."

"Okay," Frenchy said, springing up from her relaxed position. "Enough about real life. Let's talk about what we're going to do in these two weeks."

Suddenly, Jolene's foot circled Sarah's as she teased her with a sly grin. "It's good to see you smile."

"It feels good to smile," Sarah said.

"It sure does," Frenchy said, slurping her drink. "My smile is going to stretch on for miles. I couldn't be any happier right now."

Jolene and Sarah shared a glance. Then, Jolene turned to Frenchy. "I worried about you after the breakup. I'm glad you didn't let my jerk of an uncle win."

Sarah reengaged Jolene's foot dance. "We're calling him The Idiot now."

"Suitable." Jolene scanned the beach bar for the server. "He's my uncle and all, but I never liked the way he treated my mom. He arrived a whole two minutes earlier at birth, and he treated her like an underling. My mother doesn't like the way he acts, either."

"Seems no one does." Frenchy fingered her gray-streaked bang and tucked it behind her ear. "I'm not going to talk about The Idiot at all on this vacation. We're here to have fun and forget the man exists."

"What did you have in mind?" Jolene asked.

"Okay, I hope I'm not stepping on anyone's toes here," Frenchy said, "but, when I snooped around the gift shop earlier, I overheard a few people talking about cliff diving. Let's cliff dive!" Her eyes twinkled.

"From baker to cliff diver," Jolene sipped her drink. "I'm kind of digging the new bold attitude."

Sarah did too. But, no way would she jump off a cliff. She didn't want to burst Frenchy's bubble, though, so she bought herself a moment. "Cliff diving is a fantastic idea."

"You like it?" Frenchy's shoulders even lifted along with the look of shock that escaped.

"I do. For you both. I will plant a big smile on my face and watch you from my beach chair."

"Either we do this together or we don't do it at all," Frenchy said.

"I'm not cliff diving."

A heaviness hung between them.

"This trip should be about us getting out of our comfort zones," Frenchy said.

"I'm already well out of comfort." Sarah spotted the server and called her over.

"We should tell her," Jolene said to Frenchy, biting her lip and drawing her foot away.

"Tell me what?"

A tension gripped them suddenly. It zapped and flickered between them like the sizzle on the end of a firework, slithering and devouring all the oxygen as it headed for extinction.

Frenchy stared at her with an arched eyebrow, while Jolene stretched her gaze to the far end of the room, avoiding eye contact altogether.

Sarah's stomach took a wild turn downhill. "What's happening here?"

The server arrived.

Sarah shifted towards her. "I'll have a sangria with ice on the side."

"You got it." The server slinked away.

"Tell me what?" Sarah asked again.

She watched the sneaky smile spread across Frenchy's face. "Jolene and I were chatting while you sold your soul to that heap of technological metal in our room."

Sarah sat back, pressing against the wooden spindles of the chair. "Not even three hours into our trip and already you're judging like you said you wouldn't."

"No, listen," Frenchy said. "We're not judging. I mean, who am I to judge? I spray-painted The Idiot's corvette with fluorescent orange. We all do things that could be judged."

"You spray-painted the corvette?" Sarah asked.

Frenchy nodded.

"So what were you going to tell me?"

"I can't believe you didn't tell her already," Jolene said to Frenchy.

"I haven't told her anything."

"I assumed you would have," Jolene said. "You told *me* about her little problem."

Frenchy shot a crazed look Jolene's way before responding to her. "Shush. It's going to freak her out that you know."

"Whoa," Sarah said. "What little problem are we talking about?"

They both shrugged. Frenchy opened her eyes wide. "Well, since you asked, I'm obliged to tell you that you don't have to hide it from me. I already know what happened, and I can't believe you didn't tell me about it yourself. I had to find out through the grapevine."

"About what?"

"About, you know," Frenchy arched her eyebrow.

The escalator fiasco?

Had they seen a picture, or worse, a video of it? Had it gone viral? Had the world seen her naked? "My God, I told that little rug rat to stop recording me."

Frenchy shrugged.

Jolene smirked.

"Was it a picture or a video?" Sarah asked, mortified.

Jolene sipped her rum swizzle.

Frenchy shrugged again.

"Unbelievable. Sam swore he didn't find any pictures or videos."

Frenchy twisted her mouth. "Sorry, I guess he missed the mark."

"Who sent it to you? And where did you see it? Facebook or YouTube?"

"I can't remember," Frenchy said. "What happened anyway?"

"Well, you must've seen. I'm so embarrassed. What a stupid, careless mistake. I never should've gotten on an escalator wearing no undies. I should've taken the elevator instead."

Frenchy nodded. "Of course."

"I'll never make that mistake ever again. Trust me. You two should never either. Though I guess you won't now that you know what can happen."

"Tell us from your angle. How did it all happen?" Jolene kept the glass pressed to her lips.

"I got caught. What can I say?"

Frenchy lowered her glass. "How?"

"I bent over to get my cell because of your call about the party and next thing I knew my skirt got stuck in the crack between the escalator steps and the top landing. It ate it. It went on a mad frenzy to swallow every last thread. I couldn't get to it and well, I'm sure you saw what happened from there. It mortified me. Old men ogled me. Kids laughed. Everyone stared."

Frenchy and Jolene's eyes grew larger. Their faces grew red.

"Now my hoo-ha is going viral apparently."

"Why didn't you wear undies?" Frenchy asked.

"My undies were giving me a wedgie. I couldn't take it anymore, so I took them off and flung them on my passenger seat before my meeting with La Chapelle."

"You were bare naked?" Frenchy asked.

"Well, yeah. That's the whole little problem."

The two busted out laughing.

"It's not funny. There's a video of me naked on the internet."

Tears streamed down both of their faces as they fought to catch their breaths.

"Why are you acting like this is the first time you've heard this?"

Frenchy flung her head back. "Because it is."

"Then, what video did you see?"

"None!" Frenchy cracked up into a new fit.

"Oh my God," Jolene dabbed at her eyes. "Priceless."

Sarah sat in a pool of shock. "I have no idea what just happened here. You told me you knew about my problem. How did you know I had a problem?"

"We didn't." Frenchy swiped her smeared mascara with her fingers. "We just wanted to have a little fun with you. Everyone has something to hide. Apparently, all you have to do is toss out an open-ended teaser and watch the truth unfold."

Jolene swallowed a giggle. "You did say you liked the teasing side of me." She struggled to straighten her face. "I'm sorry, but I'm still caught on the fact that you stood in the middle of the mall naked, showcasing your, well your—"

"—my what? My hoo-ha?" Sarah asked, filling it in for them.

Suddenly the three of them fell into hysterics, slapping the table, their legs, their chairs, anything they could find to absorb their laughter.

~ ~

Several hours later, tired from the travels and wanting to get settled into their suite and in bed by a decent hour to be fresh for their dive adventure the next day, they hobbled out of the beach bar and landed on the paved pathway with residual chuckles.

The sky opened and it began to pour, and the evocative smell of fresh rain fell upon them. Reluctantly, they said quick goodbyes to Jolene as she dashed off in the opposite direction. Sarah and Frenchy stomped like children through the puddles, giggling and splashing until drenched in joy.

Chapter Fifteen

The next morning, Sarah woke with nervous flutters. That day she would step off the side of a boat in the middle of the ocean and go with the flow. First, they had to be tested at the docks to ensure they could stay buoyant so they wouldn't destroy the fragile coral. They had to fin through a stationary hoop at twenty-five feet. If they could do that, they'd get the thumbs-up to get on that boat and test their courage.

Sarah checked the voicemail she missed from Tom the night before. He thanked her for being so flexible and apologized for the canceled meeting with Zak's.

As she began to type a response back to him, Jolene texted her. "I'm going to set up the boats this morning while a fellow dive master named Will tests you and Frenchy at the docks."

"You can't test us?"

"It's Will's day. We alternate. You're not nervous, are you?"

"Not at all. Why would I be nervous? I'm a certified diver now. Certified to go to sixty feet. I'm not nervous. Nope."

An hour later, they arrived at the testing site. A long plastic dock floated on top of the aqua shore, bouncing and shifting with each small wake.

Will greeted them with a wide grin, sun-highlighted hair and golden skin. He looked like someone who spent his days ignoring the rules of life and seeking fun and adventure instead. Everything about him screamed fearless and laid back. He probably strolled through life one carefree stride at a time, soaking up sunrays and good times by the gallon.

On his instruction, they geared up.

Too nervous to remember what hose connected to what gadget, Sarah wanted to cry. Flustered, she followed Frenchy's lead until she found herself ready to dunk into the big, blue body of water waiting to swallow her.

They walked into the water instead of using the dock, something that eased the entry for Sarah. "Let's have some fun," Frenchy said with a glimmering grin before sticking her regulator into her mouth.

Fun. Yes, she was fun. She would die proving it to herself. So, taking a large breath, she stuck the regulator in her mouth and stumbled further into the water, following Frenchy and Will until their heads all left the safety of the sun and air. When Sarah took in the view, she could see far and wide unlike in the darkness of the quarry. She spotted tiny fish and white sand. Less intimidated, she proceeded to the bottom of the sandy beach floor feeling like an astronaut might on the moon. Frenchy struggled with keeping her feet on the ground. She kept floating up then dropping like on an amusement ride. At twenty-five feet, they arrived at the circle. Sarah pumped her inflator hose to lift and fin through it. That proved a little harder than expected. Using her breaths to keep her buoyant, she managed though. When she cleared through, she glanced back and noticed Frenchy signaling her *okay* as she sailed through, too.

They high-fived each other under the water, and when they ascended back to the surface, Will congratulated them. "You're good to go."

"We're good to go," Sarah said to Frenchy. Bring on the cicadas, the green algae, and the deep blue sea!

Minutes later, after they geared down, they headed over to the boats where they'd meet up with Jolene and the rest of the divers.

When they arrived, they secured their tanks and gear along with the other divers in their group. Then, the engine started.

Sarah's heart rolled.

Jolene put the boat into gear. They reversed out of their spot and eased out of the cove, past the suites and palm trees, Coconuts, the docks, and out into the open waters of the Caribbean.

Jolene fired up the engine once they hit the open water. The wind rushed at them, knocking Sarah off-balance. She gripped the boat railing and held on for dear life.

About twenty minutes into their ride, the boat came to a sudden stop as the engine cut off. The boat rocked, causing Sarah's heart to buck.

Sarah liked comfort. She liked seeing the next step. Looking at the turquoise water, she had no idea what would happen. She scanned the water, wondering what lurked below. More dangerous threats than that of a man-made quarry lurked. An entire world existed underwater, parts of which had never been explored by humans. Sharks and other creatures lived in it. She could destroy coral by finning incorrectly. She could drown in a single giggle. What if she giggled? She'd choke. How did one cough underwater without filling her lungs? What if she panicked again?

"I'm not doing this," she whispered to Frenchy.

Frenchy whipped her head in her direction. "Like hell, you're not. We came to scuba dive, not act like two helpless women afraid of adventure. Besides, do you expect me to go into that water without a dive buddy?"

Sarah glanced at Jolene with her shiny mocha hair, sun-kissed skin, and confidence. "I'm sure she'll be happy to show you around down there."

"Don't do this," Frenchy said, cradling a tone of warning.

She hated when Frenchy got all dictator-like. What if she got lost down there? Or what if something ate her? What if she ran out of air? What if her mask filled? "I'm not ready for this."

The passengers began squirting defogger onto their masks.

"Okay folks," Will called out, "gear up. Let's go diving!" He swung towards his equipment and began putting on his BCD vest.

Frenchy stood and began putting her arms through her wetsuit. "Stand up," she ordered.

Sarah looked around at the others, gearing up and fiddling with their air tanks and regulator hookups. A tumultuous fight ensued inside her, causing her to shiver despite the balmy eighty-degree temperatures that day.

Frenchy lifted the armhole of Sarah's new BCD. "I'm not letting you chicken out. This is a life-changing opportunity to experience something only a very small fraction of the world population will ever get to."

"You're breaking the cardinal rule of diving. Dive buddies never force a dive on the other."

Frenchy fumed. "Suit yourself."

If Sarah didn't know Frenchy better, she looked about ready to wind up and punch her in the face. Frenchy did come with a soft side, though. So, no doubt, after she dove in and saw all that pretty ocean life, she'd come back and not care that Sarah did in fact chicken out on the opportunity of a lifetime.

Could she do it? She'd practiced the panic attack prevention breathing tips since her certification dive malfunction. Surely, if it set in, she could pull herself from the red zone of panic and work through it. Deep, slow breaths and tense and relax muscle moves engrained themselves in her brain. She had put the remedy to muscle memory. Besides, according to every website known to scuba diving, the leading and most credible ones, too, most divers experienced at least one, and generally, at most one, significant panic attack while on a dive. She already survived hers.

She had to do it. She couldn't turn back now. Not with the thousands of dollars Frenchy tossed into the fancy new equipment. She stood and began practicing her deep breathing as she fit her shaky arms into the BCD.

Frenchy just smiled.

After a few long minutes of gearing up, Sarah sat and waited for their turn at the boat's back deck. "Ready?" Frenchy asked once everyone else had jumped in.

Gentle waves kissed the rocky shore in the distance, creating white foamy crests that spilled from the core of its turquoise womb. Cottony puffs drifted in the blue skies, casting shadows on the orange roofs of the sprawling homes that dotted the horizon. The wind whispered a song in between its gusts, salting the space under the fiery sun with a tingle capable of waking even the soundest of sleepwalkers. Wide-awake to the moment, Sarah inhaled deeply and trembled at the hands of nature and all its potential.

Then, Sarah's heart abandoned her, dashing away on the sparkling ripples below. Her arms and legs went numb. Her tummy rolled some more. She gulped a mouthful of air, wobbling behind Frenchy. They headed towards Jolene at the back of the boat. For the first dive, Jolene would stay on board and watch for bubbles as Will took them out.

Frenchy walked right to the edge and clasped her mask and BCD while Jolene checked her air valve. Frenchy tossed Sarah a glance. "I'll see you in there."

Sarah stared out at the other divers waiting on her to get her butt in that water. What did she get herself into? Jolene checked her air, and tapped her back. "You're all set, dear."

Panic coursed its way through every morsel of her veins. "Are you sure? The air is definitely on?"

Jolene leaned in. "I wouldn't let you jump otherwise."

She had to believe her. She had to trust in the process of the crazy venture. What other choice did she have? Turn around and sit with a pout on her face for the next four hours as she waited on all of them to pursue their passion?

She stared at Frenchy who cheered her on with a click of her GoPro camera. She floated like a natural.

"This is much harder than I imagined."

"The time is never going to be perfect," Jolene said. "If you wait for that, the moment's gone and all you've gained is regret. You know how to handle regret, and quite well, so go handle it," she whispered.

She envied everyone's bravery.

So what if she died? She would die doing something brave and adventurous, and something few people had the courage to do. She could dive in, see the colorful world, and if she died, wouldn't that be an awesome place to live out her last breaths? Better than a disease or car accident. At least here they could say she died pursuing something pretty fucking awesome. With that, she secured her mask and BCD and jumped in.

In the moments after breaking through the water and lifting her head out of it to catch a lungful of fresh sea air, Sarah's heart stopped racing. A strange and welcoming calm blanketed her. She waded in the water like a real live scuba diver, and Jolene cocked her head and smiled with pride at her.

She'd dreamed of how the water would respond when she entered it. Never in those dreams had she considered it would soothe her. Despite the challenge of staying afloat with her gear, she managed to tread like a pro.

The water challenged her to keep her head upright, and her breathing started to speed up. She kicked her feet more. "I can do this," she murmured, careful not to expel too much energy on talking.

She pointed her gaze to Frenchy and smiled as she clicked her camera.

A moment later, Will dove in. "Everyone ready to dive?"

There went Sarah's heart again, galloping out of her chest. She tugged on her BCD straps to secure them as tight as they would go. Then, she swallowed an enormous amount of air before sticking her regulator in her mouth. She inhaled, and the compressed air coated her mouth and throat in staleness.

"We're going to go against the current on the way out to the coral site about twenty minutes or so. Then, we'll turn around and head back with the current. Maximum time is sixty minutes." He stuck his regulator back in his mouth, so calm and collected.

Everyone signaled to their buddies and began their descent, letting the air out of their BCDs. People's heads began to disappear below the surface, all except hers and Frenchy's.

Sarah kicked to stay afloat, waiting on Frenchy to descend. Her friend kept her finger pressed to her air tube, and attempted diving under the surface with no luck. Meanwhile Sarah didn't know how much longer she could last with kicking her feet. She began pumping air into her BCD to see if that would help alleviate some of the work, but it worsened things.

Panic started to seep in. She'd have to descend without Frenchy or risk running out of breath before even breaking water. She let herself sink a little, and continued to descend, watching as Frenchy struggled to get underway. Frenchy disappeared from her sight. Sarah fell to the sandy bottom much too fast. Luckily, they anchored in a shallow enough area, only twenty feet from the surface. She landed on a thud, and caught her balance. She breathed, and the air entered her lungs.

She admired all the bright life. Tiny tufts of sea grass swayed as small transparent fish darted in and out of it. She glanced at the pearly white sand. She bent to greet it in awe. It softened in her hand. She picked some up and marveled at how it gracefully funneled its way back to its home.

She would be okay. She could do this.

She spotted Frenchy, hanging like a doll all the way at the boat's ladder. Her feet balanced on one of the ladder's rungs. She should've been up there with her, but she enjoyed the peace of being glued to the sandy bottom of the ocean. She looked around and saw all sorts of beautiful silky flounder and colorful rainbow angelfish circling her legs. They swam in peace, accepting of her presence in their domain. She smiled and bubbles floated from her lips.

She was diving!

She looked up again and Frenchy's feet hadn't moved from the rung. Great dive buddy Sarah turned out to be, leaving her friend hanging off the boat while she toured the land of flounder and rainbow-colored fish. She attempted to lift off the ground, kicking her feet and getting some altitude from that maneuver. She had to push herself to fin upwards and get momentum. Her equipment weighed her down, like gravity pushed against her and kept her captive in the calm water. It didn't matter how close that boat appeared to her, a panic leaked into her veins the harder she had to push to get off the ground. She pumped more air into her BCD, but none entered. *My God, have I run out of air?*

If I make it out of this alive, I swear to God I will change things. I'm going to get highlights. I'm going to stop saying yes to everything. I'm going to downsize my house. I'm going to stop working eighty hours a week. Serious changes! I'm going to start living like a normal fucking person. Do you hear me, God? I promise.

She wrestled with getting buoyant and still no luck.

Sarah remembered her training. Dump the weights from her pockets and kick like hell to the surface. That she did. She kicked and kicked until the blessing of the sweet mother air hit her face. She tore the regulator from her mouth and gasped, reaching for the rope attached to the boat.

"Help!" Sarah shouted.

Jolene pulled the rope and Frenchy scooted off the ladder rung to clear space for her. Sarah clung to the ladder and tried to catch a full breath.

"I had to…do an…emergency…ascent."

Jolene pulled her out of the water, guiding her safely up the ladder and over to the bench.

"What happened?" she asked her.

Trying to catch her breath, she said, "I couldn't stay afloat and I sank too fast. Nothing is happening when I pump my BCD."

"Perhaps you have too much weight in your pockets. We can fix that. Frenchy had too little and couldn't sink."

"Mine are at the bottom. I dropped them for the ascent."

Jolene's eyebrows arched. She analyzed her BCD, then, "Wow. Your inflator hose is broken."

"My hose?"

"Yeah, it's broken off at a weird angle, too."

"This is brand new. It's only the second time I've worn it here."

"It's the last time you'll be wearing it, too, if we don't fix it. Once we get back to shore, I can see what we've got in the equipment room. I might be able to repair it."

"Might?"

~ ~

Frenchy and Sarah had to sit out the first dive. Will would've been too far gone by then to guide them. Frenchy stood at the helm of the ship, taking in the view of the southwestern corner of Bonaire.

Jolene stared out in the direction Will had planned to dive, searching for their bubbles. Sarah joined her.

"You're scared shitless, aren't you?" Jolene placed her foot on the bench for more leverage against the gentle sea rolls.

Sarah shrugged and wiped the salt water from her forehead with the back of her hand. Her lips quivered. "It doesn't matter. I'm here." She shook her head in defiance of her fear, tucking a piece of her wet hair behind her petite ear. "I'm going to do this."

Jolene noticed the lightest shade of blue hazing over her lips. She'd seen many frightened newbies since beginning her diving career, and Sarah topped most of them. Many needed coaxing and more training in shallower water. Jolene glanced out at the calm turquoise water. Diving was a dangerous sport. One had to be motivated to do it. Typically, if not a natural desire, that motivation stemmed from anger, frustration, or sheer determination to prove courage.

Jolene gripped the railing, keeping her eyes focused on the bubbles in the distance. "Are you sure you want to do this?"

Sarah released a hesitant chuckle. "Maybe I should stick with snorkeling." She bowed her head. "How stupid, right? Here I am in Bonaire, one of the best dive islands in the world and I want to snorkel. I can't just snorkel. That'd be like going to a wine festival and drinking water."

"Will you let me help you through this?"

Sarah stretched her gaze out to the open water. "I want to do this. I can't get on that plane until I do. While I hung out on the bottom, I saw a whole new world open up to me. I spotted flounder and these little triangle-shaped colorful fish. And the sand is so white."

"I won't let anything happen to you," Jolene said, cupping her hand over Sarah's. "I'll take you down for the second dive. You can wear Will's BCD. You'll be safe with me."

The gloom of unease spilled into the tiny pores on Sarah's sun-kissed face. "I felt safe down there because of the shallow depth. I could come up fast enough if something went wrong. But way out there," she glanced to the region of the bubbles. "They're so far and so deep."

Jolene wanted Sarah to like diving. She wanted her to fall in love with it. She wanted her to live and breathe it and want to visit as often as possible. But, she couldn't force what wasn't meant to fit.

"What do you say later on today I take you out to the shallow water by the restaurant dock and we snorkel using our tanks? We'll get in the water, get you comfortable, and see some amazing creatures."

Sarah eased back into a smile. "That sounds doable. I like doable. Doable means I can take something back with me. It'll be like diving, right? There are still lots of coral and fish, I'm assuming."

Jolene kept her hand over Sarah's, imagining all the dives they could've shared and watching in sadness as they disappeared into the fog of fear that waited on the horizon for Sarah's surrender.

~ ~

Sarah waited out their second dive by sitting and staring out at the gorgeous horizon decorated in stucco roofs and palm trees. A wave of envy toppled her. She sat like a coward frying in the blazing sun.

Later on, when the divers emerged, excited and wet, the jealousy outgrew her heart. It ripped right through it, tearing it open and causing its edges to

227

curl, frazzled from the explosion of her own device.

Jolene drove the boat back to the dock and chatted with one of the guest divers, Toby. They laughed and pointed at things back on land, and carried on oblivious to the storm Sarah fought against herself. Frenchy talked with Will and her new friends by the water bucket as they cleaned their cameras and compared clicks.

When they arrived back at the docks, Jolene took a closer look at Sarah's BCD. "Let me take this to the back and see if I have a replacement hose."

Sarah dunked her mask, regulator, and wetsuit in the dump sinks to rinse the seawater from them. Frenchy stepped up beside her. "I'm not mad at you."

Sarah gulped back a cry. She pressed her wetsuit deeper into the sink, focusing on it. "I plan to do this. I promise. I just need some space and time."

"You got it."

A few minutes later, Jolene walked over to her with the BCD. "I fixed it."

Sarah took it from her, sweeping her eyes over it. She wanted to trust her. She had to trust her.

"I promise. It's safe and good as new."

Sarah smiled. "Thank you."

"So, after lunch, I'll be taking the group back out on the afternoon dive. After that, I'll take you to the shore dive site near the restaurant. We'll take it very slow and only snorkel if that's all you want to do. Want to meet me at three-thirty?"

Sarah didn't argue, which only added to the pileup of distress.

While Frenchy and the other divers got ready to head back out for their afternoon dive, Sarah retreated to the safety of her suite as a complete failure. The grit rubbed against her, exfoliating all the surety she had won at the quarry and test dive, replacing it with ugly fear.

While back inside, she received a new message from Tom. "Once again, I'm sorry about yesterday. They want to reschedule. I know I'm asking a lot, but can you possibly do today at five?"

She typed back faster than her mind could work. "I'm in Bonaire, Tom. You realize what you're asking?"

Within a minute, he replied. "I do. And I'm begging you. I've secured a two-thousand-dollar bonus for you if you can do the call today."

~ ~

"Do you want to snorkel with us?" Sarah asked Frenchy once she returned from the afternoon dive.

Frenchy placed her dive computer and regulator on the small table in the suite's foyer, and then she opened up into a yoga stretch. "I'm going to meet up with Will for a drink at the bar. He says they have a band playing."

"Will is like twenty-five."

Frenchy grabbed a towel and headed towards the bathroom. "Your point is?"

Sarah laughed. "I stand corrected."

~ ~

The snorkel dive resembled her test dive, relaxing and graceful. They eased into the water and stayed on the surface for a few hundred yards. Then, they began to descend to a comfortable level of twenty feet. They hugged the coral bank, floating above it. Sarah witnessed small turtles, parrotfish, and colorful coral in many sizes and shapes, some even resembling a brain.

At one point, Jolene looped her arm in hers and pointed to a moray eel swimming past. Buoyant and in control, Sarah forgot about the compressed air and panic, and focused on being in that moment with the sea creatures and

229

coral. They spent an hour combing the beauty, and when they surfaced, Sarah's entire spirit smiled. "Thank you," she whispered.

Jolene's lips curled up. "That's all there is to it. With functioning equipment, you'll be this relaxed, even out there in the deeper sea."

"I could've died out there."

"You could die if an asteroid falls on top of you right now, too."

Sarah laughed, and it released all the strain from earlier.

"Come on," Jolene said, latching onto her arm. "Let's get the gear rinsed off. Then, maybe we can all grab dinner?"

"First I have to make a quick Skype call for work."

"I've never met someone as dedicated as you."

"I'll take that as a compliment."

Jolene nodded, not denying it would be anything but that.

When they got back to the lockers by the docks, Sarah panicked when she saw the clock. They'd spent much more time below than she realized. "I've only twenty minutes to get back and get on Skype."

"I'll help you carry some of the equipment; this way we can run to get you there faster."

"Okay," Sarah said, breathless. "Let's do it."

They tore through the paths between the suites, carrying her equipment on their backs. They leaped over shrubs to take shortcuts and landed at her suite with seven minutes to spare.

Sarah dropped her bag in the foyer and sailed over to her laptop.

"I'll hang your stuff so it can dry."

Sarah assessed the space and angled herself against the only area of the room not covered in some piece of random clothing or diving gear. Then, she peeked at herself. Her hair hung messy and she still had sand crystals clinging to her cheeks. She pulled her hair back into a ponytail, rubbed her face, and tore off her T-shirt. Then, she put on a dress shirt right over her bathing suit.

Jolene stared at her from the foyer.

"How's this for spontaneous?" Sarah opened her arms.

"It definitely suits you," Jolene said in a sultry tone.

"Wish me luck. I'm going in."

Jolene laughed. "You look radiant."

"Are you making fun of me?"

"I'm absolutely not making fun of you."

Sarah liked the way Jolene's eyes danced. "I'm entertainment value right now."

"You most certainly are."

Sarah nodded then logged onto Skype wearing a huge smile. With Jolene as her witness, she met up with her power, plugging into a network where she couldn't mess up a major account. In her arena, Sarah showed off her fearless side.

Jolene grabbed a seat on the bench in the foyer gazing at Sarah as she met the management team at Zak's wearing a smart button-down blouse and a set of bikini bottoms only Jolene was privy to see.

"Thanks for meeting us on such short notice," Mr. Saunders, the VP of their corporate relations said. "I'm assuming you've been briefed?"

Sarah stared at Jolene who flirted with a sultry grin. She snapped her attention back on the screen. "I have, yes. What happened was unacceptable, and we will make it up to you. What can we do to make it better?"

Mr. Saunders folded his hands on the table, and spoke at her, "We lost an entire week's worth of momentum because of Ashley's mistake. We want to be compensated for that loss."

Sarah dropped her hands to her lap, straightening herself and blocking out the tease radiating off Jolene's face from across the room. "Although we can't make up for this in actual dollars, what we can do is offer a better package at no additional cost to you."

"What exactly would that look like?"

"I'd have to work out the details of course, but we'd be looking at premium placements, full page ads, extra banner advertising and higher impressions at no extra cost. If I put together a package, will you review and consider it?"

"I'd be willing to review it, yes. It's going to take more than a few banner ads."

Sarah glanced back over at Jolene. Her finger lingered in between her pouty lips. Sarah gained an edge from wearing that smart button-down blouse and bikini bottoms. She shifted back to Mr. Saunders. "You've got a partner in us. I hope all the years we've worked together won't be diminished by one bad move on the part of someone who's no longer affiliated with The Ascension Group. We're truly sorry about what happened."

"Well, I can tell you take this seriously. I understand you're out of the country and still willing to chat with us. So, thank you for that. I eagerly await your proposal. I'd like to talk about some specifics."

In the foyer, Jolene untied her ponytail and shook out her long, wet strands of hair. Then, she relaxed back against the wall, knees up near her chest, eyes finding their way down to Sarah's bikini bottoms.

Sarah glanced back at the screen. "Yes, of course, sir," she said on a faint breath.

Mr. Saunders continued to set his demands, and Sarah did her best to focus and be that smart executive everyone thought her to be. She tried to block out Jolene's curvaceous appeal, but to no avail. By the time the meeting ended, Sarah was mush.

"Thank you for your time," he said once he finished voicing his specifics. "Enjoy yourself, and we'll look forward to hearing back from you."

Sarah closed the cover to her laptop, sealing herself off from anyone not Jolene Aster.

They remained in their respective spots, daring each other with hungry eyes. Jolene traveled her gaze around Sarah, pausing along her neckline, collarbone, cleavage, and down to that edgy area that craved attention.

Sarah closed her eyes to take in the mounting desire, dropping her hands back in her lap. Then, her fingers slipped in between her legs and into her bikini bottoms. She teased herself with the tips of her very wet fingers. Then, she heard Jolene get up from the bench.

Sarah opened her eyes.

Jolene walked towards her, one hip flick after another. When she landed next to her, Jolene leaned down and delivered one of the most passionate kisses of Sarah's life. They breathed as one, sharing a piece of themselves with each tender pass.

"I'm thrilled you're here," Jolene whispered.

Sarah reached up and supported Jolene's soft cheeks in her hands, kissing her more deeply. "Me, too."

"This is very dangerous what we're doing here," Jolene said as she traced Sarah's lips with the tip of her velvety tongue.

"It is dangerous. It's incredibly dangerous. But it feels so right. Doesn't it? It feels so—"

"—stop talking," Jolene said. "I just want to kiss you."

Sarah escaped into Jolene, riding along the curve of her passion with no fear of falling off its edge. She opened and let Jolene's breath sweep her into a dance that woke her up to the thrill of letting go of the noise and embracing the fullness of the calm.

Sarah wanted to remain in that euphoric high, and she did for a few intoxicating minutes until she heard the sound of the beep on the door. It brought their kiss to an abrupt stop. A blink later, in walked Frenchy carrying an empty glass with an umbrella in it. "I'm popping in for a quick nap, and then Will is taking me salsa dancing." She went into the closet and pulled out a pair of dress sandals.

Sarah and Jolene shared a smile.

"You missed one hell of a time," she said.

Sarah rose from her chair, revealing her naked legs.

"Or maybe not," Frenchy said.

Jolene stepped forward. "I'll head back to my place and shower. Then, I'll meet you back here in an hour to grab drinks and dinner?"

Sarah's body still pulsed. "Sure thing."

Jolene swung towards the door and waved. "Until then."

"Until then," Frenchy and Sarah said in unison.

Chapter Sixteen

An hour later, Jolene arrived. They meandered down the cobblestone pathway leading to Coconuts. Sarah swung her arms with a bit more spunk than usual. She wore a pale pink dress, and stepped with a weightless, freeing bounce. The early evening breeze tickled her bare arms and legs. For the slightest moment, she roamed around the resort with an air of nakedness, free from restrictions.

She walked past a patch of vibrant red and green plants and stopped at the sight of their heart-shaped leaves. She headed over to them, and Jolene followed. She fingered one of the leaves and enjoyed its soft, velvety surface. "I've walked by these plants for two days and only now noticed the heart shape."

Jolene laughed. "Those are flamingo lilies. They're everywhere."

Sarah glanced down the path and, sure enough, heart-shaped leaves danced in the breeze. "Well, isn't that something?"

They strolled some more then arrived at Coconuts in time for happy hour. "I'll grab us some drinks, if you want to get that seat near the edge of the deck," Sarah motioned.

"Of course." Jolene turned and headed towards the small round table, glancing back once over her shoulder and offering Sarah one of those contagious smiles of hers.

A few minutes later, drinks in hand, Sarah stared out at the calm water.

"What did you promise yourself when you considered you might die down there today?" Jolene asked, taking a sip of her piña colada.

Sarah chuckled and sighed.

Jolene bathed her in a knowing glance.

"You've been in a similar circumstance?" Sarah asked.

"Uh-uh. I asked you first." Jolene tossed her a playful look.

Sarah stole a view of the painted pastel sky. "I promised to change some things."

Out of her peripheral, Sarah caught the curiosity spreading across Jolene's face. "What kind of things?"

Sarah rubbed her forehead and drew a deep breath. "The rat race. I'm in the rat race. I heard other people talk about it all my life. I promised myself, I'd never end up there. How can someone be so careless to end up living life on someone else's orders? Then, one day I woke up and there I sat on a clogged highway that never moves anymore."

"The rat race," Jolene repeated matter-of-factly.

"Yeah. It's a silent killer." Sarah sipped her drink. "It's an endless loop, and I'm running from one end of the track to the other, hoping that on the next return something will change, the answer will be there, the thing I've been waiting for will arrive, and the cycle will end with a brilliant twist."

Jolene blanketed her in ease.

Sarah continued to share her discovery. "Here's the real tragedy in participating in it—you can't exit. It's like being on the New Jersey Turnpike between those long exits that are like thirty miles apart and arriving at one only to find a closed sign. So you have no choice but to keep driving, hoping the next one will arrive and be open. That hope is what keeps you going. When that hope is taken away, it weakens your spirit for the open road.

Momentum starts to die out. After a while, that shiny new engine that accompanied you at the beginning, the one that purred, begins to get muddled and tired. So then you start looking for doses of quick fixes, like a shot of adrenaline to the heart of the engine, and each time you take one, it has less power than the one before it. So now you need more to keep moving. It's a dependency thing. A total dependency. You look for those breaks and treats along the way, and when they appear, they're like a magic pill fashioned to replenish. Then, when it's gone and all traces of its original hope fade, you're back to square one, running that damn loop again, trying to find a way out."

"Why not create your own exit?"

Sarah hung onto Jolene's wise question. "I have no idea where to exit. I've been in the race so long. I've pigeonholed myself into a life that's hard, if not impossible to escape. The company I work for, they're so good to me. It'd be irresponsible of me to take any random exit."

"It'd be more irresponsible not to, wouldn't it?"

The question caught Sarah off guard. She dribbled some of her drink down the front of her dress. "I'm very clumsy." She dabbed the spot with a napkin. "Good thing the drink is white."

Jolene leaned over and helped her wipe the spot. "You told me once that you loved your job. Then, you told me that you didn't love your job. So where does that leave you?"

Sarah rested on the silence in between the breaking of waves on the coral below, weighing through the choices. "I hate my job." Sarah sat back. "There. I said it. I hate my job."

"You hate it?"

"I flat out hate it."

"Why not leave your work to pursue something that makes you happier?"

Sarah twisted under Jolene's stare. "I'd be peddling backwards. I hate going backwards. It took me so long to go forward."

Sarah regarded the water, at how it flowed so easily, no effort or reassurances needed. Just the sun and the moon and some rain from time to time. Whereas she required a lot. She was high-maintenance. She liked the comforts of having plush carpeting and organic fruits in her artistic hand-painted pottery bowl on her granite countertops. She liked wearing designer clothes and being able to go out to eat without fear she'd blow her bank account for the week. "I'm very comfortable."

"It's hard to leave comfort. I get it." Jolene nodded.

Sarah idled on that statement. Jolene was lucky. She had everything figured out. She had a job she loved. She lived in paradise. She didn't fear things. She stood her ground and lived her life as she wanted. "You're lucky. You seem happy. Really happy."

"I am. I've got what I need."

Jolene glowed. She thrived in her life, needing only the sea and her scuba gear. She didn't have a car, a house of her own, a house cleaner, a landscaper, yet, her smile radiated brighter and more natural than any she'd seen in a long time.

"You're so free."

Jolene offered her a sideways glance. "That's worth everything to me."

"How did you get this free?"

Jolene wrestled with the question, pulling in her lower lip. "A lot of soul-searching, reading, and reflecting. I'm still in learning mode."

They sat staring out over the railings of the deck, watching as the horizon swallowed the remains of the pink sky. Even in the shadows, Sarah sat in a halo of new light that shined life back into her heart. That day, she faced a fear of death and woke back up to life again. In the warm, tropical breeze that brushed along her skin, Sarah rooted herself in the dynamic soil of self-propelled hope, spreading herself tall and wide as she soaked up the nutrients of a profound moment in time when the unstable forces of mystery helped her see that life offered not just one way to live, but many.

Empowered by the new view, she felt free of work demands for the first time since chasing that carrot her boss dangled in front of her so many years ago. For the moment, she feasted only on the delicacy of her own circumstances, right then and there.

A genuine lightness shone within her, creating a wondrous wave of carefree whim. "I feel so alive right now," Sarah whispered, closing her eyes and basking in the glow of a grateful vibe.

Then, Jolene traced her soft finger across Sarah's cheek, causing it to lift. She released the slightest murmur before opening her eyes and landing in the affectionate cushion of Jolene's gaze.

"You know what the secret to carving your own exit is?" Jolene whispered.

"Tell me."

"The secret is to take action on something of your own every single day of your life and watch it grow."

"Like what? Tell me." Sarah scooted closer to the table. "Tell me how to grow something different."

"Whatever you plant, as long as you water and feed it, will grow."

"So philosophical." Sarah reached out for her hand. "I do love to hear you talk. Tell me more about this planting and feeding thing."

"I'll tell you a little secret."

Sarah caressed her hand. "You and I seem to love sharing secrets, don't we? Go ahead, tell me."

"When I first arrived back on the island, I felt empty and kind of lost. I came back a different person. I missed my mother a lot this time around. She had grown on me."

"Because you watered her?"

"Yeah, I guess in a way."

"You're lucky to have your mother still. Mine died of breast cancer when I was eighteen and my father a heart attack less than two years later."

"I'm so sorry."

"I've had plenty of time to adjust."

"Is that why you work so hard? You're empty too?"

"I'd rather talk about you. I talk too much as it is," Sarah said with a wave of her hand.

Jolene laughed. "You do talk a lot. Good thing I enjoy being a listener."

"Well tonight you're the talker. I'm the listener. So talk. Continue."

"Well, okay. Getting back to what I learned. I'm a loner. No surprise, I'm sure. I mean I like to be in the water with the tourists, but at the end of the day, I'm a very simple person. I like the quietness of my small apartment. I read and listen to meditative music. My mother is a loner, too. She spends her days wrapped in the minds of her characters, and comes to the surface to eat, sleep, and hang with Frenchy on her patio on Mondays and Wednesdays. I saw her go from a wilted state to full bloom in the matter of time I spent with her. Her hair carried less gray, her eyes twinkled and she laughed more as the weeks turned into months. She needed some watering and sunlight. I guess in a way, I provided that to her."

"I can see that."

"When I returned here, I returned with a sense of loss. I missed watering her. I didn't realize how much until I came home to my dead plant. It was this dried twig that had one little shoot coming off its tip. I watered it. Then, I read about using Epsom salt to help keep the soil balanced. By the second day, I noticed the shoot had grown. I know this will sound crazy, but I felt this sense of gratitude from it. So, I began to play classical music because I learned plants like that. Then, all of a sudden, new shoots began popping up the full length of the twig's body. It came back to life. It needed me, and I needed it. Together we healed each other. It's grown twenty-two leaves as of this morning. It's all about finding something greater outside ourselves then offering it our love and attention. I began using this same philosophy with the dive clients. I see them arrive all stressed and anxious, and I devote myself to helping them to relax and be present, even if for just a short week."

Sarah reclined back in her chair, taking in the full beauty of her statement. Then, she cradled Jolene's hand with more presence. "That's beautiful and profound."

Jolene leaned back in her chair, closed her eyes, and squeezed Sarah's hand.

"Do you ever miss watering Shannon?" Sarah asked.

Jolene stared out at the sea. "Honestly, no. I didn't love her. As it turned out, I only loved the idea of loving her. Does that make sense?"

Sarah had never loved anyone. She'd lusted after women, plenty of them. The only ones she ever seemed to attract were married women. "How did you know you didn't love her?"

"My heart didn't ache for her. Besides, I forced her into being with me."

"You don't strike me as the forcing type."

"You do crazy things when you think you're in love. I loved having someone around. I loved protecting her. I wanted to be the one who made her

241

happy. Of course, her heart didn't reciprocate. She had one foot here and the other back home. She missed her family, her friends, and her ex-boyfriend."

"Oh," Sarah said.

"When you've put so much time into someone, you want validation. You know? So, I kept too tight of a grip on her."

Sarah did the same in business. "I can see how that can happen. At least you're not gripping to a life where you're trapped in an office with light fixtures that produce fake sunlight, hoping the sleep in your brain goes away fast so you can get focused and get through the day."

"Is that really your life?"

Sarah looked out at the sparkling waves. "More or less. You know what the problem with taking a vacation is?"

"That you end up putting the word problem and vacation in the same sentence?"

Sarah laughed. "It points out the deep contrast between reality and fiction."

"Not if you write your own story."

"You've got one hell of a pen," Sarah said. "I bet that pen has a lot of stories."

"That it does. As soon as I picked it up, the story began writing itself. I couldn't ignore it."

"Except your story has a problem that you don't seem to be able to get past."

"Enlighten me," Jolene said.

Sarah bit her lip. "Every story needs that one character who pokes a hole into it. A story needs conflict, needs tension to keep the pages from falling flat on each other."

"Where do I find this page turner?" Jolene asked.

"Maybe we should let the story reveal itself."

"A nice, slow build up, you're saying?"

"I'm not saying anything. I'm not the writer." Sarah sipped her drink.

"So what are you then?"

"Dare I say the spark that elicits your creativity?"

Jolene turned back to the water on a moan.

~ ~

After drinks at Coconuts, as Sarah and Jolene dined at the resort's restaurant on flounder, specialty rice, roasted vegetables and sugary treats, Frenchy, Will and a few of the other divers from their boat group joined them.

"We should've eaten here instead." Frenchy stole Sarah's fork and plucked a piece of her blackened fish. "The music is better here too."

"There's no music," Sarah said.

"Exactly." Frenchy rolled her eyes. "Hey, we're heading to Coconuts. Come with us, please."

Less than ten minutes later, Sarah and Jolene went back to Coconuts with them. Jolene sat at the head of the table, smiling and chatting with Will. In between Jolene's laughs, she'd glance at Sarah and heat the space between them. Her sidelong glances played on Sarah.

They laughed and had a few more drinks then decided to call it a night. As Sarah and Jolene lingered on their goodbye, Frenchy rushed to her.

"I need the room."

"Oh for goodness' sake. How old are you?" Sarah whispered.

"Old enough to know I need to have fun while I have the chance."

"What am I supposed to do?"

Frenchy arched her eyebrow at Jolene.

Sarah arched hers back at Frenchy.

Jolene stepped in. "Sarah and I can take a stroll."

"See," Frenchy said. "Problem solved."

~ ~

They strolled through the resort under the golden hue of quiet lights. "You can sleep at my place tonight," Jolene said.

Sarah's inner thighs twitched. "I'm sure Will and Frenchy will clear out soon enough."

Jolene stopped walking and reached for her hands. "Do you not want to spend the night?

"I do," Sarah paused. "And, to be honest, that scares me."

Jolene nodded as if struggling with her own fears. "What are you afraid of?"

Of ruining the fullness in my soul? Of finding myself craving a woman who lives in a different country? "We've got such different lives."

Jolene moved in closer and kissed her softly. "We do."

"That frightens me," Sarah said on a whisper.

"Me, too."

Sarah stared into her eyes and they pulled her in. She reached up and held Jolene's face in the palm of her hands. Then, she kissed her with tender passes. "I can't fall for someone who lives on an island a thousand miles away from me."

"Have you fallen?" Jolene asked, breathless.

"I've never met anyone like you."

Jolene hugged her. "There's no pressure here. Let's just enjoy the night."

Sarah took Jolene's hand and walked onward with her, in a silence that both comforted and sent her tumbling.

When they entered her apartment, Jolene closed the blinds. Sarah analyzed the room. It was tidy, bathed in a soft glow, and smelled like lemon and spice. A bedroom lay to the far right of the room. A small kitchen area with a miniature-sized fridge and a two-burner stove sat to the left. In the center of the room, sat a leather couch and a recliner.

Simple. Cozy. Home.

Sarah indulged in the warmth of the citrusy, golden space, drawing a deep breath and spinning in its earthy blend. On the windowsill sat a small plant with green leaves and a tall twig at its center. She walked over to it and massaged one of the leaves. "Is this the plant?"

Jolene came up beside her and fingered an adjacent leaf. Their fingers met. "Beautiful, isn't she?"

Sarah glanced at the smoothness of her cheeks and the soft contour of her jaw. "She sure is."

Still glancing at the leaf, a lonely tear rolled down Jolene's cheek.

Sarah wiped it with the back of her hand, drawn to its birth.

"I need you to kiss me right now," Jolene whispered.

Sarah kissed her wet cheek, inhaling her and savoring the lingering scent of her vulnerability. She gazed into Jolene's watery eyes, wanting to bathe in that moment for an eternity. "Why are you sad?"

"I'm going to miss you," Jolene whispered. "It already hurts."

Sarah smoothed her finger over Jolene's trembling eyelid.

She didn't want to leave disappointed. She wanted to take home with her the sweet memory of Jolene. She didn't care that it might hurt to not be able to reach out and hold her hand again or kiss her salty cheek. She didn't care that she might cry herself to sleep every night knowing Jolene slid under the covers of a bed in a land far-off from her own. She didn't care about any of that in the moment. She wanted to hug and kiss her tenderly, root her in her heart, so on those cold Maryland nights when she lay alone under her ceiling fan and with the shadows of the moon casting their darkness, she'd find light in the memory of their time together.

Sarah traced Jolene's cheek, enjoying the softness. She placed her lips against hers and drank from what she had to offer her in that moment, savoring every last drop so as not to waste any of its preciousness.

With the ocean breeze as their companion, they surrendered to the wave of passion between them, sealing off the island, the worries, the fears, and escaping into their own paradise, one powered by their beating hearts and hungry desires to join as one under the soft, warm sheets.

They headed over to Jolene's bedroom.

Sarah traced her hand down Jolene's exquisite contours, diving in deep to the sultry sway of her hips as she neared her waist and inched lower. Their breaths danced together like two feathers caught on a melody suited only for them. Teasing, provocative, and focused on the movement of the other, they glided on a journey towards harmony where the light of their love shone even as they dove deeper, risking all to explore the depths of their interests.

They lowered onto the bed and underneath the warm sheets.

Sarah connected with Jolene on a soulful level, one that opened her to a new existence, a freeing, uninhibited, and safe one. The closer she came to her heat, the more intense the desire to connect. When she landed on Jolene's mound, she relished in its softness and velvety comfort. As she traveled further, she melted in the heat of her wetness. Staring into her eyes, Sarah continued her journey into Jolene's paradise, a paradise where tenderness wrapped itself in love and drove her further into the ecstasy of her caress. Jolene's body swayed with hers, as Sarah entered her intimate domain where the earthy scents of her pleasure drifted between, blurring the line they had originally drawn.

Jolene's wetness, silky and playing a more delicious melody with each of Sarah's strokes, dizzied her and sent her on a beautiful ride where sky and ground reversed, where air and water blended, where flight and dive became one. Jolene sought out Sarah's pulsing desire, too, and as one they brought each other to the extremes of pleasure where the air cradled them in a comforting rock, one that sent them reeling together towards that place where freedom and love waited.

~ ~

Jolene cradled Sarah and sank at their reality. She already ached for Sarah, and she still lay in her arms. How much would that void hurt when Sarah returned home and she found herself empty of any real chance she'd ever be that loved and satiated again?

Jolene rolled over. "One of these mornings, I want to take you on a transition dive at sunrise and blow your mind open wide."

"My mind can't be blown any wider." Sarah chuckled and kissed her.

"Yeah. Just wait and see," Jolene spoke, edging against the corner of her lips.

They lay gazing at each other.

Sarah opened her mouth slightly then closed it.

"What was that?" Jolene asked, pulling her in tighter.

"This is going to hurt like hell in a few days."

Jolene brushed that thought aside. She'd have the rest of her life to contemplate things. For now, she didn't have to. "That's the future. That has nothing at all to do with this very second."

A look of recognition washed over Sarah's face, dislodging the tension.

"I wish you didn't move back here."

"I never moved from here. This is home. It has been from the moment I first dove in those waters."

Sarah buried her head against Jolene's chest.

Jolene wanted to steal the smell of earth from her hair; the earth that had been kissed by her drizzle and drenched with joy, capable of leaving an everlasting smile on her face.

"Hey," Jolene said, kissing the top of her head, protecting them from her own selfish fears. "Let's enjoy this for what it is."

"What is this?" Sarah mumbled.

"It's now."

Sarah nodded against her chest. "It's now."

Chapter Seventeen

The next morning, Sarah snuck in and found Frenchy sleeping alone. She tucked herself into her blankets for another few minutes of shut-eye.

Less than an hour later, Sarah woke to Frenchy's singsong voice. "Rise and shine, beautiful." She carried a tray of coffee cups and fruits past the beds and into the living room space. "I figure we can eat a light snack before we get on the boat today." She placed the tray on the table and stretched her skinny arms over her mass of dark hair. Those signature streaks of silver found their way to her bangs, highlighting a sophisticated, mature look a person couldn't find in a bottle of hair dye.

Sarah got up and went over to the desk to check her email.

"My body repels the electrostatic forces from that thing," Frenchy said. "The radiation molecules stick to me like annoying dust mites. They're clouding my mind and causing my skin to get hot and clammy."

Sarah understood. Those molecules, invisible to her naked eye, ravaged her inner harmony with their heavy presence. She closed the laptop and focused on her best friend.

"How was last night?" Sarah asked.

"Will and I walked the beach then came back here." Frenchy peered up at her from behind her coffee mug, her eyes brimming with energy.

"Did you behave yourself?"

"If I said yes, would you wipe away that look of warning?"

249

"I'm not judging you," Sarah said, coming over to her side with her fresh cup of coffee. "I'm just asking."

Frenchy's face grew an intense shade of crimson. "I was a very bad girl."

"Are you sure that's a good idea?"

"Are you sure it's a good idea to be falling for a woman who lives in a different country than you?"

"I'm not the one who just came out of a long-term relationship."

Frenchy stood, placing herself in the power position with one hand on the desk. "But Jolene did."

Sarah glared at Frenchy. "Jolene wasn't happy with Shannon. Yes, that's right. She told me."

Frenchy sipped her coffee, and sighed. "You know, this trip is causing me to do some deep soul-searching. I discovered something."

"What's that?"

"I was never happy with Johnny."

"You're still hurting from him."

"Well, it's not my fault I'm sensitive. I didn't get a happy-go-lucky personality to take with me everywhere like you." She pointed her eyes back at Sarah. "I'm an ordinary person trying to carve out a life that clicks. You hook up, get married, and live happily ever after." She sighed again. "I guess I took a wrong turn."

"Well, so did I."

"Are you finally admitting that?" Frenchy asked.

"I don't know what I'm admitting. I'm very confused. My mind is going in circles, screaming at me to run, to run as fast as I can to avoid something dangerous."

"Kiddo, you need to get out of your head," Frenchy said.

"How?"

"You need to eat your fruit, put on your swimsuit, get on that boat, and dive like your life depends on it."

"She took me shallow diving yesterday afternoon."

"And you're still alive." Frenchy smiled.

"I'm still alive."

Frenchy pointed at her. "You better get in that water today."

"Oh, I'm going to get in that water today. You watch and see."

~ ~

Jolene started the engine and took off to the first dive site.

The nausea rose again as the wind whipped Sarah's face.

Will advanced towards Jolene who stood at the front of the boat. He whispered something to her then looked back at the divers.

Could something already be wrong? Sarah turned to Frenchy. "I hate this."

"You've got to do this."

The engine sped. Sarah glanced around at everyone acting so calm and unlike people ready to dive into the mysterious potential dangers that lurked below them. Will reassumed his position at the back of the boat, staring out at the sea without concern.

The ride to the first site happened in a blink. Soon, Jolene cut the engine and the boat rocked. Everyone began putting gel in their masks again as they chatted, undeterred by the risks of equipment malfunctions or decompression illness. They could dive in those turquoise waters and never return. That could be the last time they swirled gel around their masks, enjoyed the sunshine warming their bare shoulders, or breathed natural oxygen from the air instead of a tank.

Like soldiers heading into battle, they faced the potential with grace, accepting the risks with nothing more than a glance to the cloudless sky.

Frenchy handed her the gel. "Squirt away."

"You're okay with this? Knowing you might not come out alive?"

"If I die, I will have died a lively and full person." Frenchy handed her the mask. "Now squirt."

"I don't want to die."

"So live." Frenchy snatched back the gel, opened it, and aimed for the mask. "If you're not going to squirt, at least smear. Get it in the grooves near the edges. You don't want it fogging on you."

"Why do you want to do this?"

"Because kiddo, I see the whole world in a different shade now." She glanced towards Will, and they shared a smile.

"How's that?"

"You'll have to go down there to find out for yourself."

Frenchy bent over and slipped her foot into her fin, signaling the end of her pep talk. "I'll be buddying up with Frank and Alex. You'll be safe with Jolene. Now get to it."

Soon, all the divers headed to the back of the boat and jumped like thrill seekers to a destination unknown. Sarah approached last. Will checked her tank valve then patted her shoulder. "You're all set."

"Are you sure? It's definitely on?"

"You're good to go."

She gripped her mask with her trembling hand, and stared out at Frenchy. *It's do or die.*

She extended one leg, and while continuing to look at Frenchy treading the water like a pro, she let the ocean pull her in.

She landed on a giant splash. Then, Jolene dropped in right after her. "I'll be right beside you." Jolene signaled her thumbs down, and Sarah gasped one last lungful of fresh air before sticking her regulator in her mouth.

She descended at a much slower pace that time. The water, warm and soft against the little skin that was exposed, cushioned her down to the white sandy bottom at twenty feet. She hovered above the seafloor taking in the view above. The sun lit the surface and penetrated down to the tiniest fleck of sand. She scanned the view, taking in the feathery plants swaying with the current, dancing to the tune of nature's pulse. Tiny yellow fish darted in and out of their graceful flow, disinterested in the divers who hovered like aliens inspecting their world.

Her deep inhales and exhales accompanied her as she finned around colorful fish and sea grass. Jolene signaled an okay sign to her. Sarah inhaled and rested on the comfort of her own breath sounds and the beautiful lull between them.

Yes, she would be okay.

Jolene linked her arm in hers and finned them towards the deeper blue.

Together, they joined with the sea.

An energy glittered inside, one that dissolved the anxiety of the unknown. They swam against the mild current, basking in the glow of the untouched. Jolene led her and the others towards the coral richness where fish in every color and shape communed around plants that glowed.

Sarah swam in peace, catching glimpses of the beauty. Dreamlike, she absorbed it all, wanting to note every sight, sound, and sense of awe she could gather.

An angelfish swam beside her, welcoming her into its world. Mesmerized by the grace of it, Sarah steadied her breaths wanting to stay in alignment with its smooth progression into the deeper world of its magical kingdom.

Beneath the sea, everything flowed in equal beauty. No one outdid the other. Income level, house size, car type, clothing brand, none of it mattered. No one competed with her for breath or for balance. Enough existed for everyone. The murky chatter of anxiety quieted and a soothing calm swam in, one that allowed her to capture the sensory delicacies.

She floated, turning and twisting with the simple flick of her fin.

An underlying sophistication draped the sea, one that couldn't be seen from above. She stretched out, hanging in suspension, motionless, in balance, with her breathing lifting her and letting her fall, graceful as a leaf in the wind.

She braved on, unlinking from Jolene. They shared a knowing glance, words unnecessary to understand the breadth of the moment when nothing else in the world mattered but that beautiful soulful dance between them and the hug of the water. Jolene finned beside her, quiet and balanced, simplified and efficient, wrapped in spellbinding elegance.

Sarah hoped she appeared as elegant to Jolene.

Free of the hustle and trap of competitiveness, Sarah relaxed to the sounds of her breaths, swaddled in the movements of the sea, exploring the depths of her curiosity by going beyond the rigidity of her comfort. Life's woes, so small and meaningless now, had no place next to the dazzling enormity of the life that surrounded her.

The noise of angry clients, of her insecurities, of her roaring inner voice barking out unrealistic demands, stopped. A pristine beat replaced them, a beat so in tune and idyllic it completed her on a level she'd never known.

The mental wheels stopped grinding as grace entered. That grace sank into every fiber, every muscle, and every dark crevice.

Disconnected from the stressors of life, Sarah thrived in the weightlessness, embracing the ride with the ease of using only her breath to glide her up and over the side of an underwater hill sprinkled in creatures and colors.

The true essence of the water, coral, and sea creatures shone through the veil of limiting expectations, carrying her along on the journey to freedom. She and the sea joined in a synergetic union. The water became her partner in an experience full of adventure. Suddenly, she wasn't obsessed with the constant bombardment of activities to get to the next step. The only step that mattered unfolded before her.

She marveled at that underwater world, a place few got to see for themselves. She saw colorful parrotfish, queen conches, and soft corals and sponges that resembled bushes in shades of purple, ochre, and green.

Free of talk, Sarah heard the call of life, whispering its secrets to her that the flow ended at the surface where expectations, deadlines, and worries about the past and future got in the way. The water dissolved her stress like a warm bath, dispersing the tightness of her limited world. Infused in calmness, with only the sound of the bubbles—glurg, blurbble, glurg—Sarah peered at Jolene only a foot away, and smiled with her entire body. They turned around and flowed back to the boat with the current as their guide, sharing the same wonders, even from within separate suits.

Joined in an intimate joy, despite their singular moves, they emerged from the warmth of the sea.

Sarah lifted her head out of the water with her soul reborn. The sun shone brighter and the air smelled fresher.

Jolene floated beside her, and one-by-one all the others surfaced. Smiles blanketed each of their faces, a smile Sarah now understood. The smile stretched throughout her body and extended out beyond.

She grabbed the rope and pulled herself towards the boat's ladder. Will reached out and helped her climb.

Sarah sat on the bench, and Jolene helped her secure the tank to its holder. She unbuckled and eased herself from the gear and stood up a free woman.

Jolene reached for her hands and swung them, offering her the beautiful silence of a smile rooted in something greater than any words could explain. She let them go and headed to the front of the boat.

As Frenchy sat on the bench, Sarah helped her secure the tank to its holder. "I did it," she said. "I went scuba diving in the middle of the ocean."

"You look ravishing." Frenchy winked.

A few minutes later, Jolene started the engine and headed off to their next site. Once cruising along, Sarah focused on the beautiful tickle of the wind. Suddenly all the problems she had wanted to solve, no longer gripped her heart. The emptiness she had carried around with her, didn't weigh on her anymore. The breeze blew in her face and wiped away the tears as they fell.

She looked over at Frenchy who didn't speak a word for the first time in their friendship. They sat together in silence, enjoying the lift to their souls and the new space in their minds.

Comfort and fullness moved into Sarah's heart, replacing the dull throb of the void from the external world.

~ ~

Life took on a new look when Sarah stepped out of comfort. Life slowed to a speed where she could open her eyes and see things with more clarity, especially when she dug deep and got past the surface. Under the water, she found out what kind of guts she had.

Over the two weeks, Sarah's mind began expanding, and no amount of money or opportunity would put it back to its former shape. She had dug up the soil, and uncovered truths about life. Time rolled by fast, too fast not to let go and have some fun. Sarah didn't care how much the memory of that fun would hurt in the end. She wanted to enjoy creating it.

For the remainder of their time, Sarah stayed with Jolene, and Frenchy welcomed Will into her bed, citing she deserved to have her sexual desires satiated by a man more than twenty-five years her junior. "It's so good to wrap myself around a body that doesn't crack when I hug him."

Frenchy beamed, and Sarah did, too, worrying about the goodbye only when the goodbye happened. She refused to waste a single moment of her time with Jolene wrapped in anything but the moment right in front of her.

When Jolene and Will worked the afternoon dives, Frenchy and Sarah drove that cute little blue pickup all over the quaint island. They visited the donkey sanctuary, and fed the animals right out of their hands. They took pictures with pink flamingos. They visited the infamous pink salt dunes and gorgeous overlook sites as they drove along the coastline towards a beautiful pier. They meandered down bumpy roads dotted with colorful stones indicating the name of dive sites. They indulged in delicious gelato at a cute little shop on the main street. Then, they shopped until they dropped later by the resort's sprawling pool.

They soaked up all they could during their time on that little piece of Caribbean heaven.

And as promised, towards the end of her time on Bonaire, Jolene treated her to an early morning transition dive. They rose at five a.m. and sank into the shore with plenty of time to grasp the awakening.

Diving at sunrise offered a front row seat to three-dimensional adventure. The world sprang to life when that first ray of light hit the water. Alive with movement, the sea expanded and receded, progressing and swaying at the hands of the sleeping moon and the waking sun.

The colossal underwater farm, tantalizing and fertile, blended into a submerged desert of sand and coral, providing nutrient-rich niches for an array of fish, sponges, turtles, and feathery sea grasses. Schools of fish welcomed them into their domain, swimming alongside of them like one of their classmates, as they went off to feed their hunger for a ride on the current where the rolling, playful sea waited for their curious perusal.

They came upon a sloping hill, a majestic work of living art, encrusted with colorful sponges and corals untouched and unspoiled. On the reef terrace, they discovered dazzling coral of vibrant colors inhabited by a glittery spectrum of reef fish.

The time evaporated along with their compressed air. Before long, they emerged with their newfound discoveries of life and surfaced once again back into the arms of reality.

Chapter Eighteen

On the last full day of their trip, Frenchy, Sarah, Jolene, Will, and several divers from the group on their boat, headed to the cliff dive site at Boka Slagbaai.

They trekked up the steep, rocky path to the top of the cliff. The water below, a beautiful watercolor display of blues and greens, looked like a painting in a museum.

Jolene approached. She exhaled a sharp breath while she looked down. "I always get a little nervous right before I do this."

Funny enough, Sarah's nerves calmed. Something different brewed. Something revved in the pit of her tummy, powering her with flight.

"You're nervous?" Frenchy asked, nearing the edge and stealing a peek over it.

"It's a bit higher than the back of the boat," Jolene said. "This gets my adrenaline spiking."

Before diving into the ocean, Sarah assumed a person would have to be an adrenaline junkie to enjoy diving daily as Jolene did. Sarah now understood that diving relaxed a person, instead of providing the fix for an adrenaline junkie.

Sarah reached out for Frenchy's hand. "Want to jump together?"

"I was hoping you'd ask that."

"Wait," Jolene joined their circle then waved the rest of the group in. "Right before you leap, it's customary to shout out a promise you will keep after you've survived the jump."

"Survived?" Sarah asked.

"Like a last wish type thing?" Frenchy asked.

"Like a beginning wish," Jolene said on a smile. "Who's first?"

"We are," Sarah shouted.

Frenchy's face turned white. "Really?"

Sarah squeezed her hand. "It's do or die time." Sarah led them to the cliff's edge and looked down. At that moment, she didn't care what would happen on the other side of that water. She wanted to break through and be a part of it. Down into the deepest parts of her soul, she craved to dive and see where the flow led her. She raised their hands in solidarity. "What's your promise?"

Frenchy licked her lips as she peeked below. Her hand trembled. "To leave The Idiot behind me once and for all, where he belongs." Her voice echoed and a smile radiated from her entire being. "And yours?"

Sarah raised her hand even higher, tilted her head back and screamed out, "I'm going to let go and just be!" On that last word, before it could even echo back to her, she let go of Frenchy's hand and leaped off the side of that cliff. She jumped with her feet first towards the surface of that mystifying water, free and light. When she broke through the water, she plummeted to that magical place where the noise stopped, worries ceased, and the full embodiment of life's beauty caught up to a person, filling her with a rich supply of appreciation and gratitude for the most spectacular gift of being alive.

Jolene stood at the top of that cliff, the last one to jump. She raised both arms in the air. The sun cast a gorgeous glow on her silhouette. She shouted her promise, and the echo reverberated so much, Sarah couldn't decipher it. Jolene's splash said enough though. It told them all she had a burning desire to do something, and no fear would ever stand in her way.

Later on, as they headed back to their trucks, Sarah caught up with Jolene. She leaned in and whispered, "What was your promise?"

Jolene stopped and gazed at her, and serenity unfolded. "I promised myself to stay open to whatever life is tossing my way."

Sarah caught her breath. "And what do you hope it tosses you?"

Jolene shrugged. "I'm hoping something remarkable."

Sarah folded into her arms. "You jumped with a lot of intensity."

"I guess we're both full of intensity. You picked up a cicada. You dove in the ocean. You jumped off a cliff. What next?"

The sun shone like a radiant beacon of hope in the mid-morning sky, forming its promise to her that all would be okay in her world now that she let go. She would view life with a different lens and find the hidden treasures of her circumstances. Just like when she moved her recliner that day that she first tried scuba, she would shift things around at work and find the happiness and balance she deserved. She would take more time off and vacation with Jolene in Bonaire. She would make time for living, for friendship, and if fate agreed, for love. If she could dive sixty feet beneath the surface and jump off a cliff, she could certainly make a long-distance relationship work.

She could do anything now.

When they got to their truck, Sarah noticed the broken window on the passenger side door. A flash of panic shot through her. "My phone." She ran over to the truck, crunching the pebbles embedded in the sand. She flung open the door. No phone.

She spun towards the group. "They stole it. They broke in and stole it."

Jolene approached her. "You locked the door?"

"Yes," Sarah snapped. "Of course I did."

Jolene backed down, biting her lip. "The rental place didn't tell you not to?"

Frenchy filtered in beside them. "I assumed the clerk was joking."

"A locked truck is like a beacon welcoming thieves to shop for free."

Frenchy reached into the side pocket of the door. "My God, they stole my phone too."

~ ~

Jolene drove with Sarah who sat next to her looking nothing like she just jumped off a cliff and proclaimed to let go. "I'm sorry that happened."

Sarah shook her head. Pain etched on her face. Jolene wished she could wipe it away. "It's just a phone, I guess," she said.

Jolene reached for her hand. "It's okay to be upset. You're human."

"I'm likely foolish for admitting this, but I'm naked without it. I'm safe and comfortable in the company of a phone. How silly, right?"

"We all seek safety and comfort. It's in our DNA. It's a basic need." She watched Sarah's face flinch. "Being safe allows us the freedom to move and take chances. We all crave that safety net."

"Even you?" Hope rose in the fine lines along her eyes.

"Let me show you something." Jolene drove faster, rounding the curves with a little more punch than usual. She drove along the shore towards the resort. "I've always had a dream of finding a home here, of laying some roots."

A calmness blanketed Sarah's face.

Jolene drove to the dead-end street just north of the resort's entrance. At the end sat the colorful home she'd dreamed of purchasing. "You asked me once what I fear. I told you being trapped. I haven't purchased this house, despite it creeping into my dreams most every night since I saw a for sale sign on it, and that's because I'm afraid."

"What're you afraid of?"

"It would mean that I'm committed to this island."

"And that's bad, how?"

"Let me explain." She squeezed Sarah's hand. "Before I met you, I almost purchased this. Then, my mother got hurt, and I let the dream simmer. When I returned, I'd drive here almost three times a week to get a look at it. I'd sit here on my bike and stare at its colorful siding and curious windows, imagining filling it with funky furniture and books. Lots of books. I still haven't called the real estate agent because I fear committing to it. I fear growing roots."

"Why would you not want to grow roots here? I mean look at it. It's so perky and vibrant. It's got you written all over it. Why wouldn't you want to grow roots in a place where you don't have to live in a jail cell like the rest of the world? Where we live fifty weeks out of the year in the jail of work we hate, commutes that sicken us, and jobs that consume our life, just to escape for two weeks a year on vacation?"

"I guess a part of me fears that by setting roots I'm finalizing my flow. I'm controlling it, telling it which way to move. I don't want to grip something too tight because I'm afraid of losing it. It happens, as we've talked about."

"It's just a house. It sells. It's replaceable. It's just stuff."

"Just stuff, huh?" Jolene smiled. "The sea has changed you."

"Yeah. I guess maybe it did."

"The house doesn't have a finished kitchen. I'd need to be patient while I wait for it to be installed."

"A kitchen? Who needs a kitchen? I swear by my microwave. It'll cook anything. Even if you want a turkey, you can cook a turkey in it."

"It won't have a kitchen faucet."

"You can use the shower," Sarah said. "Showers are great for washing dishes, so I've heard."

"The pace here is slow," Jolene continued. "It might take me three months to have a sink installed."

"Then, it's a damn good thing you're a patient person." Sarah lingered on a smile.

Jolene drank the fullness of her words. "I wanted to make it work in Maryland. I wanted to make my mom and Gerry happy. I couldn't and that saddened me. It tore me up to be reminded that home isn't where home used to be. This is home."

"So Maryland could never be home for you?"

"When I'm in Maryland, I depend on the future too much. I find myself saying, one day when this happens I'll be happy. But, when I'm here, I'm already happy. I'm at peace, I'm still, and I'm thrilled to be alive."

"So why are you so hesitant to lay your roots?"

Tears began to fill her eyes.

Sarah smoothed her hand over her arm. "Tell me."

"It's lonely. Look at that house. What if I'm always the only one to romp through it in my pajamas or cook in it? So you see, you're not the only one who's stuck. We're all stuck in some capacity at varying degrees."

"I'd love a colorful house like that. I'd love to curl up on the couch and read books and magazines with you. And eat popcorn. Lots of popcorn drizzled in butter and salt."

"You're welcome to curl up with me and eat all the popcorn your belly can handle."

"I couldn't."

"Why not?"

Sarah nestled against her. "Come on. You know I can't do that."

"Sure you can. You can hold your meetings on Skype and fly back to Maryland once in a while to meet in person."

"I'd love that. I would absolutely love that. But, it's not possible in my position. Not possible at all. I manage a bunch of people and the company requires me to be there in the flesh."

"Then, become a scuba instructor and dive with me. Or freelance your design skills on the island. Or better yet, buy a boat with me and open a little dive shop."

Sarah looked up into her watery eyes and wiped the tears as they rolled down her cheeks. "I wish it could be that easy. Life doesn't work that way, though. I've already settled in life. I have a job and a house. I can't just walk away from that. You know?"

"It's just a job. It can be replaced."

"Not this one." Sarah eased against her, filling Jolene with a deep sense of longing and loss.

~ ~

Later on, the whole gang took Frenchy and Sarah out to a restaurant overlooking the bay. They sat on the deck and feasted on stuffed halibut, calamari, and mussels dripping in butter and herbs.

When they finished, Frenchy came up to Sarah. "It's our last night. Will and I are going to sleep on the beach. So, the room's all yours." She turned to him. "Let's go, Will." She opened her arm out to him. "Let's take a stroll."

Jolene gazed at Sarah and smirked. Sarah rose and extended her arm. "Let's take a stroll, too."

They left the restaurant and headed towards Sarah's suite.

When they entered, Sarah led her to the bed.

She spent the better part of their last night together slowly undressing Jolene, taking in every bit of her contours. Sarah leaned into her, enjoying the life in that moment.

"How will I ever say goodbye to you?" Jolene asked on a kiss.

Jolene's lips warmed her. "I don't want to think about that right now." Sarah mounted herself on top of Jolene. "I just want to be right here, right now, with you."

Jolene responded on a delicious moan, arching her back and filling Sarah with a deep sense of love.

~ ~

The next morning, Jolene walked Frenchy and Sarah to their truck. She hugged Frenchy. "I'm counting on you to help get my mother on a plane to visit."

"You got it. Maybe I'll even sneak Sarah into one of my suitcases for you." She winked, and scuttled over to the driver's side of the truck.

Sarah swallowed her sadness, meeting up with life's current and letting go of all fear as she trusted in its flow. "One day soon," she whispered, "we'll meet up again. Who knows, maybe I'll show up one day with just a suitcase at my side, and surprise you."

"That would be the sexiest thing in the world, if you did."

"I'm going to miss you like crazy," Sarah whispered. "I don't know how I'm going to go back to my reality now that I've experienced all I did."

"Promise me something." Jolene pulled her in closer.

266

Sarah closed her eyes and enjoyed the tickle of Jolene's fresh breath for one last moment. Then, she opened her eyes again and landed in the loving embrace of Jolene's earnestness. "Anything."

"Promise me this isn't the last time I get to hold you in my arms."

Sarah pulled in her lower lip. "It sincerely better not be." She landed softly on Jolene's lips one last time before the world swooped in and sent them in opposite directions.

Chapter Nineteen

As Sarah and Frenchy stood in line at the security checkpoint with their matching carry-ons, Sarah's heart ached. She gripped the handle of hers and rolled it towards the security woman. She placed it onto the rolling platform and watched it enter the point-of-no-return.

Then, an alarm beeped. The security woman unzipped her case, poking her stick into Frenchy's undies and bras.

"Oh no," Frenchy whispered behind her.

Sarah turned. "Oh no what?"

"They're going to find my secret stash."

"What do you mean?"

"Wait for it," she whispered even lower.

The security woman pulled out a pink Bonaire hoodie wrapped into a ball. Then, the coral began to fall from it, landing in a pile on the platform. "Is this your coral?" the woman asked, pointing her eyes at Sarah.

Sarah shot Frenchy a look of warning.

Frenchy stepped up. "That's my suitcase, and those are my undies. They give me a terrible wedgie. Take them and throw them in the trash for all I care."

Sarah stiffened at the sight of the woman's thin lips.

"It's against the law to take coral or any other living creature from the island." The woman poked around some more. She pulled out another wad wrapped in a T-shirt, and then she began to swipe the pile into a trashcan. She dug deeper and found more, dumping the remainder of it.

"What a waste of good coral," Frenchy said under her breath.

"Excuse me?" the woman asked.

Sarah kicked Frenchy's shin. "Nothing. She said nothing."

The woman zipped the carry-on and moved her along. "Next time, you leave everything right here on the island."

Sarah nodded, understanding all too well.

~ ~

On the never-ending, dreadful taxi ride back to her home, Sarah's breath became weak and the car began to spin. She wrestled for control over her emotions for as long as possible, but they unraveled, sending her into a swift and toxic spiral that carved a hole smack dab in the middle of her life.

"I hate this," Sarah said.

"You've got choices."

Sarah's heart pumped too hard for logic to form. Tired and bleary-eyed, she glared at Frenchy. "Do you think I enjoy this stress? I can't go pee without checking my messages first. When I look and see that I have messages, I die a little. This large boulder of panic sits right in the middle of my chest. I have to deal with it. I don't have a big divorce settlement or a booming business to fall back on here. I've just got my savings, which would dissolve in a blink if I ignore those messages."

Her friend's face, at first shadowed in pity, grew softer. Frenchy's eyes glossed. She fidgeted with her fingers the way she did whenever overwhelmed. "It shouldn't be this way," she said softly. "Not for either one of us."

A fire grew inside Sarah. Tears began spilling out the sides of her eyes.

"I'd be a better person if I traveled on the right path. I'm not supposed to be where I am, but I'm stuck with it. I fill up on things. When the blues sail in, I buy a new piece of furniture. When I end up finding out that I'm dating a married woman, I buy a new wardrobe. When a fever sets in, I buy a new pill to wipe it out. The longer I try poking myself back into life, the more I trap myself. You're the lucky one."

"Excuse me?"

"You know what you want out of life. I wish I did. I wish I could wake up in the morning and do something that matters."

"You matter a great deal."

"I'm stuck keeping my position in the rat race. How fucked up is that? I race around my life like an out of control cicada, bumping into everything in my path, unaware of which way I'm supposed to go. I'm up, down, sideways, backwards, everywhere but straightforward. I'm super focused one second, the next my phone rings, pulling my attention to one of fifty other things that vie for my time. Yet, I can't let go of it."

"I'm so sorry." Frenchy wrapped her hand in hers.

"Do you know how painful it is to have put everything you've got into one thing, only to find out that at the end of the day, it doesn't amount to much of anything? It's still not enough. It's too empty. There's never enough money, benefits, or recognition for all the effort. In fact, a scary void seeps in, one that steals the breath right out of my chest; one that's so empty I can hear the blankness beating on my heart like a drumroll, warning me that at any moment it could stop and create deadness. What if everything I've done is a total waste?"

"It's not a waste."

"I look at my goal board and am amazed at the things I've accomplished in one year's time. I don't know anyone who puts that kind of energy into getting things done. I worked my ass off, and now wonder why. None of it matters because you know what?"

"What, kiddo?"

"I've beaten this path to a pulp, beaten the living crap out of it because it's what I've always done, and god dammit I want it to work not because I love crunching numbers but because I put it on my board, because it fell in place as the next logical step after everything I've already done. I've taken so many steps towards these goals that I can't abandon them."

"You can do whatever the heck you want to do."

Sarah sighed. "I always imagined if I got a job in advertising, I'd be happy. If I got a promotion to a team lead, I'd have something to smile about. If I climbed all the way up to a director, I might wake up in the morning wanting to be awake instead of tossing the pillow back over my head. You know what I did when I became a marketing executive? Nothing. I didn't celebrate. I stepped up another rung on the ladder. Big deal. It meant nothing. I already began planning the next big thing. All that complication and for what? I'm never satisfied, and I fear that I never will be."

Frenchy said nothing. Just listened.

"Do you know that in order to make it to the level I'm at, I had to trample on someone else's dreams? I had to stomp on someone. I had to kill someone else's dream, someone who might actually enjoy the view."

"You worked hard for those promotions."

"I'm standing on top of a large mountain, and when I look out, I see nothing but complicated tangles. I no longer derive joy from any of it. My stomach hurts. I've turned into a road rage maniac screaming at strangers who are driving too slow or in the wrong lane. I pass elderly people in the grocery store who aren't pushing their carts fast enough and flick them a dirty look. I stomp my feet when someone is taking too long at the ATM. I have no patience with the world. For the first time in my life, I want to slow down and ride the current instead of demanding it go faster, only now I can't find the brake."

"You have been kind of impatient."

"This scares me because I can't go back to the rat race and pretend it doesn't bother me anymore. I've seen something that scares me. I've seen freedom. I've seen happiness. And I fear I'll never see it again once I go back to that rushing world."

"You're tired. You're heartbroken. You envisioned that customs clerk was going to throw your butt in a Bonaire jail cell. Just cut yourself some slack."

"The fast lane, it's all I know. It's what I've groomed for my entire life. I wouldn't know what to do without it. Now I don't even know what to do with it. So, you see, I'm in a bad position."

"What's the goal you're trying so hard to achieve?" Frenchy asked.

"I don't know. I ran out of them. I raced to get so many; I forgot why I wanted them. I raced past everything in my twenties and half of my thirties. In all my chasing, I've forgotten to pause and take life in."

"You're always trying to get somewhere."

"I am, and it's always somewhere different than where I am right now."

They sat silent, letting the truth marinate.

Her fulfillment was based on the next turn, only when she rounded the turn, she was still going too fast, so fast she never met up with it."

"I never stop running," Sarah said, exasperated. She never took the time to sit still and let life lure her into its presence. She squinted too far ahead for happiness.

"Under the water, something woke up in me, a sense that the answer to life's meaning isn't some goal I put on my board that I get to one day in the future. It's in the depth of the actions I take, the breaths, the blinks, the smiles, the awareness that we affect everything and everyone around us by our actions and inactions, by how fast we run and walk, drive, eat, and talk. No wonder I ramble. My words are always ten paces ahead of my next thought."

"I love your rambling, though."

Frenchy opened her arms, and Sarah fell against her chest. Frenchy combed her fingers through her hair the way her mother used to do when she had a fever or cold. It soothed her.

"I keep thinking when I get to my destination, wherever that is, that I'll finally free-fall into the arms of joy. You know what dawned on me that day I emerged reborn from the sea?"

Frenchy continued to soothe her achy head. "What's that?"

"I don't see the potential in the space I occupy and I've worked so hard to occupy it." Sarah found it impossible to let go because she feared she wouldn't know who she was without it. A lump formed in her throat and the emotions caught up with her. She buckled in her best friend's arms.

"When you're in a constant state of flux, meaning can't fit," Frenchy said. "So, make some room, kiddo. Take a simple, long deep drag of air. Open up some space. Breathe and allow yourself to find the meaning beneath everything."

"You make it sound so simple."

"This trip has taught me something. It's helped me to discover that my purpose is about slipping into these simple pockets right here; pockets of friendship, of baking bread, of indulging in new things. In these pockets, I forget about what I've lost, and focus on what I've gained, which is a deep respect and love for everything new and promising. That's where joy lives, and you can access it at any time."

Sarah envied her optimism.

As the taxi pulled up in front of Sarah's house, Frenchy turned to her. "The hurt will go away eventually. It did for me. It can for you too."

Frenchy's hurt disappeared because she didn't have a choice. Sarah did have a choice, and that's what made it so hard to accept. "I hope you're right."

Sarah slipped out of the backseat and landed on her street, back into the arms of what she used to consider home sweet home. She regarded her white colonial, a mere stranger in the darkness. The cold chill of the November air seeped deep into her bones. Reality pointed its finger at her, and she had to deal with it.

She rolled her suitcase up her front walk, turned and waved to her newly healed best friend.

Chapter Twenty

Sarah returned to work the following day, and her assistant handed her a new cell phone. "Tom and the rest of the leadership team are waiting in the conference room for you. Something about a big merger and new initiative."

The familiar churning of life began again.

Sarah wanted to jump back on an airplane and protect what she'd discovered in Bonaire. She didn't want to sit in a meeting and pretend she cared about mergers and acquisitions or how to spread marketing dollars to bridge together increased sales and revenue. Everything in her told her to sabotage her current reality so she could call Jolene and tell her she discovered she didn't want that old life. She wanted off the beaten path. She wanted out of the rat race.

Tom beamed from the head of the table. "We've got news."

Sarah grabbed her usual seat to the right of him. "My trip was great, thank you." She sat and beamed back at him with her best sarcastic grin.

He nodded. "Right. Sorry, I slip right into work, don't I?"

"It's what we do." Sarah wrote the date on the top of her fresh notepad. "What's this news?"

"We've landed a new account with Tonya Designs. They want us to begin brainstorming campaign ideas for their spring release. We need to act quickly."

"Right, quick." Sarah took in the news.

277

"We'll draft a plan."

"Draft a plan?" The stress began its slow and murky swim through her.

"Yes, we'll put some structure behind this and make it another win for us all."

"Another win," Sarah repeated. The weight of her words slammed her against the foundation set long before she understood the complexities of rigid structure.

"We're also going to promote you. They're likely going to need their own dedicated designers and social media specialists. Whatever you need to get the ball rolling."

Sarah ground her jaw, and forced an uneasy smile. "Of course."

Tom clapped his hands together. "Great. Thank you," he said with gracious warmth. "Thank you for everything you do for us. You make a difference here. It wouldn't be the same without you."

~ ~

After her meeting, Sarah went back to her office and stared at the pile of paperwork waiting for her review. Gone two weeks and she fell behind a month. It never ended.

Her efforts would never be enough. There would always be another merger, another account, another team to bring up to speed. She needed air. She needed lots of fresh air. She needed to escape the confines of her office, take a walk, and breathe in a large gulp of freshness instead of the staleness that already began to curl up under her door and snuff out her peaceful vibe.

Sarah's stomach turned. She didn't want to dig into another complicated plateful of tasks, business meetings, projections, and stress.

She wanted to stand on that gorgeous beach, hand in hand with Jolene, and create a new life where everything fell into breathtaking place. But that was not reality. She needed to focus on reality. She had bills, responsibilities, and people who depended on her. She had so many things to deal with.

Sarah had little choice but to swipe her hands and proceed right back on set as if she had just taken a small commercial break. She would have to fire up her computer, run reports, lead meetings, get the movers and shakers on point, conquer the world right on the surface of where she'd carved that path.

Eventually the pain would end as Frenchy said it would. Frenchy was always right. Well except for her choice to force Johnny into marriage with an ultimatum. He never would've been happy to be wedged into a life that didn't fit him. Eventually the fabric would've ripped and fallen to the ground, exposing the ill-fitted situation for what it was, a façade. No matter how much she tried to fit him into her life, he simply couldn't fit. The seams eventually wore out and broke, and no amount of thread could ever patch it back to its original shape. Frenchy was smart to see that. The truth had expanded and grown too large to fit back together into the confinement of a space never designed for growth.

Free from the grip, Frenchy could grow into someone unafraid to dig and discover new fertile ground to plant new seeds, seeds capable of growing deeper, more vibrant roots that would support her and help her grow far better harvests than ever possible in the containment of her former life.

Frenchy had embraced her new landscape by not getting stuck on the surface and peeking over the edge with fear. She let go of the fear and dove into the unknown.

Hope blossomed in the unknown.

The unknown scared Sarah. Yet, it also exhilarated her. Anything was possible in it.

Sarah wanted to be as brave as Frenchy, taking back control and leaving fear behind. She wanted to enjoy the empowerment of jumping off a cliff, diving into an ocean, and petting a cicada. She wanted to untangle from the web of an old, tired path and plant something new.

She wanted a lot of things; things that required her to let go of the comfort of the known.

Letting go challenged her. It required her to trust that if she allowed the currents of circumstance to carry her along, she'd end up home eventually. In letting go, she would have choices.

Life always came down to a choice of deciding on what to focus. Whatever the choice, something would always grow from it.

With proper perspective, she could learn to endure most anything. She could learn to endure traffic jams. She could learn to endure staring at reports all day. She could learn to endure eating dinners at her office desk.

Sarah didn't want to endure life, though. She wanted to love it.

~ ~

"They gave me a promotion," Sarah told Jolene on their morning call.

"Are you happy?"

"It gives me more leverage to run the game the way I want, I suppose."

"You didn't answer my question."

"Does it add another layer of complication to life? Yes. Am I conflicted? Yes."

"You should take it."

"Take it?" Sarah asked. "That's your advice?"

"Get lost in it for some time. Dig deep and figure out what's truly important. It's the only way you're going to find yourself. Otherwise, you're just flirting with the surface, and nothing is as it appears there. Go get your hands dirty, Sarah. Like I did with my twig, figure out if you already have what you need to grow new leaves. Take the time to discover what you really want. Take six months and give it a try, otherwise you'll always wonder what-if."

"Then, after six months, what happens if I discover I'm still not happy?"

"You come surprise me. You show up like we talked about already, with nothing but a suitcase and a hunger for something new. That's when we'll know."

"What will we know?"

"That you're ready to let go."

~ ~

Some of Sarah's best decisions happened while under the light of spontaneity, when she went with the flow without any expectation. In those moments, she had no plan and no idea of where she'd end up. Life always worked out in the end. As long as air traveled into her lungs, and her heart kept beating, she had life on her side.

Beneath everything, that's all that truly mattered.

When she planned too rigidly, she lost sight of everything around her and got stuck in the muck of what she expected to happen instead of what could happen if she learned to let go.

She wanted to let go. She wanted not to worry for once what her next step would be. She wanted to close her eyes, take a deep breath, and dive beyond the surface of her existence to where mystery woke up her soul and to where she started to feed her hunger to taste more than the banality of what she'd always known.

She didn't know what that meant for her future, and for the first time, she didn't care about the future. She only concerned herself with that moment, right then, and she didn't want to waste it being caught up in what-ifs and fearful ideologies of potential outcomes. She only cared about the beauty of standing in the light of possibility, ready to toss her hands in the air and let life take her on an unpredictable ride.

~ ~

That night, Sarah went to her closet and began to rake through her clothes and toss them into *keep* and *donate* piles. She stacked hangers upon hangers of clothes onto the donation pile, freeing herself from the clutter. When she emptied her closet, she turned to her storage bins and began the process of letting go of belts, hats, costume jewelry, and worn-out shoes and boots from years past.

She spent the entire night purging her closets, drawers, and shelves of useless items.

She needed to shed the layers to move forward in a solid decision.

She had clung to comfort and familiarity for too long. They robbed her from discovering new pathways. They prevented her from losing herself so she could find herself.

She rummaged through a bin of old awards and certificates and came across one certifying her as a project management specialist. That certificate hung in her home office for years until she hired someone to repaint. It went into the bin, and she never hung it back up. It represented a time when she stumbled to figure out her next step. She always searched ahead, operating under the guise that she'd eventually run into that ah-ha moment.

A part of Sarah enjoyed the game she played with life, always hopeful that around the next curve an adventure would surprise her and remind her that she hadn't wasted all that time looping an endless track that led nowhere.

In all her running, she missed something critical. She had choices. She could choose to dip out of the race, change the direction of it, or accept it. To take back the wheel, she had to choose. No one could do it for her. Whatever her choice, she had to stand by it with full acceptance, honoring it, trusting it, and keeping her fear at bay.

She dragged bins of items out into the hallway, and one by one, she dragged them down the winding staircase that opened into her foyer, a foyer no one ever entered but her and the house cleaner.

She studied the big space filled with stuff and asked herself what she wanted. More money? A bigger house? A more luxurious car? How much longer could she argue that one day she'd arrive, when she never even decided where she wanted to land? She had just gotten on that first road and gripped the steering wheel on a drive she didn't even control, stuck behind a line of others who also reduced the journey to a means to an end, waiting on life to change lanes so they could speed up, get ahead, and arrive somewhere other than the current moment with all its potential quality.

She stood amidst a heaviness. Everything weighed her down. None of it mattered.

Could she leave it all behind? To leave everything behind would require her to trust that life existed outside of the rat race. To experience it and find out what stirred inside, she'd have to eventually exit and reroute onto a new path. She'd have to put her fears aside, and be willing to take new turns so she could discover new sights, new scents, and new experiences that would pry open the rusty lid to her existence and open her view.

What did she have to lose but her grip on a life lacking meaning beyond files and reports; a life tarnished by the illusion that the same road would yield new insights?

She could fall and get hurt.

She might end up crying in the corner of an even emptier house.

She could stumble and never find her footing again.

She turned on some music and poured herself a glass of wine. She wished Frenchy would show up with a plate of those brownies. Maybe they would help her figure out the next step. She swayed to the vibes of Michael Bublé singing his famous song, *Home*. She sang along with him, belting out the verse and listening for its echo against the harshness of her vaulted two-story ceiling.

What if she leaped and didn't fall or get hurt? What if she triumphed? What if all roads leading away from the rat race offered something far better? Maybe she would soar. Maybe, just maybe, by taking that exit ramp, she could eventually find her way to a place she could call home.

She called Jolene after drinking three glasses of wine. "When you said six months, you didn't actually mean we shouldn't talk for six months, did you?"

"How are you going to know for sure if you don't let go of this and test it?"

"You're asking me to let go of you?"

"You need space. That's where freedom flies. When you let go and embrace that freedom, you're more open to the possibilities of life and where it can take you."

"You're willing to let me go?"

"I care for you too much to hang on. When and if you're ready, you'll know what to do."

~ ~

Sarah knew exactly what to do.

She hired and trained the newest members of the team to work the new account. They caught on quickly, and soon fell right into place like a well-oiled machine. It had broken down when Ashley left, and Sarah and her team put it back together again with replaceable parts. Everything was replaceable. Things, houses, cars, bank accounts, funding sources, careers, even people.

Nothing remained permanent, regardless of how much a person clung to it. The job, the money, the security, all of it just sat on the surface of a world that rotated and flowed. Sarah didn't want to stand by idle, watching life rotate around her anymore. She wanted to leap onto the moving parts and be the one rotating.

So, in the week following the new team's first successful campaign launch for the newest client of Ascension, Sarah walked into Tom's office and handed over her letter of resignation. She wanted to get back to the basics, create a simpler life, and remove herself from the distractions that stole her focus from reality and the precious present moment.

"What will it take to keep you here?" Tom asked. "An upgrade to your car? A spot in the rewards trip to Hawaii? I could probably get you a ten percent merit increase."

None of that stirred her soul. No amount of money or material possessions could make her happy. It never did. It never would. Even if he allowed her to work remotely from Bonaire, he'd still steal her joy with his constant demands. Sarah put up her hand. "Stop, Tom. I've made up my mind."

She readied herself to escape the rat race and get onto a new road, one where she would write simpler goals, and enjoy the intimate process of achieving them one breath, one blink, one moment at a time.

A month later, after finishing her time at Ascension, she snuck one last look at her old life before grabbing the one and only picture she had on her desk, one of her and Frenchy making sweet rolls with dough all over their faces and hair. She cradled it against her chest then crossed the threshold.

She would figure things out. She always did before. She had everything in her to succeed with whatever life wanted to toss at her.

Sarah pushed through the double doors of her former office building and refused to look back. From then on, her life would improve. No matter what it took, she would find her purpose and finally live the life she always envisioned, one where she woke up and never wanted to fall back asleep.

She had been functioning on autopilot her entire adult life, meandering through traffic jams, pointless business meetings, and endless routines in a daze, trying to survive the greatest of all death sentences to the human spirit, the dreaded rat race.

She needed to taste the zest for life and let it marinate until it bubbled over in sinful delight. To do that, she had to leave behind what she'd always known and start fresh.

Her first step, a trip to get her faded hair layered and highlighted. Her second step, wipe away her endless list of impossible goals from her dry-erase board and replace them with a simple smiley face. Before she embarked on her journey to a future unknown, she had to take her third and final step. She would put everything she owned up for sale on eBay.

Time to lighten the load and reassess.

Time to get living.

~ ~

"Here," Sarah said, handing Frenchy the key to her empty house. "Make sure the realtor sets the alarm, will you?"

"You bet." Frenchy's chin began buckling.

"I remember back when I bought this place," Sarah said, looking around the empty space. "I pranced around the house, never imagining I could ever

286

be that happy again."

Frenchy nodded in recognition. "I remember."

"It was so big. So empty. So, I kept buying things to fill it. I'd get high from shopping. Then, the high would disappear in a flash."

"It's all just stuff, isn't it?"

"I don't need it anymore." Sarah wrapped her arms across her chest. "Everything is amplified now. The brightness of the sun. The chirping of the birds. Beneath everything is the fullness and beauty of now. I'm present. I'm totally and completely present."

"It's all that matters."

"It's all we truly have," Sarah said.

"All we've ever had."

"Everything else is surface stuff," Sarah said, staring into her best friend's eyes. "It's a façade set up to force us into chasing something we can't achieve unless we stop and admire it when it's right in front of us."

Frenchy started to cry. "I'm going to miss you, kiddo."

"You better come visit."

"Jack and I are already planning a strategy to get Maureen on the plane. He bought us all tickets for her birthday in May. We'll make it happen. Even if I have to bake a little something special into, say, some delicious brownies." Frenchy winked.

"You're crazy."

"And resourceful. Don't leave out resourceful, kiddo."

"Resourceful. That you are."

They stared at each other with watery eyes. "I broke my promise," Sarah said finally. "I said I'd never leave you."

"You're not leaving me. You'll always be with me." Frenchy's chin quivered. She opened her arms, and Sarah fell into them. "You better tell Will when I arrive. I wouldn't want to miss out on diving with him."

"Diving, huh?"

They laughed.

"You're a cougar," Sarah said.

"And damned proud of it." Frenchy stepped back, still gripping Sarah's shoulders. "So, you're going to just show up with a suitcase and surprise her?"

"She loves the victory of surprises, and she's taught me that life's all about capturing those little victories."

"But you're such a planner."

"No. I'm more than that. I'm a woman who handles cicadas, dives into the middle of the ocean, jumps off cliffs, and embraces the spontaneous side of life now."

"What do you say we get you to the airport, then?" Frenchy hugged her then kissed her forehead before leading her out the front door and into the arms of the unknown, their footsteps echoing against the cement walkway.

~ ~

Sarah took a shuttle to the resort, handed the driver a tip and wheeled her single suitcase down the path towards the dock where she knew Jolene would be. The afternoon dive would have ended by then, and she'd be in the gear room filling tanks for the next day.

She rounded the corner to the open dock area, and saw her, bent over the filling station. A peaceful glow radiated from her, the kind that emanated from deep within.

The fragrance of the ocean breeze danced in the air. Divers rinsed their gear in the dump buckets, silent and thoughtful, full with an experience few understood.

Will emerged from the boat, carrying his BCD and a grin. He headed over to Jolene and whispered something. She laughed. Her whole face lightened the shadows in that darkened room of air tanks.

Sarah gripped the handle of her suitcase, not out of fear, but out of a new confidence that no matter what happened in the future, for that one moment of time, she engaged with life. She stared at the woman she fell quickly in love with, ready to start fresh, ready to get out of the comfort zone in search of something more zestful.

The comfort zone had always been a place of security. To stand at the edge of that circle and gaze wantonly into its center only served to layer the seeds of change into an impenetrable womb at one's feet. Just like with Jolene's twig, those seeds wanted to come alive and experience their full-unbridled potential, bursting through the surface of their imposed limits and reaching heights that offered spectacular sights.

Sarah stationed herself, gripping her suitcase handle, overjoyed with the sight before her. With the same delicate slow-motion sway of sea grass, Jolene turned towards her and an obvious joy sprang from her smiling eyes. She dropped the hose, pushed past Will and headed over to her, one giant stride at a time, scanning the full length of her all the way down to her one suitcase.

"Would you still consider this the sexiest thing in the world?" Sarah let go of the suitcase, and opened herself to that moment at hand, the only moment that existed, the moment when nothing else in the world mattered but the love resting on Jolene's lips as they connected under the bright blue skies of a beautiful Bonaire afternoon.

"It truly is the sexiest thing in the world," Jolene said softly.

Sarah gazed into her eyes, happy to have learned sooner than later, that when she finally let go, let go of all the limiting weight dragging her down, she became buoyant beneath the surface of life's fertile ground and everything flowed.

Jolene was her prism, and her invisible light vibrated beyond the outer shell of distorted reality with all its limiting distractions. Her light emanated from a deeper place, one connected to the root of all that mattered in life, to that very moment, that very breath, that very step they took on their journey to a destination unknown and full of promise.

NOTE FROM SUZIE CARR

As with all of my books, I enjoy giving a portion of proceeds back to the community by donating to the NOH8 Campaign www.noh8campaign.com and Hearts United for Animals www.hua.org. Thank you for being a part of this special contribution.

A SPECIAL REQUEST

If you enjoyed reading this story, I'd be so grateful for your honest review of it. Just a sentence or two will help others discover *Beneath Everything* and help me to serve you better with future books!

(www.amazon.com/author/suziecarr)

www.ingramcontent.com/pod-product-compliance
Lightning Source LLC
Chambersburg PA
CBHW030031180626
46810CB00001B/313